GOOD INDIAN

B. M. BOWER

1st WORLD
LIBRARY
Literary Society

Good Indian

B. M. Bower

© 1st World Library, 2006
PO Box 2211
Fairfield, IA 52556
www.1stworldlibrary.com
First Edition

LCCN: 2007920622

Softcover ISBN: 978-1-4218-3930-1
Hardcover ISBN: 978-1-4218-3830-4
eBook ISBN: 978-1-4218-4030-7

Purchase *"Good Indian"*
as a traditional bound book at:
www.1stWorldLibrary.com/purchase.asp?ISBN=978-1-4218-3930-1

1st World Library is a literary, educational organization
dedicated to:

- Creating a free internet library of downloadable ebooks

- Hosting writing competitions and offering book
publishing scholarships.

Interested in more 1st World Library books?
contact: literacy@1stworldlibrary.com
Check us out at: www.1stworldlibrary.com

1st World Library Literary Society

Giving Back to the World

"If you want to work on the core problem, it's early school literacy."

- James Barksdale, former CEO of Netscape

"No skill is more crucial to the future of a child, or to a democratic and prosperous society, than literacy."

- Los Angeles Times

Literacy... means far more than learning how to read and write... The aim is to transmit... knowledge and promote social participation."

- UNESCO

"Literacy is not a luxury, it is a right and a responsibility. If our world is to meet the challenges of the twenty-first century we must harness the energy and creativity of all our citizens."

- President Bill Clinton

"Parents should be encouraged to read to their children, and teachers should be equipped with all available techniques for teaching literacy, so the varying needs and capacities of individual kids can be taken into account."

- Hugh Mackay

CONTENTS

CHAPTER I

PEACEFUL HART RANCH

It was somewhere in the seventies when old Peaceful Hart woke to a realization that gold-hunting and lumbago do not take kindly to one another, and the fact that his pipe and dim-eyed meditation appealed to him more keenly than did his prospector's pick and shovel and pan seemed to imply that he was growing old. He was a silent man, by occupation and by nature, so he said nothing about it; but, like the wild things of prairie and wood, instinctively began preparing for the winter of his life. Where he had lately been washing tentatively the sand along Snake River, he built a ranch. His prospector's tools he used in digging ditches to irrigate his new-made meadows, and his mining days he lived over again only in halting recital to his sons when they clamored for details of the old days when Indians were not mere untidy neighbors to be gossiped with and fed, but enemies to be fought, upon occasion.

They felt that fate had cheated them—did those five sons; for they had been born a few years too late for the fun. Not one of them would ever have earned the title of "Peaceful," as had his father. Nature had played a joke upon old Peaceful Hart; for he, the mildest-mannered man who ever helped to tame the West when it really needed taming, had somehow fathered five riotous young males to whom fight meant fun—and the fiercer, the funnier.

He used to suck at his old, straight-stemmed pipe and regard them with a bewildered curiosity sometimes; but he never tried to put his puzzlement into speech. The nearest he ever came to elucidation, perhaps, was when he turned from them and let his pale-blue eyes dwell speculatively upon the face of his wife, Phoebe. Clearly he considered that she was responsible for their dispositions.

The house stood cuddled against a rocky bluff so high it dwarfed the whole ranch to pygmy size when one gazed down from the rim, and so steep that one wondered how the huge, gray bowlders managed to perch upon its side instead of rolling down and crushing the buildings to dust and fragments. Strangers used to keep a wary eye upon that bluff, as if they never felt quite safe from its menace. Coyotes skulked there, and tarantulas and "bobcats" and snakes. Once an outlaw hid there for days, within sight and hearing of the house, and stole bread from Phoebe's pantry at night—but that is a story in itself.

A great spring gurgled out from under a huge bowlder just behind the house, and over it Peaceful had built a stone milk house, where Phoebe spent long hours in cool retirement on churning day, and where one went to beg good things to eat and to drink. There was fruit cake always hidden away in stone jars, and cheese, and buttermilk, and cream.

Peaceful Hart must have had a streak of poetry somewhere hidden away in his silent soul. He built a pond against the bluff; hollowed it out from the sand he had once washed for traces of gold, and let the big spring fill it full and seek an outlet at the far end, where it slid away under a little stone bridge. He planted the pond with rainbow trout, and on the margin a rampart of Lombardy poplars, which grew and grew until they threatened to reach up and tear ragged holes in the drifting clouds. Their slender shadows lay, like gigantic fingers, far up the bluff when the sun sank low in the afternoon.

Behind them grew a small jungle of trees-catalpa and locust among them—a jungle which surrounded the house, and in summer hid it from sight entirely.

With the spring creek whispering through the grove and away to where it was defiled by trampling hoofs in the corrals and pastures beyond, and with the roses which Phoebe Hart kept abloom until tho frosts came, and the bees, and humming—birds which somehow found their way across the parched sagebrush plains and foregathered there, Peaceful Hart's ranch betrayed his secret longing for girls, as if he had unconsciously planned it for the daughters he had been denied.

It was an ideal place for hammocks and romance—a place where dainty maidens might dream their way to womanhood. And Peaceful Hart, when all was done, grew old watching five full-blooded boys clicking their heels unromantically together as they roosted upon the porch, and threw cigarette stubs at the water lilies while they wrangled amiably over the merits of their mounts; saw them drag their blankets out into the broody dusk of the grove when the nights were hot, and heard their muffled swearing under their "tarps" because of the mosquitoes which kept the night air twanging like a stricken harp string with their song.

They liked the place well enough. There were plenty of shady places to lie and smoke in when the mercury went sizzling up its tiny tube. Sometimes, when there was a dance, they would choose the best of Phoebe's roses to decorate their horses' bridles; and perhaps their hatbands, also. Peaceful would then suck harder than ever at his pipe, and his faded blue eyes would wander pathetically about the little paradise of his making, as if he wondered whether, after all, it had been worth while.

A tight picket fence, built in three unswerving lines from the post planted solidly in a cairn of rocks against a bowlder on the eastern rim of the pond, to the road which cut straight through the ranch, down that to the farthest tree of the grove, then back to the bluff again, shut in that tribute to the sentimental side of Peaceful's nature. Outside the fence dwelt sturdier,

Western realities.

Once the gate swung shut upon the grove one blinked in the garish sunlight of the plains. There began the real ranch world. There was the pile of sagebrush fuel, all twisted and gray, pungent as a bottle of spilled liniment, where braided, blanketed bucks were sometimes prevailed upon to labor desultorily with an ax in hope of being rewarded with fruit new-gathered from the orchard or a place at Phoebe's long table in the great kitchen.

There was the stone blacksmith shop, where the boys sweated over the nice adjustment of shoes upon the feet of fighting, wild-eyed horses, which afterward would furnish a spectacle of unseemly behavior under the saddle.

Farther away were the long stable, the corrals where broncho-taming was simply so much work to be performed, hayfields, an orchard or two, then rocks and sand and sage which grayed the earth to the very skyline.

A glint of slithering green showed where the Snake hugged the bluff a mile away, and a brown trail, ankle-deep in dust, stretched straight out to the west, and then lost itself unexpectedly behind a sharp, jutting point of rocks where the bluff had thrust out a rugged finger into the valley.

By devious turnings and breath-taking climbs, the trail finally reached the top at the only point for miles, where it was possible for a horseman to pass up or down.

Then began the desert, a great stretch of unlovely sage and lava rock and sand for mile upon mile, to where the distant mountain ridges reached out and halted peremptorily the ugly sweep of it. The railroad gashed it boldly, after the manner of the iron trail of modern industry; but the trails of the desert dwellers wound through it diffidently, avoiding the rough crest of lava rock where they might, dodging the most aggressive sagebrush and dipping tentatively into hollows, seeking always the easiest way to reach some remote settlement or ranch.

Of the men who followed those trails, not one of them but could have ridden straight to the Peaceful Hart ranch in black darkness; and there were few, indeed, white men or Indians, who could have ridden there at midnight and not been sure of blankets and a welcome to sweeten their sleep. Such was the Peaceful Hart Ranch, conjured from the sage and the sand in the valley of the Snake.

CHAPTER II

GOOD INDIAN

There is a saying—and if it is not purely Western, it is at least purely American—that the only good Indian is a dead Indian. In the very teeth of that, and in spite of tho fact that he was neither very good, nor an Indian—nor in any sense "dead" —men called Grant Imsen "Good Indian" to his face; and if he resented the title, his resentment was never made manifest—perhaps because he had grown up with the name, he rather liked it when he was a little fellow, and with custom had come to take it as a matter of course.

Because his paternal ancestry went back, and back to no one knows where among the race of blue eyes and fair skin, the Indians repudiated relationship with him, and called him white man—though they also spoke of him unthinkingly as "Good Injun."

Because old Wolfbelly himself would grudgingly admit under pressure that the mother of Grant had been the half-caste daughter of Wolfbelly's sister, white men remembered the taint when they were angry, and called him Injun. And because he stood thus between the two races of men, his exact social status a subject always open to argument, not even the fact that he was looked upon by the Harts as one of the family, with his own bed always ready for him in a corner of the big room set apart for the boys, and with a certain place at the table which was called his—not even his assured position there could keep him from sometimes feeling quite alone, and perhaps a trifle bitter over his loneliness.

Phoebe Hart had mothered him from the time when his father had sickened and died in her house, leaving Grant there with twelve years behind him, in his hands a dirty canvas bag of gold coin so heavy he could scarce lift it, which stood for the mining claim the old man had just sold, and the command to invest every one of the gold coins in schooling.

Old John Imsen was steeped in knowledge of the open; nothing of the great outdoors had ever slipped past him and remained mysterious. Put when he sold his last claim—others he had which promised little and so did not count—he had signed his name with an X. Another had written the word John before that X, and the word Imsen after; above, a word which he explained was "his," and below the word "mark." John Imsen had stared down suspiciously at the words, and he had not felt quite easy in his mind until the bag of gold coins was actually in his keeping. Also, he had been ashamed of that X. It was a simple thing to make with a pen, and yet he had only succeeded in making it look like two crooked sticks thrown down carelessly, one upon the other. His face had gone darkly red with the shame of it, and he had stood scowling down at the paper.

"That boy uh mine's goin' to do better 'n that, by God!" he had sworn, and the words had sounded like a vow.

When, two months after that, he had faced—incredulously, as is the way with strong men—the fact that for him life was over, with nothing left to him save an hour or so of labored breath and a few muttered sentences, he did not forget that vow. He called Phoebe close to the bed, placed the bag of gold in Grant's trembling hands, and stared intently from one face to the other.

"Mis' Hart, he ain't got—anybody—my folks—I lost track of 'em years ago. You see to it—git some learnin' in his head.

When a man knows books—it's—like bein' heeled—good gun—plenty uh ca't'idges— in a fight. When I got that gold— it was like fightin' with my bare hands—against a gatlin' gun. They coulda cheated me—whole thing—on paper—I wouldn't know—luck—just luck they didn't. So you take it— and git the boy schoolin'. Costs money—I know that—git him all it'll buy. Send him—where they keep—the best. Don't yuh let up—n'er let him—whilst they's a dollar left. Put it all—into his head—then he can't lose it, and he can—make it earn more. An'—I guess I needn't ask yuh—be good to him. He ain't got anybody—not a soul—Injuns don't count. You see to it—don't let up till—it's all gone."

Phoebe had taken him literally. And Grant, if he had little taste for the task, had learned books and other things not mentioned in the curriculums of the schools she sent him to— and when the bag was reported by Phoebe to be empty, he had returned with inward relief to the desultory life of the Hart ranch and its immediate vicinity.

His father would probably have been amazed to see how little difference that schooling made in the boy. The money had lasted long enough to take him through a preparatory school and into the second year of a college; and the only result apparent was speech a shade less slipshod than that of his fellows, and a vocabulary which permitted him to indulge in an amazing number of epithets and in colorful vituperation when the fancy seized him.

He rode, hot and thirsty and tired, from Sage Hill one day and found Hartley empty of interest, hot as the trail he had just now left thankfully behind him, and so absolutely sleepy that it seemed likely to sink into the sage-clothed earth under the weight of its own dullness. Even the whisky was so warm it burned like fire, and the beer he tried left upon his outraged palate the unhappy memory of insipid warmth and great bitterness.

He plumped the heavy glass down upon the grimy counter in

the dusty far corner of the little store and stared sourly at Pete Hamilton, who was apathetically opening hatboxes for the inspection of an Indian in a red blanket and frowsy braids.

"How much?" The braided one fingered indecisively the broad brim of a gray sombrero.

"Nine dollars." Pete leaned heavily against the shelves behind him and sighed with the weariness of mere living.

"Huh! All same buy one good hoss." The braided one dropped the hat, hitched his blanket over his shoulder in stoical disregard of the heat, and turned away.

Pete replaced the cover, seemed about to place the box upon the shelf behind him, and then evidently decided that it was not worth the effort. He sighed again.

"It is almighty hot," he mumbled languidly. "Want another drink, Good Injun?"

"I do not. Hot toddy never did appeal to me, my friend. If you weren't too lazy to give orders, Pete, you'd have cold beer for a day like this. You'd give Saunders something to do beside lie in the shade and tell what kind of a man he used to be before his lungs went to the bad. Put him to work. Make him pack this stuff down cellar where it isn't two hundred in the shade. Why don't you?"

"We was going to get ice t'day, but they didn't throw it off when the train went through."

"That's comforting—to a man with a thirst like the great Sahara. Ice! Pete, do you know what I'd like to do to a man that mentions ice after a drink like that?"

Pete neither knew nor wanted to know, and he told Grant so. "If you're going down to the ranch," he added, by way of changing the subject, "there's some mail you might as well take along."

"Sure, I'm going—for a drink out of that spring, if nothing else. You've lost a good customer to-day, Pete. I rode up here prepared to get sinfully jagged—and here I've got to go on a still hunt for water with a chill to it—or maybe buttermilk. Pete, do you know what I think of you and your joint?"

"I told you I don't wanta know. Some folks ain't never satisfied. A fellow that's rode thirty or forty miles to get here, on a day like this, had oughta be glad to get anything that looks like beer."

"Is that so?" Grant walked purposefully down to the front of the store, where Pete was fumbling behind the rampart of crude pigeonholes which was the post-office. "Let me inform you, then, that—"

There was a swish of skirts upon the rough platform outside, and a young woman entered with the manner of feeling perfectly at home there. She was rather tall, rather strong and capable looking, and she was bareheaded, and carried a door key suspended from a smooth-worn bit of wood.

"Don't get into a perspiration making up the mail, Pete," she advised calmly, quite ignoring both Grant and the Indian. "Fifteen is an hour late—as usual. Jockey Bates always seems to be under the impression he's an undertaker's assistant, and is headed for the graveyard when he takes fifteen out. He'll get the can, first he knows—and he'll put in a month or two wondering why. I could make better time than he does myself." By then she was leaning with both elbows upon the counter beside the post-office, bored beyond words with life as it must be lived—to judge from her tone and her attitude.

"For Heaven's sake, Pete," she went on languidly, "can't you scare up a novel, or chocolates, or gum, or—ANYTHING to kill time? I'd even enjoy chewing gum right now—it would give my jaws something to think of, anyway."

Pete, grinning indulgently, came out of retirement behind the pigeonholes, and looked inquiringly around the store.

"I've got cards," he suggested. "What's the matter with a game of solitary? I've known men to put in hull winters alone, up in the mountains, jest eating and sleeping and playin' solitary."

The young woman made a grimace of disgust. "I've come from three solid hours of it. What I really do want is something to read. Haven't you even got an almanac?"

"Saunders is readin' 'The Brokenhearted Bride'—you can have it soon's he's through. He says it's a peach."

"Fifteen is bringing up a bunch of magazines. I'll have reading in plenty two hours from now; but my heavens above, those two hours!" She struck both fists despairingly upon the counter.

"I've got gumdrops, and fancy mixed—"

"Forget it, then. A five-pound box of chocolates is due—on fifteen." She sighed heavily. "I wish you weren't so old, and hadn't quite so many chins, Pete," she complained. "I'd inveigle you into a flirtation. You see how desperate I am for something to do!"

Pete smiled unhappily. He was sensitive about all those chins, and the general bulk which accompanied them.

"Let me make you acquainted with my friend, Good In—er—Mr. Imsen." Pete considered that he was behaving with great discernment and tact. "This is Miss Georgie Howard, the new operator." He twinkled his little eyes at her maliciously. "Say, he ain't got but one chin, and he's only twenty-three years old." He felt that the inference was too plain to be ignored.

She turned her head slowly and looked Grant over with an air of disparagement, while she nodded negligently as an acknowledgment to the introduction. "Pete thinks he's awfully witty," she remarked. "It's really pathetic."

Pete bristled—as much as a fat man could bristle on so hot a day. "Well, you said you wanted to flirt, and so I took it for granted you'd like—"

Good Indian looked straight past the girl, and scowled at Pete.

"Pete, you're an idiot ordinarily, but when you try to be smart you're absolutely insufferable. You're mentally incapable of recognizing the line of demarcation between legitimate persiflage and objectionable familiarity. An ignoramus of your particular class ought to confine his repartee to unqualified affirmation or the negative monosyllable." Whereupon he pulled his hat more firmly upon his head, hunched his shoulders in disgust, remembered his manners, and bowed to Miss Georgie Howard, and stalked out, as straight of back as the Indian whose blanket he brushed, and who may have been, for all he knew, a blood relative of his.

"I guess that ought to hold you for a while, Pete," Miss Georgie approved under her breath, and stared after Grant curiously. "'You're mentally incapable of recognizing the line of demarcation between legitimate persiflage and objectionable familiarity.' I'll bet two bits you don't know what that means, Pete; but it hits you off exactly. Who is this Mr. Imsen?"

She got no reply to that. Indeed, she did not wait for a reply. Outside, things were happening—and, since Miss Georgie was dying of dullness, she hailed the disturbance as a Heaven-sent blessing, and ran to see what was going on.

Briefly, Grant had inadvertently stepped on a sleeping dog's paw—a dog of the mongrel breed which infests Indian camps, and which had attached itself to the blanketed buck inside. The dog awoke with a yelp, saw that it was a stranger who had perpetrated the outrage, and straightway fastened its teeth in the leg of Grant's trousers. Grant kicked it loose, and when it

B. M. Bower

came at him again, he swore vengeance and mounted his horse in haste.

He did not say a word. He even smiled while he uncoiled his rope, widened the loop, and, while the dog was circling warily and watching for another chance at him, dropped the loop neatly over its front quarters, and drew it tight.

Saunders, a weak-lunged, bandy-legged individual, who was officially a general chore man for Pete, but who did little except lie in the shade, reading novels or gossiping, awoke then, and, having a reputation for tender-heartedness, waved his arms and called aloud in the name of peace.

"Turn him loose, I tell yuh! A helpless critter like that—you oughta be ashamed—abusin' dumb animals that can't fight back!"

"Oh, can't he?" Grant laughed grimly.

"You turn that dog loose!" Saunders became vehement, and paid the penalty of a paroxysm of coughing.

"You go to the devil. If you were an able-bodied man, I'd get you, too—just to have a pair of you. Yelping, snapping curs, both of you." He played the dog as a fisherman plays a trout.

"That dog, him Viney dog. Viney heap likum. You no killum, Good Injun." The Indian, his arms folded in his blanket, stood upon the porch watching calmly the fun. "Viney all time heap mad, you killum," he added indifferently.

"Sure it isn't old Hagar's?"

"No b'long-um Hagar—b'long-um Viney. Viney heap likum."

Grant hesitated, circling erratically with his victim close to the steps. "All right, no killum—teachum lesson, though. Viney heap bueno squaw—heap likum Viney. No likum dog, though. Dog all time come along me." He glanced up, passed over the fact that Miss Georgie Howard was watching him and clapping her hands enthusiastically at the spectacle, and settled an unfriendly stare upon Saunders.

"You shut up your yowling. You'll burst a blood vessel and go to heaven, first thing you know. I've never contemplated hiring you as my guardian angel, you blatting buck sheep. Go off and lie down somewhere." He turned in the saddle and looked down at the dog, clawing and fighting the rope which held him fast just back of the shoulder—blades. "Come along, doggie—NICE doggie!" he grinned, and touched his horse with the spurs. With one leap, it was off at a sharp gallop, up over the hill and through the sagebrush to where he knew the Indian camp must be.

Old Wolfbelly had but that morning brought his thirty or forty followers to camp in the hollow where was a spring of clear water—the hollow which had for long been known locally as "the Indian Camp," because of Wolfbelly's predilection for the spot. Without warning save for the beat of hoofs in the sandy soil, Grant charged over the brow of the hill and into camp, scattering dogs, papooses, and squaws alike as he rode.

ShriLL clamor filled the sultry air. Sleeping bucks awoke, scowling at the uproar; and the horse of Good Indian, hating always the smell and the litter of an Indian camp, pitched furiously into the very wikiup of old Hagar, who hated the rider of old. In the first breathing spell he loosed the dog, which skulked, limping, into the first sheltered spot be found, and laid him down to lick his outraged person and whimper to himself at the memory of his plight. Grant pulled his horse to a restive stand before a group of screeching squaws, and laughed outright at the panic of them.

"Hello! Viney! I brought back your dog," he drawled. "He tried to bite me—heap kay bueno* dog. Mebbyso you killum. Me no hurtum—all time him Hartley, all time him try hard

B. M. Bower

bite me. Sleeping Turtle tell me him Viney dog. he likum Viney, me no kill Viney dog. You all time mebbyso eat that dog—sabe? No keep—Kay bueno. All time try for bite. You cookum, no can bite. Sabe?"

*AUTHOR'S NOTE.—The Indians of southern Idaho spoke a somewhat mixed dialect. Bueno (wayno), their word for 'good,' undoubtedly being taken from the Spanish language. I believe the word "kay" to be Indian. It means "no', and thus the "Kay bueno" so often used by them means literally 'no good," and is a term of reproach On the other hand, "heap bueno" is "very good," their enthusiasm being manifested merely by drawing out the word "heap." In speaking English they appear to have no other way of expressing, in a single phrase, their like or dislike of an object or person.

Without waiting to see whether Viney approved of his method of disciplining her dog, or intended to take his advice regarding its disposal, he wheeled and started off in the direction of the trail which led down the bluff to the Hart ranch. When he reached the first steep descent, however, he remembered that Pete had spoken of some mail for the Harts, and turned back to get it.

Once more in Hartley, he found that the belated train was making up time, and would be there within an hour; and, since it carried mail from the West, it seemed hardly worthwhile to ride away before its arrival. Also, Pete intimated that there was a good chance of prevailing upon the dining-car conductor to throw off a chunk of ice. Grant, therefore, led his horse around into the shade, and made himself comfortable while he waited.

CHAPTER III

OLD WIVES TALES

Down the winding trail of Snake River bluff straggled a blanketed half dozen of old Wolfbelly's tribe, the braves stalking moodily in front and kicking up a gray cloud of dust which enveloped the squaws behind them but could not choke to silence their shrill chatter; for old Hagar was there, and Viney, and the incident of the dog was fresh in their minds and tickling their tongues.

The Hart boys were assembled at the corral, halter-breaking a three-year-old for the pure fun of it. Wally caught sight of the approaching blotch of color, and yelled a wordless greeting; him had old Hagar carried lovingly upon her broad shoulders with her own papoose when he was no longer than her arm; and she knew his voice even at that distance, and grinned—grinned and hid her joy in a fold of her dingy red blanket.

"Looks like old Wolfbelly's back," Clark observed needlessly. "Donny, if they don't go to the house right away, you go and tell mum they're here. Chances are the whole bunch'll hang around till supper."

"Say!" Gene giggled with fourteen-year-old irrepressibility. "Does anybody know where Vadnie is? If we could spring 'em on her and make her believe they're on the warpath—say, I'll gamble she'd run clear to the Malad!"

B. M. Bower

"I told her, cross my heart, this morning that the Injuns are peaceful now. I said Good Injun was the only one that's dangerous—oh, I sure did throw a good stiff load, all right!" Clark grinned at the memory. "I've got to see Grant first, when he gets back, and put him wise to the rep he's got. Vad didn't hardly swallow it. She said: 'Why, Cousin Clark! Aunt Phoebe says he's perfectly lovely!'" Clark mimicked the girl's voice with relish.

"Aw—there's a lot of squaws tagging along behind!" Donny complained disgustedly from his post of observation on the fence. "They'll go to the house first thing to gabble—there's old Hagar waddling along like a duck. You can't make that warpath business stick, Clark—not with all them squaws."

"Well, say, you sneak up and hide somewhere till yuh see if Vadnie's anywhere around. If they get settled down talking to mum, they're good for an hour—she's churning, Don—you hide in the rocks by the milk-house till they get settled. And I'll see if—Git! Pikeway, while they're behind the stacks!"

Donny climbed down and scurried through the sand to the house as if his very life depended upon reaching it unseen. The group of Indians came up, huddled at the corral, and peered through the stout rails.

"How! How!" chorused the boys, and left the horse for a moment while they shook hands ceremoniously with the three bucks. Three Indians, Clark decided regretfully, would make a tame showing on the warpath, however much they might lend themselves to the spirit of the joke. He did not quite know how he was going to manage it, but he was hopeful still. It was unthinkable that real live Indians should be permitted to come and go upon the ranch without giving Evadna Ramsey, straight from New Jersey, the scare of her life.

The three bucks, grunting monosyllabic greetings' climbed, in all the dignity of their blankets, to the top rail of the corral, and roosted there to watch the horse-breaking; and for the present Clark held his peace.

The squaws hovered there for a moment longer, peeping through the rails. Then Hagar—she of much flesh and more temper—grunted a word or two, and they turned and plodded on to where the house stood hidden away in its nest of cool green. For a space they stood outside the fence, peering warily into the shade, instinctively cautious in their manner of approaching a strange place, and detained also by the Indian etiquette which demands that one wait until invited to enter a strange camp.

After a period of waiting which seemed to old Hagar sufficient, she pulled her blanket tight across her broad hips, waddled to the gate, pulled it open with self-conscious assurance, and led the way soft-footedly around the house to where certain faint sounds betrayed the presence of Phoebe Hart in her stone milk-house.

At the top of the short flight of wide stone steps they stopped and huddled silently, until the black shadow of them warned Phoebe of their presence. She had lived too long in the West to seem startled when she suddenly discovered herself watched by three pair of beady black eyes, so she merely nodded, and laid down her butter-ladle to shake hands all around.

"How, Hagar? How, Viney? How, Lucy? Heap glad to see you. Bueno buttermilk—mebbyso you drinkum?"

However diffident they might be when it came to announcing their arrival, their bashfulness did not extend to accepting offers of food or drink. Three brown hands were eagerly outstretched—though it was the hand of Hagar which grasped first the big tin cup. They not only drank, they guzzled, and afterward drew a fold of blanket across their milk-white lips, and grinned in pure animal satisfaction.

"Bueno. He-e-ap bueno!" they chorused appreciatively, and squatted at the top of the stone steps, watching Phoebe manipulate the great ball of yellow butter in its wooden bowl.

After a brief silence, Hagar shook the tangle of unkempt, black hair away from her moonlike face, and began talking in a soft monotone, her voice now and then rising to a shrill singsong.

"Mebbyso Tom, mebbyso Sharlie, mebbyso Sleeping Turtle all time come along," she announced. "Stop all time corral, talk yo' boys. Mebbyso heap likum drink yo' butter water. Bueno."

When Phoebe nodded assent, Hagar went on to the news which had brought her so soon to the ranch—the news which satisfied both an old grudge and her love of gossip.

"Good Injun, him all time heap kay bueno," she stated emphatically, her sloe black eyes fixed unwaveringly upon Phoebe's face to see if the stab was effective. "Good Injun come Hartley, all time drunk likum pig.

"All time heap yell, heap shoot—kay bueno. Wantum fight Man-that-coughs. Come all time camp, heap yell, heap shoot some more. I fetchum dog—Viney dog—heap dragum through sagebrush—dog all time cry, no can get away—me thinkum kill that dog. Squaws cry—Viney cry—Good Injun"—Hagar paused here for greater effect—"makum horse all time buck—ridum in wikiup—Hagar wikiup—all time breakum—no can fix that wikiup. Good Injun, hee-e-ap kay bueno!" At the last her voice was high and tremulous with anger.

"Good Indian mebbyso all same my boy Wally." Phoebe gave the butter a vicious slap. "Me heap love Good Indian. You no call Good Indian, you call Grant. Grant bueno. Heap bueno all time. No drunk, no yell, no shoot, mebbyso"—she hesitated, knowing well the possibilities of her foster son—"mebbyso catchum dog—me think no catchum. Grant all same my boy. All time me likum—heap bueno."

Viney and Lucy nudged each other and tittered into their

blankets, for the argument was an old one between Hagar and Phoebe, though the grievance of Hagar might be fresh. Hagar shifted her blanket and thrust out a stubborn under lip.

"Wally boy, heap bueno," she said; and her malicious old face softened as she spoke of him, dear as her own first-born. "Jack bueno, mebbyso Gene bueno, mebbyso Clark, mebbyso Donny all time bueno." Doubt was in her voice when she praised those last two, however, because of their continual teasing. She stopped short to emphasize the damning contrast. "Good Injun all same mebbyso yo' boy Grant, hee-ee-eap kay bueno. Good Injun Grant all time DEBBIL!"

It was at this point that Donny slipped away to report that "Mamma and old Hagar are scrappin' over Good Injun again," and told with glee the tale of his misdeeds as recounted by the squaw.

Phoebe in her earnestness forgot to keep within the limitations of their dialect.

"Grant's a good boy, and a smart boy. There isn't a better-hearted fellow in the country, if I have got five boys of my own. You think I like him better than I like Wally, is all ails you, Hagar. You're jealous of Grant, and you always have been, ever since his father left him with me. I hope my heart's big enough to hold them all." She remembered then that they could not understand half she was saying, and appealed to Viney. Viney liked Grant.

"Viney, you tell me. Grant no come Hartley, no drunk, no yell, no catchum you dog, no ride in Hagar's wikiup? You tell me, Viney."

Viney and Lucy bobbed their heads rapidly up and down. Viney, with a sidelong glance at Hagar, spoke softly.

"Good Injun Grant, mebbyso home Hartley," she admitted reluctantly, as if she would have been pleased to prove Hagar a liar in all things. "Me thinkum no drunk. Mebbyso ketchum dog—dog kay bueno, mebbyso me killing. Good Injun Grant no heap yell, no shoot all time—mebbyso no drunk. No breakum wikiup. Horse all time kay bueno, Hagar—"

"Shont-isham!" (big lie) Hagar interrupted shrilly then, and Viney relapsed into silence, her thin face growing sullen under the upbraiding she received in her native tongue. Phoebe, looking at her attentively, despaired of getting any nearer the truth from any of them.

There was a sudden check to Hagar's shrewish clamor. The squaws stiffened to immobility and listened stolidly, their eyes alone betraying the curiosity they felt. Off somewhere at the head of the tiny pond, hidden away in the jungle of green, a voice was singing; a girl's voice, and a strange voice—for the squaws knew well the few women voices along the Snake.

"That my girl," Phoebe explained, stopping the soft pat—pat of her butter-ladle.

"Where ketchum yo' girl?" Hagar forgot her petulance, and became curious as any white woman.

"Me ketchum 'way off, where sun come up. In time me have heap boys—mebbyso want girl all time. My mother's sister's boy have one girl, 'way off where sun come up. My mother's sister's boy die, his wife all same die, that girl mebbyso heap sad; no got father, no got mother—all time got nobody. Kay bueno. That girl send one letter, say all time got nobody. Me want one girl. Me send one letter, tell that girl come, be all time my girl. Five days ago, that girl come. Her heap glad; boys all time heap glad, my man heap glad. Bueno. Mebbyso you glad me have one girl." Not that their approval was necessary, or even of much importance; but Phoebe was accustomed to treat them like spoiled children.

Hagar's lip was out-thrust again. "Yo' ketchum one girl, mebbyso yo' no more likum my boy Wally. Kay bueno."

"Heap like all my boys jus' same," Phoebe hastened to assure her, and added with a hint of malice, "Heap like my boy Grant all same."

"Huh!" Hagar chose to remain unconvinced and antagonistic. "Good Injun kay bueno. Yo' girl, mebbyso kay bueno."

"What name yo' girl?" Viney interposed hastily.

"Name Evadna Ramsey." In spite of herself, Phoebe felt a trifle chilled by their lack of enthusiasm. She went back to her butter-making in dignified silence.

The squaws blinked at her stolidly. Always they were inclined toward suspicion of strangers, and perhaps to a measure of jealousy as well. Not many whites received them with frank friendship as did the Hart family, and they felt far more upon the subject than they might put into words, even the words of their own language.

Many of the white race looked upon them as beggars, which was bad enough, or as thieves, which was worse; and in a general way they could not deny the truth of it. But they never stole from the Harts, and they never openly begged from the Harts. The friends of the Harts, however, must prove their friendship before they could hope for better than an imperturbable neutrality. So they would not pretend to be glad. Hagar was right—perhaps the girl was no good. They would wait until they could pass judgment upon this girl who had come to live in the wikiup of the Harts. Then Lucy, she who longed always for children and had been denied by fate, stirred slightly, her nostrils aquiver.

"Mebbyso bueno yo' girl,'," she yielded, speaking softly. "Mebbyso see yo' girl."

Phoebe's face cleared, and she called, in mellow crescendo: "Oh, Va-ad-NIEE?" Immediately the singing stopped.

B. M. Bower

"Coming, Aunt Phoebe," answered the voice.

The squaws wrapped themselves afresh in their blankets, passed brown palms smoothingly down their hair from the part in the middle, settled their braids upon their bosoms with true feminine instinct, and waited. They heard her feet crunching softly in the gravel that bordered the pond, but not a head turned that way; for all the sign of life they gave, the three might have been mere effigies of women. They heard a faint scream when she caught sight of them sitting there, and their faces settled into more stolid indifference, adding a hint of antagonism even to the soft eyes of Lucy, the tender, childless one.

"Vadnie, here are some new neighbors I want you to get acquainted with." Phoebe's eyes besought the girl to be calm. "They're all old friends of mine. Come here and let me introduce you—and don't look so horrified, honey!"

Those incorrigibles, her cousins, would have whooped with joy at her unmistakable terror when she held out a trembling hand and gasped faintly: "H-how do you—do?"

"This Hagar," Phoebe announced cheerfully; and the old squaw caught the girl's hand and gripped it tightly for a moment in malicious enjoyment of her too evident fear and repulsion.

"This Vincy."

Viney, reading Evadna's face in one keen, upward glance, kept her hands hidden in the folds of her blanket, and only nodded twice reassuringly.

"This Lucy."

Lucy read also the girl's face; but she reached up, pressed her hand gently, and her glance was soft and friendly. So the ordeal was over.

"Bring some of that cake you baked to-day, honey—and do brace up!" Phoebe patted her upon the shoulder.

Hagar forestalled the hospitable intent by getting slowly upon her fat legs, shaking her hair out of her eyes, and grunting a command to the others. With visible reluctance Lucy and Viney rose also, hitched their blankets into place, and vanished, soft-footed as they had come.

"Oo-oo!" Evadna stared at the place where they were not. "Wild Indians—I thought the boys were just teasing when they said so—and it's really true, Aunt Phoebe?"

"They're no wilder than you are," Phoebe retorted impatiently.

"Oh, they ARE wild. They're exactly like in my history—and they don't make a sound when they go—you just look, and they're gone! That old fat one—did you see how she looked at me? As if she wanted to—SCALP me, Aunt Phoebe! She looked right at my hair and—"

"Well, she didn't take it with her, did she? Don't be silly. I've known old Hagar ever since Wally was a baby. She took him right to her own wikiup and nursed him with her own papoose for two months when I was sick, and Viney stayed with me day and night and pulled me through. Lucy I've known since she was a papoose. Great grief, child! Didn't you hear me say they're old friends? I wanted you to be nice to them, because if they like you there's nothing they won't do for you. If they don't, there's nothing they WILL do. You might as well get used to them—"

Out by the gate rose a clamor which swept nearer and nearer until the noise broke at the corner of the house like a great wave, in a tumult of red blanket, flying black hair, the squalling of a female voice, and the harsh laughter of the man who carried the disturbance, kicking and clawing, in his arms. Fighting his way to the milk-house, he dragged the squaw along beside the porch, followed by the Indians and all the

Hart boys, a yelling, jeering audience.

"You tell her shont-isham! Ah-h—you can't break loose, you old she-wildcat. Quit your biting, will you? By all the big and little spirits of your tribe, you'll wish—"

Panting, laughing, swearing also in breathless exclamations, he forced her to the top of the steps, backed recklessly down them, and came to a stop in the corner by the door. Evadna had taken refuge there; and he pressed her hard against the rough wall without in the least realizing that anything was behind him save unsentient stone.

"Now, you sing your little song, and be quick about it!" he commanded his captive sternly. "You tell Mother Hart you lied. I hear she's been telling you I'm drunk, Mother Hart—didn't you, you old beldam? You say you heap sorry you all time tellum lie. You say: 'Good Injun, him all time heap bueno.' Say: 'Good Injun no drunk, no heap shoot, no heap yell—all time bueno.' Quick, or I'll land you headforemost in that pond, you infernal old hag!"

"Good Injun hee-eap kay bueno! Heap debbil all time." Hagar might be short of breath, but her spirit was unconquered, and her under lip bore witness to her stubbornness.

Phoebe caught him by the arm then, thinking he meant to make good his threat—and it would not have been unlike Grant Imsen to do so.

"Now, Grant, you let her go," she coaxed. "I know you aren't drunk—of course, I knew it all the time. I told Hagar so. What do you care what she says about you? You don't want to fight an old woman, Grant—a man can't fight a woman—"

"You tell her you heap big liar!" Grant did not even look at Phoebe, but his purpose seemed to waver in spite of himself. "You all time kay bueno. You all time lie." He gripped her more firmly, and turned his head slightly toward Phoebe. "You'd be tired of it yourself if she threw it into you like she does into me, Mother Hart. It's got so I can't ride past this old hag in the trail but she gives me the bad eye, and mumbles into her blanket. And if I look sidewise, she yowls all over the country that I'm drunk. I'm getting tired of it!" He shook the squaw as a puppy shakes a shoe—shook her till her hair quite hid her ugly old face from sight.

"All right—Mother Hart she tellum mebbyso let you go. This time I no throw you in pond. You heap take care next time, mebbyso. You no tellum big lie, me all time heap drunk. You kay bueno. All time me tellum Mother Hart, tellum boys, tellum Viney, Lucy, tellum Charlie and Tom and Sleeping Turtle you heap big liar. Me tell Wally shont-isham. Him all time my friend—mebbyso him no likum you no more.

"Huh. Get out—pikeway before I forget you're a lady!"

He laughed ironically, and pushed her from him so suddenly that she sprawled upon the steps. The Indians grinned unsympathetically at her, for Hagar was not the most popular member of the tribe by any means. Scrambling up, she shook her witch locks from her face, wrapped herself in her dingy blanket, and scuttled away, muttering maledictions under her breath. The watching group turned and followed her, and in a few seconds the gate was heard to slam shut behind them. Grant stood where he was, leaning against the milk-house wall; and when they were gone, he gave a short, apologetic laugh.

"No need to lecture, Mother Hart. I know it was a fool thing to do; but when Donny told me what the old devil said, I was so mad for a minute—"

Phoebe caught him again by the arm and pulled him forward. "Grant! You're squeezing Vadnie to death, just about! Great grief, I forgot all about the poor child being here! You poor little—"

"Squeezing who?" Grant whirled, and caught a brief glimpse of a crumpled little figure behind him, evidently too scared to cry, and yet not quite at the fainting point of terror. He backed, and began to stammer an apology; but she did not wait to hear a word of it. For an instant she stared into his face, and then, like a rabbit released from its paralysis of dread, she darted past him and deaf up the stone steps into the house. He heard the kitchen-door shut, and the click of the lock. He heard other doors slam suggestively; and he laughed in spite of his astonishment.

"And who the deuce might that be?" he asked, feeling in his pocket for smoking material.

Phoebe seemed undecided between tears and laughter. "Oh, Grant, GRANT! She'll think you're ready to murder everybody on the ranch—and you can be such a nice boy when you want to be! I did hope—"

"I don't want to be nice," Grant objected, drawing a match along a fairly smooth rock.

"Well, I wanted you to appear at your best; and, instead of that, here you come, squabbling with old Hagar like—"

"Yes—sure. But who is the timid lady?"

"Timid! You nearly killed the poor girl, besides scaring her half to death, and then you call her timid. I know she thought there was going to be a real Indian massacre, right here, and she'd be scalped—"

Wally Hart came back, laughing to himself.

"Say, you've sure cooked your goose with old Hagar, Grant! She's right on the warpath, and then some. She'd like to burn yuh alive—she said so. She's headed for camp, and all the rest of the bunch at her heels. She won't come here any more till you're kicked off the ranch, as near as I could make out her jabbering. And she won't do your washing any more, mum—she said so. You're kay bueno yourself, because you take Good Indian's part. We're all kay bueno—all but me. She wanted me to quit the bunch and go live in her wikiup. I'm the only decent one in the outfit." He gave his mother an affectionate little hug as he went past, and began an investigative tour of the stone jars on the cool rock floor within. "What was it all about, Grant? What did yuh do to her, anyway?"

"Oh, it wasn't anything. Hand me up a cup of that buttermilk, will you? They've got a dog up there in camp that I'm going to kill some of these days—if they don't beat me to it. He was up at the store, and when I went out to get my horse, he tried to take a leg off me. I kicked him in the nose and he came at me again, so when I mounted I just dropped my loop over Mr. Dog. Sleeping Turtle was there, and he said the dog belonged to Viney, So I just led him gently to camp."

He grinned a little at the memory of his gentleness. "I told Viney I thought he'd make a fine stew, and, they'd better use him up right away before he spoiled. That's all there was to it. Well, Keno did sink his head and pitch around camp a little, but not to amount to anything. He just stuck his nose into old Hagar's wikiup—and one sniff seemed to be about all he wanted. He didn't hurt anything."

He took a meditative bite of cake, finished the buttermilk in three rapturous swallows, and bethought him of the feminine mystery.

"If you please, Mother Hart, who was that Christmas angel I squashed?"

"Vad? Was Vad in on it, mum? I never saw her." Wally straightened up with a fresh chunk of cake in his hand. "Was she scared?"

"Yes," his mother admitted reluctantly, "I guess she was, all right. First the squaws—and, poor girl, I made her shake hands all round—and then Grant here, acting like a wild hyena—"

"Say, PLEASE don't tell me who she is, or where she belongs, or anything like that," Grant interposed, with some sarcasm. "I smashed her flat between me and the wall, and I scared the daylights out of her; and I'm told I should have appeared at my best. But who she is, or where she belongs—"

"She belongs right here." Phoebe's tone was a challenge, whether she meant it to be so or not. "This is going to be her home from now on; and I want you boys to treat her nicer than you've been doing. She's been here a week almost; and there ain't one of you that's made friends with her yet, or tried to, even. You've played jokes on her, and told her things to scare her—and my grief! I was hoping she'd have a softening influence on you, and make gentlemen of you. And far as I can make out, just having her on the place seems to put the Old Harry into every one of you! It isn't right. It isn't the way I expected my boys would act toward a stranger—a girl especially. And I did hope Grant would behave better."

"Sure, he ought to. Us boneheads don't know any better—but Grant's EDUCATED." Wally grinned and winked elaborately at his mother's back.

"I'm not educated up to Christmas angels that look as if they'd been stepped on," Grant defended himself.

"She's a real nice little thing. If you boys would quit teasing the life out of her, I don't doubt but what, in six months or so, you wouldn't know the girl," Phoebe argued, with some heat.

"I don't know the girl now." Grant spoke dryly. "I don't want to. If I'd held a tomahawk in one hand and her flowing locks in the other, and was just letting a war-whoop outa me, she'd look at me—the way she did look." He snorted in contemptuous amusement, and gave a little, writhing twist of his slim body into his trousers. "I never did like blondes," he added, in a tone of finality, and started up the steps.

"You never liked anything that wore skirts," Phoebe flung after him indignantly; and she came very close to the truth.

B. M. Bower

CHAPTER IV

THE CHRISTMAS ANGEL

Phoebe watched the two unhappily, sighed when they disappeared around the corner of the house, and set her bowl of butter upon the broad, flat rock which just missed being overflowed with water, and sighed again.

"I'm afraid it isn't going to work," she murmured aloud; for Phoebe, having lived much of her life in the loneliness which the West means to women, frequently talked to herself. "She's such a nice little thing—but the boys don't take to her like I thought they would. I don't see as she's having a mite of influence on their manners, unless it's to make them act worse, just to shock her. Clark USED to take off his hat when he come into the house most every time. And great grief! Now he'd wear it and his chaps and spurs to the table, if I didn't make him take them off. She's nice—she's most too nice. I've got to give that girl a good talking to."

She mounted the steps to the back porch, tried tho kitchen door, and found it locked. She went around to the door on the west side, opposite the gate, found that also secured upon the inside, and passed grimly to the next.

"My grief! I didn't know any of these doors COULD be locked!" she muttered angrily. "They never have been before that I ever heard of." She stopped before Evadna's window, and saw, through a slit in the green blind, that the old-fashioned bureau had been pulled close before it. "My grief!" she whispered disgustedly, and retraced her steps to the east side, which, being next to the pond, was more secluded. She surveyed dryly a window left wide open there, gathered her brown-and-white calico dress close about her plump person, and crawled grimly through into the sitting- room, where, to the distress of Phoebe's order-loving soul, the carpet was daily well-sanded with the tread of boys' boots fresh from outdoors, and where cigarette stubs decorated every window-sill, and the stale odor of Peaceful's pipe was never long absent.

She went first to all the outer rooms, and unlocked every one of the outraged doors which, unless in the uproar and excitement of racing, laughing boys pursuing one another all over the place with much slamming and good-natured threats of various sorts, had never before barred the way of any man, be he red or white, came he at noon or at midnight.

Evadna's door was barricaded, as Phoebe discovered when she turned the knob and attempted to walk in. She gave the door an indignant push, and heard a muffled shriek within, as if Evadna's head was buried under her pillow.

"My grief! A body'd think you expected to be killed and eaten," she called out unsympathetically. "You open this door! Vadnie Ramsey. This is a nice way to act with my own boys, in my own house! A body'd think—"

There was the sound of something heavy being dragged laboriously away from tho barricaded door; and in a minute a vividly blue eye appeared at a narrow crack.

"Oh, I don't see how you dare to L-LIVE in such a place, Aunt Phoebe!" she cried tearfully, opening the door a bit wider. "Those Indians—and that awful man—"

"That was only Grant, honey. Let me in. There's a few things I want to say to you, Vadnie. You promised to help me teach my boys to be gentle—it's all they lack, and it takes gentle

B. M. Bower

women, honey—"

"I am gentle," Evadna protested grievedly. "I've never once forgotten to be gentle and quiet, and I haven't done a thing to them—but they're horrid and rough, anyway—"

"Let me in, honey, and we'll talk it over. Something's got to be done. If you wouldn't be so timid, and would make friends with them, instead of looking at them as if you expected them to murder you—I must say, Vadnie, you're a real temptation; they can't help scaring you when you go around acting as if you expected to be scared. You—you're TOO—" The door opened still wider, and she went in. "Now, the idea of a great girl like you hiding her head under a pillow just because Grant asked old Hagar to apologize!"

Evadna sat down upon the edge of the bed and stared unwinkingly at her aunt. "They don't apologize like that in New Jersey," she observed, with some resentment in her voice, and dabbed at her unbelievably blue eyes with a moist ball of handkerchief.

"I know they don't, honey." Phoebe patted her hand reassuringly. "That's what I want you to help me teach my boys—to be real gentlemen. They're pure gold, every one of them; but I can't deny they're pretty rough on the outside sometimes. And I hope you will be—"

"Oh, I know. I understand perfectly. You just got me out here as a—a sort of sandpaper for your boys' manners!" Evadna choked over a little sob of self-pity. "I can just tell you one thing, Aunt Phoebe, that fellow you call Grant ought to be smoothed with one of those funny axes they hew logs with."

Phoebe bit her lips because she wanted to treat the subject very seriously. "I want you to promise me, honey, that you will be particularly nice to Grant; PARTICULARLY nice. He's so alone, and he's very proud and sensitive, because he feels his loneliness. No one understands him as I do—"

"I hate him!" gritted Evadna, in an emphatic whisper which her Aunt Phoebe thought it wise not to seem to hear.

Phoebe settled herself comfortably for a long talk. The murmur of her voice as she explained and comforted and advised came soothingly from the room, with now and then an interruption while she waited for a tardy answer to some question. Finally she rose and stood in the doorway, looking back at a huddled figure on the bed.

"Now dry your eyes and be a good girl, and remember what you've promised," she admonished kindly. "Aunt Phoebe didn't mean to scold you, honey; she only wants you to feel that you belong here, and she wants you to like her boys and have them like you. They've always wanted a sister to pet; and Aunt Phoebe is hoping you'll not disappoint her. You'll try; won't you, Vadnie?"

"Y—yes," murmured Vadnie meekly from the pillow. "I know you will." Phoebe looked at her for a moment longer rather wistfully, and turned away. "I do wish she had some spunk," she muttered complainingly, not thinking that Evadna might hear her. "She don't take after the Ramseys none—there wasn't anything mushy about them that I ever heard of."

"Mushy! MUSHY!" Evadna sat up and stared at nothing at all while she repeated the word under her breath. "She wants me to be gentle—she preached gentleness in her letters, and told how her boys need it, and then—she calls it being MUSHY!"

She reached mechanically for her hair-brush, and fumbled in a tumbled mass of shining, yellow hair quite as unbelievable in its way as were her eyes—Grant had shown a faculty for observing keenly when he called her a Christmas angel—and drew out a half-dozen hairpins, letting them slide from her lap to the floor. "MUSHY!" she repeated, and shook down her hair so that it framed her face and those eyes of hers. "I suppose that's what they all say behind my back. And how can a girl be nice WITHOUT being mushy?" She drew the brush meditatively through her hair. "I am scared to death of Indians," she admitted, with analytical frankness, "and tarantulas and snakes—but—MUSHY!"

Grant stood smoking in the doorway of the sitting-room, where he could look out upon the smooth waters of the pond darkening under the shade of the poplars and the bluff behind, when Evadna came out of her room. He glanced across at her, saw her hesitate, as if she were meditating a retreat, and gave his shoulders a twitch of tolerant amusement that she should be afraid of him. Then he stared out over the pond again. Evadna walked straight over to him.

"So you're that other savage whose manners I'm supposed to smooth, are you?" she asked abruptly, coming to a stop within three feet of him, and regarding him carefully, her hands clasped behind her.

"Please don't tease the animals," Grant returned, in the same impersonal tone which she had seen fit to employ—but his eyes turned for a sidelong glance at her, although he appeared to be watching the trout rise lazily to the insects skimming over the surface of the water.

"I'm supposed to be nice to you—par-TIC-ularly nice— because you need it most. I dare say you do, judging from what I've seen of you. At any rate, I've promised. But I just want you to understand that I'm not going to mean one single bit of it. I don't like you—I can't endure you!—and if I'm nice, it will just be because I've promised Aunt Phoebe. You're not to take my politeness at its face value, for back of it I shall dislike you all the time."

Grant's lips twitched, and there was a covert twinkle in his eyes, though he looked around him with elaborate surprise.

"It's early in the day for mosquitoes," he drawled; "but I was sure I heard one buzzing somewhere close."

"Aunt Phoebe ought to get a street roller to smooth your manners," Evadna observed pointedly.

"Instead it's as if she hung her picture of a Christmas angel up before the wolf's den, eh?" he suggested calmly, betraying his Indian blood in the unconsciously symbolic form of expression. "No doubt the wolf's nature will be greatly benefited—his teeth will be dulled for his prey, his voice softened for the nightcry—if he should ever, by chance, discover that the Christmas angel is there."

"I don't think he'll be long in making the discovery." The blue of Evadna's eyes darkened and darkened until they were almost black. "Christmas angel,—well, I like that! Much you know about angels."

Grant turned his head indolently and regarded her.

"If it isn't a Christmas angel—they're always very blue and very golden, and pinky-whitey—if it isn't a Christmas angel, for the Lord's sake what is it?" He gave his head a slight shake, as if the problem was beyond his solving, and flicked the ashes from his cigarette.

"Oh, I could pinch you!" She gritted her teeth to prove she meant what she said.

"It says it could pinch me." Grant lazily addressed the trout. "I wonder why it didn't, then, when it was being squashed?"

"I just wish to goodness I had! Only I suppose Aunt Phoebe—"

"I do believe it's got a temper. I wonder, now, if it could be a LIVE angel?" Grant spoke to the softly swaying poplars.

"Oh, you—there now!" She made a swift little rush at him, nipped his biceps between a very small thumb and two fingers, and stood back, breathing quickly and regarding him in a

B. M. Bower

shamed defiance. "I'll show you whether I'm alive!" she panted vindictively.

"It's alive, and it's a humming-bird. Angels don't pinch." Grant laid a finger upon his arm and drawled his solution of a trivial mystery. "It mistook me for a honeysuckle, and gave me a peck to make sure." He smiled indulgently, and exhaled a long wreath of smoke from his nostrils. "Dear little humming-birds—so simple and so harmless!"

"And I've promised to be nice to—THAT!" cried Evadna, in bitterness, and rushed past him to the porch.

Being a house built to shelter a family of boys, and steps being a superfluity scorned by their agile legs, there was a sheer drop of three feet to the ground upon that side. Evadna made it in a jump, just as the boys did, and landed lightly upon her slippered feet.

"I hate you—hate you—HATE YOU!" she cried, her eyes blazing up at his amused face before she ran off among the trees.

"It sings a sweet little song," he taunted, and his laughter followed her mockingly as she fled from him into the shadows.

"What's the joke, Good Injun? Tell us, so we can laugh too." Wally and Jack hurried in from the kitchen and made for the doorway where he stood.

From under his straight, black brows Grant sent a keen glance into the shade of the grove, where, an instant before, had flickered the white of Evadna's dress. The shadows lay there quietly now, undisturbed by so much as a sleepy bird's fluttering wings.

"I was just thinking of the way I yanked that dog down into old Wolfbelly's camp," he said, though there was no tangible reason for lying to them. "Mister!" he added, his eyes still searching the shadows out there in the grove, "we certainly did go some!"

B. M. Bower

CHAPTER V

"I DON'T CARE MUCH ABOUT GIRLS"

"There's no use asking the Injuns to go on the warpath," Gene announced disgustedly, coming out upon the porch where the rest of the boys were foregathered, waiting for the ringing tattoo upon the iron triangle just outside the back door which would be the supper summons. "They're too lazy to take the trouble—and, besides, they're scared of dad. I was talking to Sleeping Turtle just now—met him down there past the Point o' Rocks."

"What's the matter with us boys going on the warpath ourselves? We don't need the Injuns. As long as she knows they're hanging around close, it's all the same. If we could just get mum off the ranch—"

"If we could kidnap her—say, I wonder if we couldn't!" Clark looked at the others tentatively.

"Good Injun might do the rescue act and square himself with her for what happened at the milk-house," Wally suggested dryly.

"Oh, say, you'd scare her to death. There's no use in piling it on quite so thick," Jack interposed mildly. "I kinda like the kid sometimes. Yesterday, when I took her part way up the bluff, she acted almost human. On the dead, she did!"

"Kill the traitor! Down with him! Curses on the man who betrays us!" growled Wally, waving his cigarette threateningly.

Whereupon Gene and Clark seized the offender by heels and shoulders, and with a brief, panting struggle heaved him bodily off the porch.

"Over the cliff he goes—so may all traitors perish!" Wally declaimed approvingly, drawing up his legs hastily out of the way of Jack's clutching fingers.

"Say, old Peppajee's down at the stable with papa," Donny informed them breathlessly. "I told Marie to put him right next to Vadnie if he stays to supper—and, uh course, he will. If mamma don't get next and change his place, it'll be fun to watch her; watch Vad, I mean. She's scared plum to death of anything that wears a blanket, and to have one right at her elbow—wonder where she is—"

"That girl's got to be educated some if she's going to live in this family," Wally observed meditatively. "There's a whole lot she's got to learn, and the only way to learn her thorough is—"

"You forget," Grant interrupted him ironically, "that she's going to make gentlemen of us all."

"Oh, yes—sure. Jack's coming down with it already. You oughta be quarantined, old-timer; that's liable to be catching." Wally snorted his disdain of the whole proceeding. "I'd rather go to jail myself."

Evadna by a circuitous route had reached the sitting-room without being seen or heard; and it was at this point in the conversation that she tiptoed out again, her hands doubled into tight little fists, and her teeth set hard together. She did not look, at that moment, in the least degree "mushy."

When the triangle clanged its supper call, however, she came slowly down from her favorite nook at the head of the pond, her hands filled with flowers hastily gathered in the dusk.

"Here she comes—let's get to our places first, so mamma can't change Peppajee around," Donny implored, in a whisper; and the group on the porch disappeared with some haste into the kitchen.

Evadna was leisurely in her movements that night. The tea had been poured and handed around the table by the Portuguese girl, Marie, and the sugar-bowl was going after, when she settled herself and her ruffles daintily between Grant and a braided, green-blanketed, dignifiedly loquacious Indian.

The boys signaled each another to attention by kicking surreptitiously under the table, but nothing happened. Evadna bowed a demure acknowledgment when her Aunt Phoebe introduced the two, accepted the sugar-bowl from Grant and the butter from Peppajee, and went composedly about the business of eating her supper. She seemed perfectly at ease; too perfectly at ease, decided Grant, who had an instinct for observation and was covertly watching her. It was unnatural that she should rub elbows with Peppajee without betraying the faintest trace of surprise that he should be sitting at the table with them.

"Long time ago," Peppajee was saying to Peaceful, taking up the conversation where Evadna had evidently interrupted it, "many winters ago, my people all time brave. A]1 time hunt, all time fight, all time heap strong. No drinkum whisky all same now." He flipped a braid back over his shoulder, buttered generously a hot biscuit, and reached for the honey." No brave no more—kay bueno. All time ketchum whisky, get drunk all same likum hog. Heap lazy. No hunt no more, no fight. Lay all time in sun, sleep. No sun come, lay all time in wikiup. Agent, him givum flour, givum meat, givum blanket, you thinkum bueno. He tellum you, kay bueno. Makum Injun lazy. Makum all same wachee-typo" (tramp). "All time eat, all time sleep, playum cards all time, drinkum whisky. Kay bueno. Huh." The grunt stood for disgust of his tribe, always something of an affectation with Peppajee.

"My brother, my brother's wife, my brother's wife's—ah—" He searched his mind, frowning, for an English word, gave it up, and substituted a phrase. "All the folks b'longum my brother's wife, heap lazy all time. Me no likum. Agent one time givum plenty flour, plenty meat, plenty tea. Huh. Them damn' folks no eatum. All time playum cards, drinkum whisky. All time otha fella ketchum flour, ketchum meat, ketchum tea—ketchum all them thing b'longum." In the rhetorical pause he made there, his black eyes wandered inadvertently to Evadna's face. And Evadna, the timid one, actually smiled back.

"Isn't it a shame they should do that," she murmured sympathetically.

"Huh." Peppajee turned his eyes and his attention to Peaceful, as if the opinion and the sympathy of a mere female were not worthy his notice. "Them grub all gone, them Injuns mebbyso ketchum hungry belly." Evadna blushed, and looked studiously at her plate.

"Come my wikiup. Me got plenty flour, plenty meat, plenty tea. Stay all time my wikiup. Sleepum my wikiup. Sun come up"—he pointed a brown, sinewy hand toward the east— "eatum my grub. Sun up there"—his finger indicated the zenith—"eatum some more. Sun go 'way, eatum some more. Then sleepum all time my wikiup. Bimeby, mebbyso my flour all gone, my meat mebbyso gone, mebbyso tea—them folks all time eatum grub, me no ketchum. Me no playum cards, all same otha fella ketchum my grub. Kay bueno. Better me playum cards mebbyso all time.

"Bimeby no ketchum mo' grub, no stopum my wikiup. Them folks pikeway. Me tellum 'Yo' heap lazy, heap kay bueno. Yo' all time eatum my grub, yo' no givum me money, no givum hoss, no givum notting. Me damn' mad all time yo'. Yo' go damn' quick!'" Peppajee held out his cup for more tea. "Me

B. M. Bower

tellum my brother," he finished sonorously, his black eyes sweeping lightly the faces of his audience, "yo' no come back, yo'—"

Evadna caught her breath, as if someone had dashed cold water in her face. Never before in her life had she heard the epithet unprintable, and she stared fixedly at the old-fashioned, silver castor which always stood in the exact center of the table.

Old Peaceful Hart cleared his throat, glanced furtively at Phoebe, and drew his hand down over his white beard. The boys puffed their cheeks with the laughter they would, if possible, restrain, and eyed Evadna's set face aslant. It was Good Indian who rebuked the offender.

"Peppajee, mebbyso you no more say them words," he said quietly. "Heap kay bueno. White man no tellum where white woman hear. White woman no likum hear; all time heap shame for her."

"Huh," grunted Peppajee doubtingly, his eyes turning to Phoebe. Times before had he said them before Phoebe Hart, and she had passed them by with no rebuke. Grant read the glance, and answered it.

"Mother Hart live long time in this place," he reminded him. "Hear bad talk many times. This girl no hear; no likum hear. You sabe? You no make shame for this girl." He glanced challengingly across the table at Wally, whose grin was growing rather pronounced.

"Huh. Mebbyso you boss all same this ranch?" Peppajee retorted sourly. "Mebbyso Peacefu' tellum, him no likum."

Peaceful, thus drawn into the discussion, cleared his throat again.

"Wel-l-l—WE don't cuss much before the women," he admitted apologetically "We kinda consider that men's talk. I reckon Vadnie'll overlook it this time." He looked across at her beseechingly. "You no feelum bad, Peppajee."

"Huh. Me no makum squaw-talk." Peppajee laid down his knife, lifted a corner of his blanket, and drew it slowly across his stern mouth. He muttered a slighting sentence in Indian.

In the same tongue Grant answered him sharply, and after that was silence broken only by the subdued table sounds. Evadna's eyes filled slowly until she finally pushed back her chair and hurried out into the yard and away from the dogged silence of that blanketed figure at her elbow.

She was scarcely settled, in the hammock, ready for a comforting half hour of tears, when someone came from the house, stood for a minute while he rolled a cigarette, and then came straight toward her.

She sat up, and waited defensively. More baiting, without a doubt—and she was not in the mood to remember any promises about being a nice, gentle little thing. The figure came close, stooped, and took her by the arm. In the half—light she knew him then. It was Grant.

"Come over by the pond," he said, in what was almost a command." I want to talk to you a little."

"Does it occur to you that I might not want to talk t to you?" Still, she let him help her to her feet.

"Surely. You needn't open your lips if you don't want to. Just 'lend me your ears, and be silent that ye may hear.' The boys will be boiling out on tho porch, as usual, in a minute; so hurry."

"I hope it's something very important," Evadna hinted ungraciously." Nothing else would excuse this high—handed proceeding."

When they had reached the great rock where the i pond had its outlet, and where was a rude seat hidden away in a clump of young willows just across the bridge, he answered her.

"I don't know that it's of any importance at all," he said calmly." I got to feeling rather ashamed of myself, is all, and it seemed to me the only decent thing was to tell you so. I'm not making any bid for your favor—I don't know that I want it. I don't care much about girls, one way or the other. But, for all I've got the name of being several things—a savage among the rest—I don't like to feel such a brute as to make war on a girl that seems to be getting it handed to her right along."

He tardily lighted his cigarette and sat smoking beside her, the tiny glow lighting his face briefly now and then.

"When I was joshing you there before supper," he went on, speaking low that he might not be overheard—and ridiculed— from the house, "I didn't know the whole outfit was making a practice of doing the same thing. I hadn't heard about the dead tarantula on your pillow, or the rattler coiled up on the porch, or any of those innocent little jokes. But if the rest are making it their business to devil the life out of you, why—common humanity forces me to apologize and tell you I'm out of it from now on."

"Oh! Thank you very much." Evadna's tone might be considered ironical. "I suppose I ought to say that your statement lessens my dislike of you—"

"Not at all." Grant interrupted her. "Go right ahead and hate me, if you feel that way. It won't matter to me—girls never did concern me much, one way or the other. I never was susceptible to beauty, and that seems to be a woman's trump card, always—"

"Well, upon my word!"

"Sounds queer, does it? But it's the truth, and so what's the use of lying, just to be polite? I won't torment you any more; and if the boys rig up too strong a josh, I'm liable to give you a hint beforehand. I'm willing to do that—my sympathies are always with the under dog, anyway, and they're five to one. But that needn't mean that I'm—that I—" He groped for words that would not make his meaning too bald; not even Grant could quite bring himself to warn a girl against believing him a victim of her fascinations.

"You needn't stutter. I'm not really stupid. You don't like me any better than I like you. I can see that. We're to be as decent as possible to each other—you from 'common humanity,' and I because I promised Aunt Phoebe."

"We-e-l!—that's about it, I guess." Grant eyed her sidelong." Only I wouldn't go so far as to say I actually dislike you. I never did dislike a girl, that I remember. I never thought enough about them, one way or the other." He seemed rather fond of that statement, he repeated it so often." The life I live doesn't call for girls. Put that's neither here nor there. What I wanted to say was, that I won't bother you any more. I wouldn't have said a word to you tonight, if you hadn't walked right up to me and started to dig into me. Of course, I had to fight back—tho man who won't isn't a normal human being."

"Oh, I know." Evadna's tone was resentful. "From Adam down to you, it has always been 'The woman, she tempted me.' You're perfectly horrid, even if you have apologized. 'The woman, she tempted me,' and—"

"I beg your pardon; the woman didn't," he corrected blandly. "The woman insisted on scrapping. That's different."

"Oh, it's different! I see. I have almost forgotten something I ought to say, Mr. Imsen. I must thank you for—well, for defending me to that Indian."

"I didn't. Nobody was attacking you, so I couldn't very well defend you, could I? I had to take a fall out of old Peppajee, just on principle. I don't get along very well with my noble red cousins. I wasn't doing it on your account, in particular."

"Oh, I see." She rose rather suddenly from the bench. "It wasn't even common humanity, then—"

"Not even common humanity," he echoed affirmatively. "Just a chance I couldn't afford to pass up, of digging into Peppajee."

"That's different." She laughed shortly and left him, running swiftly through the warm dusk to the murmur of voices at the house.

Grant sat where she left him, and smoked two cigarettes meditatively before he thought of returning to the house. When he finally did get upon his feet, he stretched his arms high above his head, and stared for a moment up at the treetops swaying languidly just under the stars.

"Girls must play the very deuce with a man if he ever lets them get on his mind," he mused. "I see right now where a fellow about my size and complexion had better watch out." But he smiled afterward, as if he did not consider the matter very serious, after all.

CHAPTER VI

THE CHRISTMAS ANGEL PLAYS GHOST

At midnight, the Peaceful Hart ranch lay broodily quiet under its rock-rimmed bluff. Down in tho stable the saddle-horses were but formless blots upon the rumpled bedding in their stalls—except Huckleberry, the friendly little pinto with the white eyelashes and the blue eyes, and the great, liver-colored patches upon his sides, and the appetite which demanded food at unseasonable hours, who was now munching and nosing industriously in the depths of his manger, and making a good deal of noise about it.

Outside, one of the milch cows drew a long, sighing breath of content with life, lifted a cud in mysterious, bovine manner, and chewed dreamily. Somewhere up the bluff a bobcat squalled among the rocks, and the moon, in its dissipated season of late rising, lifted itself indolently up to where it could peer down upon the silent ranch.

In the grove where the tiny creek gurgled under the little stone bridge, someone was snoring rhythmically in his blankets, for the boys had taken to sleeping in the open air before the earliest rose had opened buds in the sunny shelter of the porch. Three feet away, a sleeper stirred restlessly, lifted his head from the pillow, and slapped half-heartedly at an early mosquito that was humming in his ear. He reached out, and jogged the shoulder of him who snored.

B. M. Bower

"Say, Gene, if you've got to sleep at the top of your voice, you better drag your bed down into the orchard," he growled. "Let up a little, can't yuh?"

"Ah, shut up and let a fellow sleep!" mumbled Gene, snuggling the covers up to his ears.

"Just what I want YOU to do. You snore like a sawmill. Darn it, you've got to get out of the grove if yuh can't—"

"Ah-h-EE-EE!" wailed a voice somewhere among the trees, the sound rising weirdly to a subdued crescendo, clinging there until one's flesh went creepy, and then sliding mournfully down to silence.

"What's that?" The two jerked themselves to a sitting position, and stared into the blackness of the grove.

"Bobcat," whispered Clark, in a tone which convinced not even himself.

"In a pig's ear," flouted Gene, under his breath. He leaned far over and poked his finger into a muffled form. "D'yuh hear that noise, Grant?"

Grant sat up instantly. "What's tho matter?" he demanded, rather ill-naturedly, if the truth be told.

"Did you hear anything—a funny noise, like—"

The cry itself finished the sentence for him. It came from nowhere, it would seem, since they could see nothing; rose slowly to a subdued shriek, clung there nerve-wrackingly, and then wailed mournfully down to silence. Afterward, while their ears were still strained to the sound, the bobcat squalled an answer from among the rocks.

"Yes, I heard it," said Grant. "It's a spook. It's the wail of a lost spirit, loosed temporarily from the horrors of purgatory. It's sent as a warning to repent you of your sins, and it's howling because it hates to go back. What you going to do about it?"

He made his own intention plain beyond any possibility of misunderstanding. He lay down and pulled the blanket over his shoulders, cuddled his pillow under his head, and disposed himself to sleep.

The moon climbed higher, and sent silvery splinters of light quivering down among the trees. A frog crawled out upon a great lily—pad and croaked dismally.

Again came the wailing cry, nearer than before, more subdued, and for that reason more eerily mournful. Grant sat up, muttered to himself, and hastily pulled on some clothes. The frog cut himself short in the middle of a deep-throated ARR-RR-UMPH and dove headlong into the pond; and the splash of his body cleaving the still surface of the water made Gene shiver nervously. Grant reached under his pillow for something, and freed himself stealthily from a blanketfold.

"If that spook don't talk Indian when it's at home, I'm very much mistaken," he whispered to Clark, who was nearest. "You boys stay here."

Since they had no intention of doing anything else, they obeyed him implicitly and without argument, especially as a flitting white figure appeared briefly and indistinctly in a shadow-flecked patch of moonlight. Crouching low in the shade of a clump of bushes, Grant stole toward the spot.

When he reached the place, the thing was not there. Instead, he glimpsed it farther on, and gave chase, taking what precautions he could against betraying himself. Through the grove and the gate and across the road he followed, in doubt half the time whether it was worth the trouble. Still, if it was what he suspected, a lesson taught now would probably insure against future disturbances of the sort, he thought, and kept stubbornly on. Once more he heard the dismal cry, and fancied it held a mocking note.

"I'll settle that mighty quick," he promised grimly, as he jumped a ditch and ran toward the place.

Somewhere among the currant bushes was a sound of eery laughter. He swerved toward the place, saw a white form rise suddenly from the very ground, as it seemed, and lift an arm with a slow, beckoning gesture. Without taking aim, he raised his gun and fired a shot at it. The arm dropped rather suddenly, and the white form vanished. He hurried up to where it had stood, knelt, and felt of the soft earth. Without a doubt there were footprints there—he could feel them. But he hadn't a match with him, and the place was in deep shade.

He stood up and listened, thought he heard a faint sound farther along, and ran. There was no use now in going quietly; what counted most was speed.

Once more he caught sight of the white form fleeing from him like the very wraith it would have him believe it. Then he lost it again; and when he reached the spot where it disappeared, he fell headlong, his feet tangled in some white stuff. He swore audibly, picked himself up, and held the cloth where the moon shone full upon it. It looked like a sheet, or something of the sort, and near one edge was a moist patch of red. He stared at it dismayed, crumpled the cloth into a compact bundle, tucked it under his arm, and ran on, his ears strained to catch some sound to guide him.

"Well, anyhow, I didn't kill him," he muttered uneasily as he crawled through a fence into the orchard. "He's making a pretty swift get-away for a fellow that's been shot."

In the orchard the patches of moonlight were larger, and across one of them he glimpsed a dark object, running wearily. Grant repressed an impulse to shout, and used the breath for an extra burst of speed. The ghost was making for the fence again, as if it would double upon its trail and reach some previously chosen refuge. Grant turned and ran also toward the fence, guessing shrewdly that the fugitive would head for the place where the wire could be spread about, and a beaten trail led from there straight out to the road which passed the house. It was the short cut from the peach orchard; and it occurred to him that this particular spook seemed perfectly familiar with the byways of the ranch. Near the fence he made a discovery that startled him a little.

"It's a squaw, by Jove!" he cried when he caught an unmistakable flicker of skirts; and the next moment he could have laughed aloud if he had not been winded from the chase. The figure reached the fence before him, and in the dim light he could see it stoop to pass through. Then it seemed as if the barbs had caught in its clothing and held it there. It struggled to free itself; and in the next minute he rushed up and clutched it fast.

"Why don't you float over the treetops?" he panted ironically. "Ghosts have no business getting their spirit raiment tangled up in a barbed-wire fence."

It answered with a little exclamation, with a sob following close upon it. There was a sound of tearing cloth, and he held his captive upright, and with a merciless hand turned her face so that the moonlight struck it full. They stared at each other, breathing hard from more than the race they had run.

"Well—I'll—be—" Grant began, in blank amazement.

She wriggled her chin in his palm, trying to free herself from his pitiless staring. Failing that, she began to sob angrily without any tears in her wide eyes.

"You—shot me, you brute!" she cried accusingly at last. "You—SHOT me!" And she sobbed again.

Before he answered, he drew backward a step or two, sat down upon the edge of a rock which had rolled out from a stone-heap, and pulled her down beside him, still holding her fast, as if he half believed her capable of soaring away over the treetops, after all.

"I guess I didn't murder you—from the chase you gave me. Did I hit you at all?"

"Yes, you did! You nearly broke my arm—and you might have killed me, you big brute! Look what you did—and I never harmed you at all!" She pushed up a sleeve, and held out her arm accusingly in the moonlight, disclosing a tiny, red furrow where the skin was broken and still bleeding. "And you shot a big hole right through Aunt Phoebe's sheet!" she added, with tearful severity.

He caught her arm, bent his head over it—and for a moment he was perilously near to kissing it; an impulse which astonished him considerably, and angered him more. He dropped the arm rather precipitately; and she lifted it again, and regarded the wound with mournful interest.

"I'd like to know what right you have to prowl around shooting at people," she scolded, seeing how close she could come to touching the place with her fingertips without producing any but a pleasurable pain.

"Just as much right as you have to get up in the middle of the night and go ahowling all over the ranch wrapped up in a sheet," he retorted ungallantly.

"Well, if I want to do it, I don't see why you need concern yourself about it. I wasn't doing it for your benefit, anyway."

"Will you tell me what you DID do it for? Of all the silly tomfoolery—"

An impish smile quite obliterated the Christmas-angel look for an instant, then vanished, and left her a pretty, abused maiden who is grieved at harsh treatment.

"Well, I wanted to scare Gene," she confessed. "I did, too. I just know he's a cowardy-cat, because he's always trying to scare ME. It's Gene's fault—he told me the grove is haunted. He said a long time ago, before Uncle Hart settled here, a lot of Indians waylaid a wagon-train here and killed a girl, and he says that when the moon is just past the full, something white walks through the grove and wails like a lost soul in torment. He says sometimes it comes and moans at the corner of the house where my room is. I just know he was going to do it himself; but I guess he forgot. So I thought I'd see if he believed his own yarns. I was going to do it every night till I scared him into sleeping in the house. I had a perfectly lovely place to disappear into, where he couldn't trace me if he took to hunting around—only he wouldn't dare." She pulled down her sleeve very carefully, and then, just as carefully, she pushed it up again, and took another look.

"My best friend TOLD me I'd get shot if I came to Idaho," she reminded herself, with a melancholy satisfaction.

"You didn't get shot," Grant contradicted for the sake of drawing more sparks of temper where temper seemed quaintly out of place, and stared hard at her drooping profile. "You just got nicely missed; a bullet that only scrapes off a little skin can't be said to hit. I'd hate to hit a bear like that."

"I believe you're wishing you HAD killed me! You might at least have some conscience in the matter, and be sorry you shot a lady. But you're not. You just wish you had murdered me. You hate girls—you said so. And I don't know what business it is of yours, if I want to play a joke on my cousin, or why you had to be sleeping outside, anyway. I've a perfect right to be a ghost if I choose—and I don't call it nice, or polite, or gentlemanly for you to chase me all over the place with a gun, trying to kill me! I'll never speak to you again as long as I live. When I say that I mean it. I never liked you from the very start, when I first saw you this afternoon. Now I hate and despise you. I suppose I oughtn't to expect you to apologize or be sorry because you almost killed me. I suppose that's just your real nature coming to the surface. Indians love to hurt and torture people! I shouldn't have expected anything else of you, I suppose. I made the mistake of treating you like a white man."

"Don't you think you're making another mistake right now?" Grant's whole attitude changed, as well as his tone. "Aren't you afraid to push the white man down into the dirt, and raise up—the INDIAN?"

She cast a swift, half-frightened glance up into his face and the eyes that glowed ominously in the moonlight.

"When people make the blunder of calling up the Indian," he went on steadily, "they usually find that they have to deal with—the Indian."

Evadna looked at him again, and turned slowly white before her temper surged to the surface again.

"I didn't call up the Indian," she defended hotly; "but if the Indian wants to deal with me according to his nature—why, let him! But you don't ACT like other people! I don't know another man who wouldn't have been horrified at shooting me, even such a tiny little bit; but you don't care at all. You never even said you were sorry."

"I'm not in the habit of saying all I think and feel."

"You were quick enough to apologize, after supper there, when you hadn't really done anything; and now, when one would expect you to be at least decently sorry, you—you—well, you act like the savage you are! There, now! It may not be nice to say it, but it's the truth."

Grant smiled bitterly. "All men are savages under the skin," he said. "How do YOU know what I think and feel? If I fail to come through with the conventional patter, I am called an Indian—because my mother was a half-breed." He threw up his head proudly, let his eyes rest for a moment upon the moon, swimming through white river of clouds just over the tall poplar hedge planted long ago to shelter the orchard from the sweeping west winds; and, when he looked down at her again, he caught a glimpse of repentant tears in her eyes, and softened.

"Oh, you're a girl, and you demand the usual amount of poor-pussy talk," he told her maliciously. "So I'm sorry. I'm heartbroken. If it will help any, I'll even kiss the hurt to make it well—and I'm not a kissing young man, either, let me tell you."

"I'd die before I'd let you touch me!" Her repentance, if it was that, changed to pure rage. She snatched the torn sheet from him and turned abruptly toward the fence. He followed her, apparently unmoved by her attitude; placed his foot upon the lower wire and pressed it into the soft earth, lifted the one next above it as high as it would go, and thus made it easier for her to pass through. She seemed to hesitate for a moment, as though tempted to reject even that slight favor, then stooped, and went through.

As the wires snapped into place, she halted and looked back at him.

"Maybe I've been mean—but you're been meaner," she summed up, in self-justification. "I suppose the next thing you will do will be to tell the boys. Well, I don't care what you do, so long as you never speak to me again. Go and tell them if you want to—tell. TELL, do you hear ? I don't want even the favor of your silence!" She dexterously tucked the bundle of white under the uninjured arm, caught the loose folds of her skirt up in her hands, and ran away up the path, not once stopping to see whether he still followed her.

Grant did not follow. He stood leaning against the fence-post, and watched her until her flying form grew indistinct in the shade of the poplar hedge; watched it reappear in a broad strip

B. M. Bower

of white moonlight, still running; saw it turn, slacken speed to a walk, and then lose itself in the darkness of the grove.

Five minutes, ten minutes, he stood there, staring across the level bit of valley lying quiet at the foot of the jagged-rimmed bluff standing boldly up against the star-flecked sky. Then he shook himself impatiently, muttered something which had to do with a "doddering fool," and retraced his steps quickly through tho orchard, the currant bushes, and the strawberry patch, jumped the ditch, and so entered the grove and returned to his blankets.

"We thought the spook had got yuh, sure." Gene lifted his head turtlewise and laughed deprecatingly. "We was just about ready to start out after the corpse, only we didn't know but what you might get excited and take a shot at us in the dark. We heard yuh shoot—what was it? Did you find out?"

"It wasn't anything," said Grant shortly, tugging at a boot.

"Ah—there was, too! What was it you shot at?" Clark joined in the argument from the blackness under the locust tree.

"The moon," Grant told him sullenly. "There wasn't anything else that I could see."

"And that's a lie," Gene amended, with the frankness of a foster-brother. "Something yelled like—"

"You never heard a screech-owl before, did you, Gene?" Grant crept between his blankets and snuggled down, as if his mind held nothing more important than sleep.

"Screech-owl my granny! You bumped into something you couldn't handle—if you want to know what *I* think about it," Clark guessed shrewdly. "I wish now I'd taken the trouble to hunt the thing down; it didn't seem worth while getting up. But I leave it to Gene if you ain't mad enough to murder whatever it was. What was it?"

He waited a moment without getting a reply.

"Well, keep your teeth shut down on it, then, darn yuh!" he growled. "That's the Injun of it—I know YOU! Screech-owl—huh! You said when you left it was an Indian—and that's why we didn't take after it ourselves. We don't want to get the whole bunch down on us like they are on you—and if there was one acting up around here, we knew blamed well it was on your account for what happened to-day. I guess you found out, all right. I knew the minute you heaved in sight that you was just about as mad as you can get—and that's saying a whole lot. If it WAS an Indian, and you killed him, you better let us—"

"Oh, for the lord's sake, WILL YOU SHUT UP!" Grant raised to an elbow, glared a moment, and lay down again.

The result proved the sort of fellow he was. Clark shut up without even trailing off into mumbling to himself, as was his habit when argument brought him defeat.

CHAPTER VII

MISS GEORGIE HOWARD, OPERATOR

"Where is the delightful Mr. Good Indian off to?" Evadna stopped drumming upon the gatepost and turned toward the person she heard coming up behind her, who happened to be Gene. He stopped to light a match upon the gate and put his cigarette to work before he answered her; and Evadna touched tentatively the wide, blue ribbon wound round her arm and tied in a bow at her elbow, and eyed him guardedly.

"Straight up, he told me," Gene answered sourly. "He's sore over something that happened last night, and he didn't seem to have any talk to give away this morning. He can go to the dickens, for all I care."

"WHAT—happened last night?" Evadna wore her Christmas-angel expression; and her tone was the sweet, insipid tone of childlike innocence.

Gene hesitated. It seemed a sheer waste of opportunity to tell her the truth when she would believe a falsehood just as readily; but, since the truth happened to be quite as improbable as a lie, he decided to speak it.

"There was a noise when the moon had just come up—didn't you hear it? The ghost I told you about. Good Injun went after it with a gun, and I guess they mixed, all right, and he got the worst of it. He was sure on the fight when he came back, and he's pulled out this morning—"

"Do you mean to tell me—did you see it, really?"

"Well, you ask Clark, when you see him," Gene hinted darkly.
"You just ask him what was in the grove last night. Ask him
what he HEARD." He moved closer, and laid his hand
impressively upon her arm. Evadna winced perceptibly. "What
yuh jumping for? You didn't see anything, did you?"

"No; but—was there REALLY something?" Evadna freed
herself as unobtrusively as possible, and looked at him with
wide eyes.

"You ask Clark. He'll tell you—maybe. Good Injun's scared
clean off the ranch—you can see that for yourself. He said he
couldn't be hired to spend another night here. He thinks it's a
bad sign. That's the Injun of it. They believe in spirits and
signs and things."

Evadna turned thoughtful. "And didn't he tell you what he—
that is, if he found out—you said he went after it—"

"He wouldn't say a blamed thing about it," Gene complained
sincerely. "He said there wasn't anything—he told us it was a
screech-owl."

"Oh!" Evadna gave a sigh of relief. "Well, I'm going to ask
Clark what it was—I'm just crazy about ghost stories, only I
never would DARE leave the house after dark if there are
funny noises and things, really. I think you boys must be the
bravest fellows, to sleep out there—without even your mother
with you!"

She smiled the credulous smile of ignorant innocence and
pulled the gate open.

"Jack promised to take me up to Hartley to-day," she
explained over her shoulder. "When I come back, you'll show

me just where it was, won't you, Gene? You don't suppose it would walk in the grove in the daytime, do you? Because I'm awfully fond of the grove, and I do hope it will be polite enough to confine its perambulations entirely to the conventional midnight hour."

Gene did not make any reply. Indeed, he seemed wholly absorbed in staring after her and wondering just how much or how little of it she meant.

Evadna looked back, midway between the gate and the stable, and, when she saw him standing exactly as she had left him, she waved her hand and smiled. She was still smiling when she came up to where Jack was giving those last, tentative twitches and pats which prove whether a saddle is properly set and cinched; and she would not say what it was that amused her. All the way up the grade, she smiled and grew thoughtful by turns; and, when Jack mentioned the fact that Good Indian had gone off mad about something, she contented herself with the simple, unqualified statement that she was glad of it.

Grant's horse dozed before the store, and Grant himself sat upon a bench in the narrow strip of shade on the porch. Evadna, therefore, refused absolutely to dismount there, though her errand had been a post-office money order. Jack was already on the ground when she made known her decision; and she left him in the middle of his expostulations and rode on to the depot. He followed disapprovingly afoot; and, when she brought her horse to a stand, he helped her from the saddle, and took the bridle reins with an air of weary tolerance.

"When you get ready to go home, you can come to the store," he said bluntly. "Huckleberry wouldn't stand here if you hog-tied him. Just remember that if you ever ride up here alone—it might save you a walk back. And say," he added, with a return of his good-natured grin, "it looks like you and Good Injun didn't get acquainted yesterday. I thought I saw mum give him an introduction to you—but I guess I made a mistake. When you come to the store, don't let me forget, and I'll do it myself."

"Oh, thank you, Jack—but it isn't necessary," chirped Evadna, and left him with the smile which he had come to regard with vague suspicion of what it might hide of her real feelings.

Two squaws sat cross-legged on the ground in the shade of the little red depot; and them she passed by hastily, her eyes upon them watchfully until she was well upon the platform and was being greeted joyfully by Miss Georgie Howard, then in one of her daily periods of intense boredom.

"My, my, but you're an angel of deliverance—and by rights you should have a pair of gauze wings, just to complete the picture," she cried, leading her inside and pushing her into a beribboned wicker rocker. "I was just getting desperate enough to haul in those squaws out there and see if I couldn't teach 'em whist or something." She sat down and fingered her pompadour absently. "And that sure would have been interesting," she added musingly.

"Don't let me interrupt you," Evadna began primly. "I only came for a money order—Aunt Phoebe's sending for—"

"Never mind what you came for," Miss Georgie cut in decisively, and laughed. "The express agent is out. You can't get your order till we've had a good talk and got each other tagged mentally—only I've tagged you long ago."

"I thought you were the express agent. Aunt Phoebe said—"

"Nice, truthful Aunt Phoebe! I am, but I'm out—officially. I'm several things, my dear; but, for the sake of my own dignity and self-respect, I refuse to be more than one of them at a time. When I sell a ticket to Shoshone, I'm the ticket agent, and nothing else. Telegrams, I'm the operator. At certain times I'm the express agent. I admit it. But this isn't one of the times."

She stopped and regarded her visitor with whimsical appraisement. "You'll wait till the agent returns, won't you?" And added, with a grimace: "You won't be in the way—I'm not anything official right now. I'm a neighbor, and this is my parlor—you see, I planted you on that rug, with the books at your elbow, and that geranium also; and you're in the rocker, so you're really and truly in my parlor. I'm over the line myself, and you're calling on me. Sabe? That little desk by the safe is the express office, and you can see for yourself that the agent is out."

"Well, upon my word!" Evadna permitted herself that much emotional relief. Then she leaned her head against the cherry-colored head-rest tied to the chair with huge, cherry-colored bows, and took a deliberate survey of the room.

It was a small room, as rooms go. One corner was evidently the telegraph office, for it held a crude table, with the instruments clicking spasmodically, form pads, letter files, and mysterious things which piqued her curiosity. Over it was a railroad map and a makeshift bulletin board, which seemed to give the time of certain trains. And small-paned windows gave one sitting before tho instruments an unobstructed view up and down the track. In the corner behind the door was a small safe, with door ajar, and a desk quite as small, with, "Express Office: Hours, 8 A.M. to 6 P.M." on a card above it.

Under a small window opening upon the platform was another little table, with indications of occasional ticket-selling upon it. And in the end of the room where she sat were various little adornments—"art" calendars, a few books, fewer potted plants, a sewing-basket, and two rugs upon the floor, with a rocker for each. Also there was a tiny, square table, with a pack of cards scattered over it.

"Exactly. You have it sized up correctly, my dear." Miss Georgie Howard nodded her—head three times, and her eyes were mirthful." It's a game. I made it a game. I had to, in self-defense. Otherwise—" She waved a hand conspicuous for its white plumpness and its fingers tapering beautifully to little, pink nails immaculately kept. "I took at the job and the place just as it stands, without anything in the way of mitigation. Can you see yourself holding it down for longer than a week? I've been here a month."

"I think," Evadna ventured, "it must be fun."

"Oh, yes. It's fun—if you make fun OF it. However, before we settle down for a real visit, I've a certain duty to perform, if you will excuse my absence for a moment. Incidentally," she added, getting lazily out of the chair, "it will illustrate just how I manage my system."

Her absence was purely theoretical. She stepped off the rug, went to the "express office," and took a card from the desk. When she had stood it upright behind the inkwell, Evadna read in large, irregular capitals:

"OUT. WILL BE BACK LATER."

Miss Georgie Howard paid no attention to the little giggle which went with the reading, but stepped across to the ticket desk and to the telegraph table, and put similar cards on display. Then she came back to the rug, plumped down in her rocker with a sigh of relief, and reached for a large, white box—the five pounds of chocolates which she had sent for.

"I never eat candy when I'm in the office," she observed soberly. "I consider it unprofessional. Help yourself as liberally as your digestion will stand—and for Heaven's sake, gossip a little! Tell me all about that bunch of nifty lads I see cavorting around the store occasionally—and especially about the polysyllabic gentleman who seems to hang out at the Peaceful Hart ranch. I'm terribly taken with him. He—excuse me, chicken. There's a fellow down the line hollering his head off. Wait till I see what he wants."

Again she left the rug, stepped to the telegraph instrument, and fingered the key daintily until she had, with the other hand, turned down the "out" card. Then she threw the switch, rattled an impatient reply, and waited, listening to the rapid clicking of the sounder. Her eyes and her mouth hardened as she read.

"Cad!" she gritted under her breath. Her fingers were spiteful as they clicked the key in answer. She slammed the current off, set up the "out" notice again, kicked the desk chair against the wall, and came back to the "parlor" breathing quickly.

"I think it must be perfectly fascinating to talk that way to persons miles off," said Evadna, eying the chittering sounder with something approaching awe. "I watched your fingers, and tried to imagine what it was they were saying—but I couldn't even guess."

Miss Georgie Howard laughed queerly. "No, I don't suppose you could," she murmured, and added, with a swift glance at the other: "They said, 'You go to the devil.'" She held up the offending hand and regarded it intently. "You wouldn't think it of them, would you? But they have to say things sometimes—in self-defense. There are two or three fresh young men along the line that can't seem to take a hint unless you knock them in the head with it."

She cast a malevolent look at the clicking instrument. "He's trying to square himself," she observed carelessly. "But, unfortunately, I'm out. He seems on the verge of tears, poor thing."

She poked investigatingly among the chocolates, and finally selected a delectable morsel with epicurean care.

"You haven't told me about the polysyllabic young man," she reminded. "He has held my heart in bondage since he said to Pete Hamilton yesterday in the store—ah—" She leaned and barely reached a slip of paper which was lying upon a row of books. "I wrote it down so I wouldn't forget it," she explained parenthetically. "He said to Pete, in the store, just after Pete had tried to say something funny with the usual lamentable failure—um—'You are mentally incapable of recognizing the line of demarcation between legitimate persiflage and objectionable familiarity.' Now, I want to know what sort of a man, under fifty and not a college professor, would—or could—say that without studying it first. It sounded awfully impromptu and easy—and yet he looks—well, cowboyish. What sort of a young man is he?"

"He's a perfectly horrid young man." Evadna leaned to help herself to more chocolates. "He—well, just to show you how horrid, he calls me a—a Christmas angel! And—"

"Did he!" Miss Georgie eyed her measuringly between bites. "Tag him as being intelligent, a keen observer, with the ability to express himself—" She broke off, and turned her head ungraciously toward the sounder, which seemed to be repeating something over and over with a good deal of insistence. "That's Shoshone calling," she said, frowning attentively. "They've got an old crank up there in the office—I'd know his touch among a million—and when he calls he means business. I'll have to speak up, I suppose." She sighed, tucked a chocolate into her cheek, and went scowling to the table. "Can't the idiot see I'm out?" she complained whimsically. "What's that card for, I wonder?"

She threw the switch, rattled a reply, and then, as the sounder settled down to a steady click-clickety-click-click, she drew a pad toward her, pulled up the chair with her foot, sat down, and began to write the message as it came chattering over the wire. When it was finished and the sounder quiet, her hand awoke to life upon the key. She seemed to be repeating the message, word for word. When she was done, she listened, got her answer, threw off the switch with a sweep of her thumb, and fumbled among the papers on the table until she found an envelope. She addressed it with a hasty scrawl of her pencil, sealed it with a vicious little spat of her hand, and then sat looking down upon it thoughtfully.

B. M. Bower

"I suppose I've got to deliver that immediately, at once, without delay," she said. "There's supposed to be an answer. Chicken, some queer things happen in this business. Here's that weak-eyed, hollow-chested Saunders, that seems to have just life enough to put in about ten hours a day reading 'The Duchess,' getting cipher messages like the hero of a detective story. And sending them, too, by the way. We operators are not supposed to think; but all the same—" She got her receipt-book, filled rapidly a blank line, tucked it under her arm, and went up and tapped Evadna lightly upon the head with the envelope. "Want to come along? Or would you rather stay here? I won't be more than two minutes."

She was gone five; and she returned with a preoccupied air which lasted until she had disposed of three chocolates and was carefully choosing a fourth.

"Chicken," she said then, quietly, "do you know anything about your uncle and his affairs?" And added immediately: "The chances are ten to one you don't, and wouldn't if you lived there till you were gray?"

"I know he's perfectly lovely," Evadna asserted warmly. "And so is Aunt Phoebe."

"To be sure." Miss Georgie smiled indulgently. "I quite agree with you. And by the way, I met that polysyllabic cowboy again—and I discovered that, on the whole, my estimate was incorrect. He's emphatically monosyllabic. I said sixteen nice things to him while I was waiting for Pete to wake up Saunders; and he answered in words of one syllable; one word, of one syllable. I'm beginning to feel that I've simply got to know that young man. There are deeps there which I am wild to explore. I never met any male human in the least like him. Did you? So absolutely—ah—inscrutable, let us say."

"That's just because he's part Indian," Evadna declared, with the positiveness of youth and inexperience. "It isn't inscrutability, but stupidity. I simply can't bear him. He's brutal, and rude. He told me—told me, mind you—that he doesn't like women. He actually warned me against thinking his politeness—if he ever is polite, which I doubt—means more than just common humanity. He said he didn't want me to misunderstand him and think he liked me, because he doesn't. He's a perfect savage. I simply loathe him!"

"I'd certainly see that he repented, apologized, and vowed eternal devotion," smiled Miss Georgie. "That should be my revenge."

"I don't want any revenge. I simply want nothing to do with him. I don't want to speak to him, even."

"He's awfully good—looking," mused Miss Georgie.

"He looks to me just like an Indian. He ought to wear a blanket, like the rest."

"Then you're no judge. His eyes are dark; but they aren't snaky, my dear. His hair is real wavy, did you notice? And he has the dearest, firm mouth. I noticed it particularly, because I admire a man who's a man. He's one. He'd fight and never give up, once he started. And I think"—she spoke hesitatingly —"I think he'd love—and never give up; unless the loved one disappointed him in some way; and then he'd be strong enough to go his way and not whine about it. I do hate a whiner! Don't you?"

A shadow fell upon the platform outside the door, and Saunders appeared, sidling deprecatingly into the room. He pulled off his black, slouched hat and tucked it under his arm, smoothed his lank, black hair, ran his palm down over his lank, unshaven face with a smoothing gesture, and sidled over to the telegraph table.

"Here's the answer to that message," he said, in a limp tone, without any especial emphasis or inflection. "If you ain't too busy, and could send it right off—it's to go C.O.D. and make 'em repeat it, so as to be sure—"

"Certainly, Mr. Saunders." Miss Georgie rose, the crisp, businesslike operator, and went to the table. She took the sheet of paper from him with her finger tips, as if he were some repulsive creature whose touch would send her shuddering, and glanced at the message. "Write it on the regular form," she said, and pushed a pad and pencil toward him. " I have to place it on file." Whereupon she turned her back upon him, and stood staring down the railroad track through the smoke-grimed window until a movement warned her that he was through.

"Very well—that is all," she said, after she had counted the words twice. "Oh—you want to wait for the repeat."

She laid her fingers on the key and sent the message in a whirl of chittering little sounds, waited a moment while the sounder spoke, paused, and then began a rapid clicking, which was the repeated message, and wrote it down upon its form.

"There—if it's correct, that's all," she told him in a tone of dismissal, and waited openly for him to go. Which he did, after a sly glance at Evadna, a licking of pale lips, as if he would speak but lacked the courage, and a leering grin at Miss Georgie.

He was no sooner over the threshold than she slammed the door shut, in spite of the heat. She walked to the window, glanced down the track again, turned to the table, and restlessly arranged the form pads, sticking the message upon the file. She said something under her breath, snapped the cover on the inkwell, sighed, patted her pompadour, and finally laughed at her own uneasiness.

"Whenever that man comes in here," she observed impatiently, "I always feel as if I ought to clean house after him. If ever there was a human toad—or snake, or—ugh! And what does he mean—sending twenty-word messages that don't make sense when you read them over, and getting others that are just a lot of words jumbled together, hit or miss? I wish—only it's unprofessional to talk about it—but, just the same, there's some nasty business brewing, and I know it. I feel guilty, almost, every time I send one of those cipher messages."

"Maybe he's a detective," Evadna hazarded.

"Maybe." Miss Georgie's tone, however, was extremely skeptical. "Only, so far as I can discover, there's never been anything around here to detect. Nobody has been murdered, or robbed, or kidnapped that I ever heard of. Pete Hamilton says not. And—I wonder, now, if Saunders could be watching somebody! Wouldn't it be funny, if old Pete himself turned out to be a Jesse James brand of criminal? Can you imagine Pete doing anything more brutal than lick a postage stamp?"

"He might want to," Evadna guessed shrewdly, "but it would be too much trouble."

"Besides," Miss Georgie went on speculating, "Saunders never does anything that anyone ever heard of. Sweeps out the store, they say—but I'd hate to swear to that. *I* never could catch it when it looked swept—and brings the mail sack over here twice a day, and gets one to take back. And reads novels. Of course, the man's half dead with consumption; but no one would object to that, if these queer wires hadn't commenced coming to him."

"Why don't you turn detective yourself and find out?" Plainly, Evadna was secretly laughing at her perturbed interest in the matter.

"Thanks. I'm too many things already, and I haven't any false hair or dark lantern. And, by the way, I'm going to have the day off, Sunday. Charlie Green is coming up to relieve me. And—couldn't we do something?" She glanced wearily around the little office. "Honest, I'd go crazy if I stayed here much longer without a play spell. I want to get clear out, away from the thing—where I can't even hear a train whistle."

"Then you shall come down to the ranch the minute you can get away, and we'll do something or go somewhere. The boys said they'd take me fishing—but they only propose things so they can play jokes on me, it seems to me. They'd make me fall in the river, or something, I just know. But if you'd like to go along, there'd be two of us—"

"Chicken, we'll go. I ought to be ashamed to fish for an invitation the way I did, but I'm not. I haven't been down to the Hart ranch yet; and I've heard enough about it to drive me crazy with the desire to see it. Your Aunt Phoebe I've met, and fallen in love with—that's a matter of course. She told me to visit her just any time, without waiting to be invited especially. Isn't she the dearest thing? Oh! that's a train order, I suppose—sixteen is about due. Excuse me, chicken."

She was busy then until the train came screeching down upon the station, paused there while the conductor rushed in, got a thin slip of paper for himself and the engineer, and rushed out again. When the train grumbled away from the platform and went its way, it left man standing there, a fish-basket slung from one shoulder, a trout rod carefully wrapped in its case in his hand, a box which looked suspiciously like a case of some bottled joy at his feet, and a loose-lipped smile upon his face.

"Howdy, Miss Georgie?" he called unctuously through the open door.

Miss Georgie barely glanced at him from under her lashes, and her shoulders indulged themselves in an almost imperceptible twitch.

"How do you do, Mr. Baumberger?" she responded coolly, and very, very gently pushed the door shut just as he had made up his mind to enter.

CHAPTER VIII

THE AMIABLE ANGLER

Baumberger—Johannes was the name he answered to when any of his family called, though to the rest of the world he was simply Baumberger—was what he himself called a true sport. Women, he maintained, were very much like trout; and so, when this particular woman calmly turned her back upon the smile cast at her, he did not linger there angling uselessly, but betook himself to the store, where his worldly position, rather than his charming personality, might be counted upon to bring him his meed of appreciation.

Good Indian and Jack, sitting side by side upon the porch and saying very little, he passed by with a careless nod, as being not worth his attention. Saunders, glancing up from the absorbing last chapter of "The Brokenhearted Bride," also received a nod, and returned it apathetically. Pete Hamilton, however, got a flabby handshake, a wheezy laugh, and the announcement that he was down from Shoshone for a good, gamy tussle with that four-pounder he had lost last time.

"And I don't go back till I get him—not if I stay here a week," he declared, with jocular savagery. "Took half my leader and my pet fly—I got him with a peacock-bodied gray hackle that I revised to suit my own notions—and, by the great immortal Jehosaphat, he looked like a whale when he jumped up clear of tho riffle, turned over, and—" His flabby, white hand made a soaring movement to indicate the manner in which the

B. M. Bower

four-pounder had vanished.

"Better take a day off and go with me, Pete," he suggested, getting an unwieldy-looking pipe from the pocket of his canvas fishing-coat, and opening his eyes at a trout-fly snagged in the mouthpiece. "Now, how did that fly come there?" he asked aggrievedly, while he released it daintily for all his fingers looked so fat and awkward. He stuck the pipe in the corner of his mouth, and held up the fly with that interest which seems fatuous to one who has no sporting blood in his veins.

"Last time I used that fly was when I was down here three weeks ago—the day I lost the big one. Ain't it a beauty, eh? Tied it myself. And, by the great immortal Jehosaphat, it fetches me the rainbows, too. Good mind to try it on the big one. Don't see how I didn't miss it out of my book—I must be getting absent-minded. Sign of old age, that. Failing powers and the like." He shook his head reprovingly and grinned, as if he considered the idea something of a joke. "Have to buck up—a lawyer can't afford to grow absent-minded. He's liable to wake up some day and find himself without his practice."

He got his fly-book from the basket swinging at his left hip, opened it, turned the leaves with the caressing touch one gives to a cherished thing, and very carefully placed the fly upon the page where it belonged; gazed gloatingly down at the tiny, tufted hooks, with their frail-looking five inches of gut leader, and then returned the book fondly to the basket.

"Think I'll go on down to the Harts'," he said, "so as to be that much closer to the stream. Daylight is going to find me whipping the riffles, Peter. You won't come along? You better. Plenty of—ah—snake medicine," he hinted, chuckling so that the whole, deep chest of him vibrated. "No? Well, you can let me have a horse, I suppose—that cow-backed sorrel will do— he's gentle, I know. I think I'll go out and beg an invitation from that Hart boy—never can remember those kids by name—Gene, is it, or Jack?"

He went out upon the porch, laid a hand upon Jack's shoulder, and beamed down upon him with what would have passed easily for real affection while he announced that he was going to beg supper and a bed at the ranch, and wanted to know, as a solicitous after-thought, if Jack's mother had company, or anything that would make his presence a burden.

"Nobody's there—and, if there was, it wouldn't matter," Jack assured him carelessly. "Go on down, if you want to. It'll be all right with mother."

"One thing I like about fishing down here," chuckled Baumberger, his fat fingers still resting lightly upon Jack's shoulder, "is the pleasure of eating my fish at your house. There ain't another man, woman, or child in all Idaho can fry trout like your mother. You needn't tell her I said so—but it's a fact, just the same. She sure is a genius with the frying-pan, my boy."

He turned and called in to Pete, to know if he might have the sorrel saddled right away. Since Pete looked upon Baumberger with something of the awed admiration which he would bestow upon the President, he felt convinced that his horses were to be congratulated that any one of them found favor in his eyes.

Pete, therefore, came as near to roaring at Saunders as his good nature and his laziness would permit, and waited in the doorway until Saunders had, with visible reluctance, laid down his book and started toward the stable.

"Needn't bother to bring the horse down here, my man," Baumberger called after him. "I'll get him at the stable and start from there. Well, wish me luck, Pete—and say! I'll expect you to make a day of it with me Sunday. No excuses, now. I'm going to stay over that long, anyhow. Promised myself three good days—maybe more. A man's got to break away from his work once in a while. If I didn't, life wouldn't be worth living. I'm willing to grind—but I've got to have my playtime, too.

B. M. Bower

Say, I want you to try this rod of mine Sunday. You'll want one like it yourself, if I'm any good at guessing. Just got it, you know—it's the one I was talking to yuh about last time I was down.

"W-ell—I reckon my means of conveyance is ready for me—so long, Peter, till Sunday. See you at supper, boys."

He hooked a thumb under the shoulder-strap of his basket, pulled it to a more comfortable position, waved his hand in a farewell, which included every living thing within sight of him, and went away up the narrow, winding trail through the sagebrush to the stable, humming something under his breath with the same impulse of satisfaction with life which sets a cat purring.

Some time later, he appeared, in the same jovial mood, at the Hart ranch, and found there the welcome which he had counted upon—the welcome which all men received there upon demand.

When Evadna and Jack rode up, they found Mr. Baumberger taking his ease in Peaceful's armchair on the porch, discussing, with animated gravity, the ins and outs of county politics; his fishing-basket lying on its flat side close to his chair, his rod leaning against the house at his elbow, his heavy pipe dragging down one corner of his loose-lipped mouth; his whole gross person surrounded by an atmosphere of prosperity leading the simple life transiently and by choice, and of lazy enjoyment in his own physical and mental well-being.

CHAPTER IX

PEPPAJEE JIM "HEAP SABES"

Peppajee Jim had meditated long in the shade of his wikiup, and now, when the sun changed from a glaring ball of intense, yellow heat to a sullen red disk hanging low over the bluffs of Snake River, he rose, carefully knocked the ashes from his little stone pipe, with one mechanical movement of his arms, gathered his blanket around him, pushed a too-familiar dog from him with a shove of moccasined foot, and stalked away through the sagebrush.

On the brow of the hill, just where the faint footpath dipped into a narrow gully at the very edge, almost, of the bluff, he stopped, and lifted his head for an unconsciously haughty stare at his surroundings.

Beneath him and half a mile or so up the river valley, the mellow green of Peaceful's orchard was already taking to itself the vagueness of evening shadows. Nearer, the meadow of alfalfa and clover lay like a soft, green carpet of velvet, lined here and there with the irrigation ditches which kept it so. And in the center of the meadow, a small inclosure marked grimly the spot where lay the bones of old John Imsen. All around the man-made oasis of orchards and meadows, the sage and the sand, pushed from the river by the jumble of placer pits, emphasized by sharp contrast what man may do with the most unpromising parts of the earth's surface, once he sets himself heart and muscle to the task.

B. M. Bower

With the deliberation of his race, Peppajee stood long minutes motionless, gazing into the valley before ho turned with a true Indian shrug and went down into the gully, up the steep slope beyond, and then, after picking his way through a jumble of great bowlders, came out eventually into the dust-ridden trail of the white man. Down that he walked, erect, swift, purposeful, his moccasins falling always with the precision of a wild animal upon the best footing among the loose rocks, stubs of sage-roots, or patches of deep dust and sand beside the wagon-road, his sharp, high-featured face set in the stony calm which may hide a tumult of elemental passions beneath and give no sign.

Where the trail curved out sharply to round the Point o' Rocks, he left it, and kept straight on through the sage, entered a rough pass through the huge rock tongue, and came out presently to the trail again, a scant two hundred yards from the Hart haystacks. When he reached the stable, he stopped and looked warily about him, but there was no sight or sound of any there save animals, and he went on silently to the house, his shadow stretching long upon the ground before him until it merged into the shade of the grove beyond the gate, and so was lost for that day.

"Hello, Peppajee," called Wally over his cigarette. "Just in time for supper."

Peppajee grunted, stopped in the path two paces from the porch, folded his arms inside his blanket, and stood so while his eyes traveled slowly and keenly around the group lounging at ease above him. Upon the bulky figure of Baumberger they dwelt longest, and while he looked his face hardened until nothing seemed alive but his eyes.

"Peppajee, this my friend, Mr. Baumberger. You heap sabe Baumberger—come all time from Shoshone, mebbyso catchum heap many fish." Peaceful's mild, blue eyes twinkled over his old meerschaum. He knew the ways of Indians, and more particularly he knew the ways of Peppajee; Baumberger, he guessed shrewdly, had failed to find favor in his eyes.

"Huh!" grunted Peppajee non-commitally, and made no motion to shake hands, thereby confirming Peaceful's suspicion. "Me heap sabe Man-that-catchum-fish." After which he stood as before, his arms folded tightly in his blanket, his chin lifted haughtily, his mouth a straight, stern line of bronze.

"Sit down, Peppajee. Bimeby eat supper," Peaceful invited pacifically, while Baumberger chuckled at the Indian's attitude, which he attributed to racial stupidity.

Peppajee did not even indicate that he heard or, hearing, understood.

"Bothered much with Injuns?" Baumberger asked carelessly, putting away his pipe. "I see there's quite a camp of 'em up on the hill. Hope you've got good watchdogs—they're a thieving lot. If they're a nuisance, Hart, I'll see what can be done about slapping 'em back on their reservation, where they belong. I happen to have some influence with the agent."

"I guess you needn't go to any trouble about it," Peaceful returned dryly. "I've had worse neighbors."

"Oh—if you're stuck on their company!" laughed Baumberger wheezily. "'Every fellow to his taste, as the old woman said when she kissed her cow.' There may be good ones among the lot," he conceded politely when he saw that his time-worn joke had met with disfavor, even by the boys, who could—and usually did—laugh at almost anything. "They all look alike to me, I must admit; I never had any truck with 'em."

"No, I guess not," Peaceful agreed in his slow way, holding his pipe three inches from his face while he eyed Peppajee quizzically. "Don't pay to have any truck with 'em while you feel that way about it." He smoothed down his snow-white beard with his free hand, pushed the pipe-stem between his teeth, and went on smoking.

"I never liked the breed, any way you look at 'em," Baumberger stated calmly.

"Say, you'll queer yourself good and plenty, if you keep on," Wally interrupted bluntly. "Peppajee's ears aren't plugged with cotton—are they, Jim?"

Neither Peppajee nor Baumberger made reply of any sort, and Peaceful turned his mild eyes reproachfully toward his untactful son. But the supper summons clanged insistently from the iron triangle on the back porch and saved the situation from becoming too awkward. Even Baumberger let his tilted chair down upon its four legs with a haste for which his appetite was not alone responsible, and followed the boys into the house as if he were glad to escape from the steady, uncompromising stare of the Indian.

"Better come and eat, Peppajee," Peaceful lingered upon the porch to urge hospitably. "You no get mad. You come eat supper."

"No!" Peppajee jerked the word out with unmistakable finality. "No eat. Bimeby mebbyso makum big talk yo'."

Peaceful studied his face, found it stern and unyielding, and nodded assent. "All right. I eat, then I talk with you." He turned somewhat reluctantly and followed the others inside, leaving Peppajee to pass the time away as pleased him best.

Peppajee stood still for a moment listening to the clatter of dishes from the kitchen, and then with dignity end deliberation seated himself upon the lowest step of the porch, and, pulling his blanket tight around him, resettled his disreputable old sombrero upon his head and stared fixedly at the crimson glow which filled all the west and made even the rugged bluff a wonderful thing of soft, rose tints and shadows of royal purple. Peaceful, coming out half an hour after with

Baumberger at his heels, found him so and made a movement to sit down beside him. But Peppajee rose and stalked majestically to the gate, then turned and confronted the two.

"I talk yo'. Mebbyso no talk Man-with-big-belly." He waited impassively.

"All right, Jim." Peaceful turned apologetically toward his guest. "Something he wants to tell me, Baumberger; kinda private, I guess. I'll be back in a minute, anyway."

"Now don't mind me at all," Baumberger protested generously. "Go ahead just as if I wasn't here—that's what'll please me best. I hope I ain't so much of a stranger you've got to stand on ceremony. Go on, and find out what the old buck wants; he's got something on his mind, that's sure. Been stealing fruit, maybe, and wants to square himself before you catch him at it." He laughed his laziest, and began leisurely to fill his pipe.

Peppajee led the way to the stable, where he stopped short and faced Peaceful, his arms folded, one foot thrust forward in the pose he affected when about to speak of matters important.

"Long time ago, when yo' hair black," he began deliberately, with a sonorous lingering upon his vowels, "yo' all time my frien'. I yo' frien' all same. Yo' no likum otha white man. Yo' all time bueno. Yo' house all same my wikiup. Me come eat at yo' house, talk yo' all same brotha. Yo' boys all same my boys—all time my frien'. Me speakum all time no lie, mebbyso."

"No," Peaceful assented unhesitatingly, "you no tell lies, Peppajee. We good friends, many years."

"Huh! Man-that-catchum-fish, him no yo' frien'. Shont-isham. All time him speakum lies—tellum frien' yo', no frien'. Yo' no more tellum stop yo' wikiup. Kay bueno. Yo' thinkum frien'. All time him have bad heart for yo'. Yo' got ranch. Got plenty hay, plenty apple, plenty all thing for eat. All time him think bad for yo'. All time him likum steal yo' ranch."

Peaceful laughed indulgently. "You no sabe," he explained. "Him like my ranch. Him say, long time ago, pay much money for my ranch. Me no sell—me like for keep all time. Baumberger good man. Him no steal my ranch. Me got one paper from government —you sabe?—one paper say ranch all time b'longum me all same. Big white chief say ranch b'longum me all time. I die, ranch b'longum my boys. You sabe?"

Peppajee considered. "Me sabe," he said at length. "Me sabe paper, sabe ranch all time b'longum yo'. All same, him like for ketchum yo' ranch. Me hear much talk, him talk Man-that-coughs, tellum him ketchum ranch. Much white man come, so—" He lifted one hand with thumb and fingers outspread, made a downward gesture, and then raised three fingers. "Catchum ranch."

Peaceful shook his head while he smiled. "No can do that. Mebbyso much men come, heap fight, mebbyso killum me, ranch all same b'longum my boys. Men that fights go to jail, mebbyso hangum." He indicated by signs his exact meaning.

Peppajee scowled, and shook his head stubbornly. "Me heap sabe. All same, ketchum yo' ranch. Man-that-catchum-fish kay bueno. Yo' thinkum frien', yo' damfool. Him all same rattlesnake. Plenty foolum yo'. Yo' see. Yo' thinkum Peppajee Jim heap big fool. Peaceful Hart, him all time one heap big damfool. Him ketchum yo' ranch. Yo' see." He stopped and stared hard at the dim bulk of the grove, whence came the faint odor of smoke from Baumberger's pipe.

"Yo' be smart man," he added grimly, "yo' all same kickum dat mans off yo' ranch." For emphasis he thrust out a foot vigorously in the direction of the house and the man he maligned, and turned his face toward camp. Peaceful watched until the blanketed form merged into the dusk creeping over the valley, and when it disappeared finally into the short cut through the sage, he shook his gray head in puzzlement over the absurd warning, and went back to talk politics with Baumberger.

B. M. Bower

CHAPTER X

MIDNIGHT PROWLERS

Came midnight and moonlight together, and with them came also Good Indian riding somewhat sullenly down the trail to the ranch. Sullen because of Evadna's attitude, which seemed to him permanently antagonistic, and for very slight cause, and which made the ranch an unpleasant abiding place.

He decided that he would not stop at the ranch, but would go on up the valley to where one Abuer Hicks lived by himself in a half-dugout, half-board shack, and by mining a little where his land was untillable, and farming a little where the soil took kindly to fruit and grasses, managed to exist without too great hardship. The pension he received for having killed a few of his fellow-men at the behest of his government was devoted solely to liquid relief from the monotony of his life, and welcome indeed was the man who brought him a bottle of joy between times. Wherefore Good Indian had thoughtfully provided himself with a quart or so and rode with his mind at ease so far as his welcome at the Hicks dwelling place was concerned.

Once again the Peaceful Hart ranch lay in brooding silence under the shadow of the bluff. A few crickets chirped shrilly along the trail, and from their sudden hush as he drew near marked unerringly his passing. Along the spring-fed creek the frogs croaked a tuneless medley before him, and, like the crickets, stopped abruptly and waited in absolute silence to take up their night chant again behind him. His horse stepped softly in the deep sand of the trail, and, when he found that his rider refused to let him stop at the stable-door, shook his head in mute displeasure, and went quietly on. As he neared the silent house, the faint creak of saddle-leather and the rattle of spur-chains against his iron stirrups were smothered in the whispering of the treetops in the grove, so that only the quick hushing of night noises alone betrayed him to any wakeful ear.

He was guilty of staring hard at that corner of the house where he knew Evadna slept, and of scowling over the vague disquiet which the thought of her caused him. No girl had ever troubled his mind before. It annoyed him that the face and voice of Evadna obtruded, even upon his thoughts of other things.

The grove was quiet, and he could hear Gene's unmistakable snore over by the pond—the only sound save the whispering of the trees, which went on, unmindful of his approach. It was evident, he thought, that the ghost was effectually laid—and on the heels of that, as he rode out from the deep shade of the grove and on past the garden to the meadows beyond, he wondered if, after all, it was again hardily wandering through the night; for he thought he glimpsed a figure which flitted behind a huge rock a few rods in advance of him, and his eyes were not used to playing him tricks.

He gave a twitch of his fingers upon the reins, and turned from the trail to investigate. He rode up to the rock, which stood like an island of shade in that sea of soft moonlight, and, peering into the shadows, spoke a guarded challenge:

"Who's that?"

A figure detached itself without sound from the blot of darkness there, and stood almost at his stirrup.

"Yo' Good Injun—me likum for talk yo'."

Good Indian was conscious of a distinct disappointment, though he kept it from his voice when he answered:

"Oh, it's you, Peppajee. What you do here? Why you no sleepum yo' wikiup?"

Peppajee held up a slim, brown hand for silence, and afterward rested it upon the saddle-fork.

"Yo' heap frien' Peaceful. Me heap frien' all same. Mebbyso we talk. Yo' get down. No can see yo', mebbyso; yo' no likum bad man for se—" He stepped back a pace, and let Good Indian dismount; then with a gesture he led him back into the shadow of the rock.

"Well, what's the row?" Good Indian asked impatiently, and curiously as well.

Peppajee spoke more hastily than was usual. "Me watchum Man-that-catchum-fish. Him hee-eeap kay bueno. Me no sabe why him walk, walk in night—me heap watchum."

"You mean Baumberger? He's all right. He comes down here to catchum many fish—trout, up in the Malad, you sabe. Heap friend Peaceful. You no likum?"

"Kay bueno." Peppajee rested a forefinger upon Good Indian's arm. "Sun up there," he pointed high in the west. "Me go all same Hartley. Come stable—Pete stable—me walkum close— no makum noise. Me hear talk. Stoppum—no can see—me hear much bad talk. All time me hear, heap likum for steal dis ranch. Me no sabe"—his tone was doubtful for a space—"all same, me hear stealum this ranch. Man, you callum—"

"Baumberger?" suggested Grant.

"Him. All same Baumberga, him talk Man-that-coughs. All time say stealum ranch. Makum much bad talk, them mans. Me come ranch, me tellum Peaceful, him all time laugh, me.

All time shakum head. Mebbyso thinkum I lie—shont-isham!"

"What more you do?" Good Indian, at least, did not laugh.

"Me go camp. Me thinkum, thinkum all time. Dat man have bad heart. Kay bueno. No can sleep—thinkum mebbyso do bad for Peaceful. Come ranch, stop all time dark, all time heap watchum. Bimeby, mebbyso man—all same yo' callum Baumberga—him come, look, so—" He indicated, by a great craning of neck in all directions, the wariness of one who goes by stealth. "Him walk still all time, go all time ova there." He swept his arm toward the meadows. "Me go still, for watchum. Yo' come, mebbyso make heap much noise—kay bueno. Dat mans, him hear, him heap scare. Me tellum, yo' mebbyso go still." He folded his arms with a gesture of finality, and stood statue-like in the deep gloom beside the rock.

Good Indian fingered his horse's mane while he considered the queer story. There must be something in it, he thought, to bring Peppajee from his blankets at midnight and to impel him, unfriendly as he usually seemed, to confide his worry to him at once and without urging. And yet, to steal the Peaceful Hart ranch—the idea was ludicrous. Still, there was no harm in looking around a bit. He sought a sagebrush that suited his purpose, tied his horse to it, stooped, and took tho clanking Mexican spurs from his heels, and touched Peppajee on the shoulder.

"All right," he murmured close to his ear, "we go see."

Without a word, Peppajee turned, and stole away toward the meadows, keeping always in the shadow of rock or bush, silent-footed as a prowling bobcat. Close behind him, not quite so silent because of his riding-boots, which would strike now and then upon a rock, however careful he was of his footing, went Good Indian.

So they circled the meadow, came into sand and sage beyond, sought there unavailingly, went on to the orchard, and skirted it, keen of eye and ear, struck quietly through it, and came at last to the place where, the night before, Grant had overtaken Evadna—and it surprised him not a little to feel his heart pounding unreasonably against his ribs when he stopped beside the rock where they had sat and quarreled.

Peppajee looked back to see why Grant paused there, and then, wrapping his blanket tightly around him, crawled through the fence, and went on, keeping to the broad belt of shade cast upon the ground by the row of poplars. Where the shade stopped abruptly, and beyond lay white moonlight with the ranch buildings blotching it here and there, he stopped and waited until Good Indian stood close beside him. Even then he did not speak, but, freeing an arm slowly from the blanket folds, pointed toward the stable.

Grant looked, saw nothing, stared harder, and so; feeling sure there must be something hidden there, presently believed that a bit of the shadow at that end which was next the corral wavered, stopped, and then moved unmistakably. All the front of the stable was distinctly visible in the white light, and, while they looked, something flitted across it, and disappeared among the sage beyond the trail.

Again they waited; two minutes, three minutes, five. Then another shadow detached itself slowly from the shade of the stable, hesitated, walked out boldly, and crossed the white sand on the path to the house. Baumberger it was, and he stopped midway to light his pipe, and so, puffing luxuriously, went on into the blackness of the grove.

They heard him step softly upon the porch, heard also the bovine sigh with which he settled himself in the armchair there. They caught the aromatic odor of tobacco smoke ascending, and knew that his presence there had all at once become the most innocent, the most natural thing in the world; for any man, waking on such a night, needs no justification for smoking a nocturnal pipe upon the porch while he gazes dreamily out upon the moon-bathed world around him.

Peppajee touched Grant's arm, and turned back, skirting the poplars again until they were well away from the house, and there was no possibility of being heard. He stopped there, and confronted the other.

"What for you no stoppum stable?" he questioned bluntly. "What for you no stoppum ranch, for sleepum?"

"I go for stoppum Hicks' ranch," said Good Indian, without any attempt at equivocation.

Peppajee grunted." What for yo' no stoppum all same Peaceful?"

Good Indian scorned a subterfuge, and spoke truly. "That girl, Evadna, no likum me. All time mad me. So I no stoppum ranch, no more."

Peppajee grinned briefly and understandingly, and nodded his head. "Me heap sabe. Yo' all time heap like for catchum that girl, be yo' squaw. Bimeby that girl heap likum yo'. Me sabe." He stood a moment staring at the stars peeping down from above the rim-rock which guarded the bluff. "All same, yo' no go stoppum Hicks," he commanded. "Yo' stoppum dis ranch all time. Yo' all time watchum man—yo' callum Baumberga." He seemed to remember and speak the name with some difficulty. "Where him go, yo' go, for heap watchum. All time mebbyso me watchum Man-that-coughs. Me no sabe catchum ranch—all same, me watchum. Them mans heap kay bueno. Yo' bet yo' life!"

A moment he stood there after he was through speaking, and then he was not there. Good Indian did not hear him go, though he had stood beside him; neither could he, catching sight of a wavering shadow, say positively that there went Peppajee.

He waited for a space, stole back to where he could hear any sound from the porch even if he could not see, and when he was certain that Baumberger had gone back to his bed, he got his horse, took him by a roundabout way to the stable, and himself slept in a haystack. At least, he made himself a soft place beside one, and lay there until the sun rose, and if he did not sleep it was not his fault, for he tried hard enough.

That is how Good Indian came to take his usual place at the breakfast table, and to touch elbows with Evadna and to greet her with punctilious politeness and nothing more. That is why he got out his fishing-tackle and announced that he thought he would have a try at some trout himself, and so left the ranch not much behind Baumberger. That is why he patiently whipped the Malad riffles until he came up with the portly lawyer from Shoshone, and found him gleeful over a full basket and bubbling with innocent details of this gamy one and that one still gamier. They rode home together, and together they spent the hot afternoon in the cool depths of the grove.

By sundown Good Indian was ready to call himself a fool and Peppajee Jim a meddlesome, visionary old idiot. Steal the Peaceful Hart ranch? The more he thought of it, the more ridiculous the thing seemed.

CHAPTER XI

"YOU CAN'T PLAY WITH ME"

Good Indian was young, which means that he was not always logical, nor much given to looking very far into the future except as he was personally concerned in what he might see there. By the time Sunday brought Miss Georgie Howard and the stir of preparation for the fishing trip, he forgot that he had taken upon himself the responsibility of watching the obviously harmless movements of Baumberger, or had taken seriously the warnings of Peppajee Jim; or if he did not forget, he at least pushed it far into the background of his mind with the assertion that Peppajee was a meddlesome old fool and Baumberger no more designing than he appeared—which was not at all.

What did interest him that morning was the changeful mood of Evadna; though he kept his interest so well hidden that no one suspected it—not even the young lady herself. It is possible that if Evadna had known that Good Indian's attitude of calm oblivion to her moods was only a mask, she might have continued longer her rigorous discipline of averted face and frigid tones.

As it was, she thawed toward him as he held himself more aloof, until she actually came to the point of addressing him directly, with a flicker of a smile for good measure; and, although he responded with stiff civility, he felt his blood pulse faster, and suddenly conceived the idea that women are like the creatures of the wild. If one is very quiet, and makes no advance whatever, the hunted thing comes closer and closer, and then a sudden pounce—he caught his breath. After that he was wary and watchful and full of his purpose.

Within ten minutes Evadna walked into the trap. They had started, and were fifty yards up the trail, when Phoebe shouted frantically after them. And because she was yet a timid rider and feared to keep the pace set by the others, it was Evadna who heard and turned back to see what was the trouble. Aunt Phoebe was standing beside the road, waving a flask.

"It's the cream for your coffee," she cried, going to meet Evadna. "You can slip it into your jacket-pocket, can't you, honey? Huckleberry is so steady—and you won't do any wild riding like the boys."

"I've got my veil and a box of bait and two handkerchiefs and a piece of soap," the girl complained, reaching down for the bottle, nevertheless. "But I can carry it in my hand till I overtake somebody to give it to."

The somebody proved to be Good Indian, who had found it necessary to stop and inspect carefully the left forefoot of his horse, without appearing aware of the girl's approach. She ambled up at Huckleberry's favorite shuffling gait, struck him with her whip—a blow which would not have perturbed a mosquito—when he showed a disposition to stop beside Grant, and then, when Huckleberry reluctantly resumed his pacing, pulled him up, and looked back at the figure stooped over the hoof he held upon his knee. He was digging into the caked dirt inside the hoof with his pocketknife, and, though Evadna waited while she might have spoken a dozen words, he paid not the slightest attention—and that in spite of the distinct shadow of her head and shoulders which lay at his feet.

"Oh—Grant," she began perfunctorily, "I'm sorry to trouble you—but do you happen to have an empty pocket?"

Good Indian gave a final scrape with his knife, and released the foot, which Keno immediately stamped pettishly into the dust. He closed the knife, after wiping the blade upon his trousers leg, and returned it to his pocket before he so much as glanced toward her.

"I may have. Why?" He picked up the bridle-reins, caught the saddle-horn, and thrust his toe into the stirrup. From under his hat-brim he saw that she was pinching her under lip between her teeth, and the sight raised his spirits considerably.

"Oh, nothing. Aunt Phoebe called me back, and gave me a bottle of cream, is all. I shall have to carry it in my hand, I suppose." She twitched her shoulders, and started Huckleberry off again. She had called him Grant, instead of the formal Mr. Imsen she had heretofore clung to, and he had not seemed to notice it even.

He mounted with perfectly maddening deliberation, but for all that he overtook her before she had gone farther than a few rods, and he pulled up beside her with a decision which caused Huckleberry to stop also; Huckleberry, it must be confessed, was never known to show any reluctance in that direction when his head was turned away from home. He stood perfectly still while Good Indian reached out a hand.

"I'll carry it—I'm more used to packing bottles," he announced gravely.

"Oh, but if you must carry it in your hand, I wouldn't dream of—" She was holding fast the bottle, and trying to wear her Christmas-angel look.

Good Indian laid hold of the flask, and they stood there stubbornly eying each other.

"I thought you wanted me to carry it," he said at last, pulling harder.

"I merely asked if you had an empty pocket." Evadna clung the tighter.

"Now, what's the use—"

"Just what I was thinking!" Evadna was so impolite as to interrupt him.

Good Indian was not skilled in the management of women, but he knew horses, and to his decision he added an amendment. Instinctively he followed the method taught him by experience, and when he fancied he saw in her eyes a sign of weakening, he followed up the advantage he had gained.

"Let go—because I'm going to have it anyway, now," he said quietly, and took the flask gently from her hands. Then he smiled at her for yielding, and his smile was a revelation to the girl, and brought the blood surging up to her face. She rode meekly beside him at the pace he himself set—which was not rapid, by any means. He watched her with quick, sidelong glances, and wondered whether he would dare say what he wanted to say—or at least a part of it.

She was gazing with a good deal of perseverance at the trail, down the windings of which the others could be seen now and then galloping through the dust, so that their progress was marked always by a smothering cloud of gray. Then she looked at Grant unexpectedly, met one of his sharp glances, and flushed hotly again.

"How about this business of hating each other, and not speaking except to please Aunt Phoebe?" he demanded, with a suddenness which startled himself. He had been thinking it, but he hadn't intended to say it until the words spoke themselves. "Are we supposed to keep on acting the fool indefinitely?"

"I was not aware that I, at least, was acting the fool," she retorted, with a washed-out primness.

"Oh, I can't fight the air, and I'm not going to try. What I've got to say, I prefer to say straight from the shoulder. I'm sick of this standing off and giving each other the bad eye over nothing. If we're going to stay on the same ranch, we might as well be friends. What do you say?"

For a time he thought she was not going to say anything. She was staring at the dust-cloud ahead, and chewing absently at the corner of her under lip, and she kept it up so long that Good Indian began to scowl and call himself unseemly names for making any overture whatever. But, just as he turned toward her with lips half opened for a bitter sentence, he saw a dimple appear in the cheek next to him, and held back the words.

"You told me you didn't like me," she reminded, looking at him briefly, and afterward fumbling her reins. "You can't expect a girl—"

"I suppose you don't remember coming up to me that first night, and calling me names, and telling me how you hated me, and—and winding up by pinching me?" he insinuated with hypocritical reproach, and felt of his arm. "If you could see the mark—" he hinted shamelessly.

Evadna replied by pushing up her sleeve and displaying a scratch at least an inch in length, and still roughened and red. "I suppose you don't remember trying to MURDER me?" she inquired, sweetly triumphant. "If you could shoot as well as Jack, I'd have been killed very likely. And you'd be in jail this minute," she added, with virtuous solemnity.

"But you're not killed, and I'm not in jail."

"And I haven't told a living soul about it—not even Aunt Phoebe," Evadna remarked, still painfully virtuous. "If I had—"

"She'd have wondered, maybe, what you were doing away

down there in the middle of the night," Good Indian finished. "I didn't tell a soul, either, for that matter."

They left the meadowland and the broad stretch of barren sand and sage, and followed, at a leisurely pace, the winding of the trail through the scarred desolation where the earth had been washed for gold. Evadna stared absently at the network of deep gashes, evidently meditating very seriously. Finally she turned to Grant with an honest impulse of friendliness.

"Well, I'm sure I'm willing to bury the tomahawk—er—that is, I mean—" She blushed hotly at the slip, and stammered incoherently.

"Never mind." His eyes laughed at her confusion. "I'm not as bad as all that; it doesn't hurt my feelings to have tomahawks mentioned in my presence."

Her cheeks grew redder, if that were possible, but she made no attempt to finish what she had started to say.

Good Indian rode silent, watching her unobtrusively and wishing he knew how to bring the conversation by the most undeviating path to a certain much-desired conclusion. After all, she was not a wild thing, but a human being, and he hesitated. In dealing with men, he had but one method, which was to go straight to the point regardless of consequences. So he half turned in the saddle and rode with one foot free of the stirrup that he might face her squarely.

"You say you're willing to bury the tomahawk; do you mean it?" His eyes sought hers, and when they met her glance held it in spite of her blushes, which indeed puzzled him. But she did not answer immediately, and so he repeated the question.

"Do you mean that? We've been digging into each other pretty industriously, and saying how we hate each other—but are you willing to drop it and be friends? It's for you to say—and you've got to say it now."

Evadna hung up her head at that. "Are you in the habit of laying down the law to everyone who will permit it?" she evaded.

"Am I to take it for granted you meant what you said?" He stuck stubbornly to the main issue. "Girls seem to have a way of saying things, whether they mean anything or not. Did you?"

"Did I what?" She was wide-eyed innocence again.

Good Indian muttered something profane, and kicked his horse in the ribs. When it had taken no more than two leaps forward, however, he pulled it down to a walk again, and his eyes boded ill for the misguided person who goaded him further. He glanced at the girl sharply.

"This thing has got to be settled right now, without any more fooling or beating about the bush," he said—and he said it so quietly that she could scarcely be blamed for not realizing what lay beneath. She was beginning to recover her spirits and her composure, and her whole attitude had become demurely impish.

"Settle it then, why don't you?" she taunted sweetly. "I'm sure I haven't the faintest idea what there is to settle—in that solemn manner. I only know we're a mile behind the others, and Miss Georgie will be wondering—"

"You say I'm to settle it, the way I want it settled?"

If Evadna did not intend anything serious, she certainly was a fool not to read aright his ominously calm tone and his tensely quiet manner. She must have had some experience in coquetry, but it is very likely that she had never met a man just like this one. At all events, she tilted her blonde head, smiled at him daringly, and then made a little grimace meant to signify her defiance of him and his unwarranted earnestness.

Good Indian leaned unexpectedly, caught her in his arms, and kissed her three times upon her teasing, smiling mouth, and while she was gasping for words to voice her amazement he drew back his head, and gazed sternly into her frightened eyes.

"You can't play with ME," he muttered savagely, and kissed her again. "This is how I settle it. You've made me want you for mine. It's got to be love or—hate now. There isn't anything between, for me and you." His eyes passed hungrily from her quivering lips to her eyes, and the glow within his own made her breath come faster. She struggled weakly to free herself, and his clasp only tightened jealously.

"If you had hated me, you wouldn't have stopped back there, and spoken to me," he said, the words coming in a rush. "Women like to play with love, I think. But you can't play with me. I want you. And I'm going to have you. Unless you hate me. But you don't. I'd stake my life on it." And he kissed her again.

Evadna reached up, felt for her hat, and began pulling it straight, and Good Indian, recalled to himself by the action, released her with manifest reluctance. He felt then that he ought never to let her go out of his arms; it was the only way, it seemed to him, that he could be sure of her. Evadna found words to express her thoughts, and her thoughts were as wholly conventional as was the impulse to straighten her hat.

"We've only known each other a week!" she cried tremulously, while her gloved fingers felt inquiringly for loosened hairpins. "You've no right—you're perfectly horrid! You take everything for granted—"

Good Indian laughed at her, a laugh of pure, elemental joy in life and in love.

"A man's heart does not beat by the calendar. Nature made the heart to beat with love, ages before man measured time, and prattled of hours and days and weeks," he retorted. "I'm not the same man I was a week ago. Nor an hour ago. What does it matter I am—the man I am NOW." He looked at her more calmly. "An hour ago," he pointed out, "I didn't dream I should kiss you. Nor you, that you would let me do it."

"I didn't! I couldn't help myself. You—oh, I never saw such a—a brute!" The tears in her eyes were, perhaps, tears of rage at the swiftness with which he had mastered the situation and turned it in a breath from the safe channel of petty argument. She struck Huckleberry a blow with her whip which sent that astonished animal galloping down the slope before them, his ears laid back and his white eyelashes blinking resentment against the outrage.

Good Indian laughed aloud, spurred Keno into a run, and passed her with a scurry of dust, a flash of white teeth and laughing black eyes, and a wave of his free hand in adieu. He was still laughing when he overtook the others, passed by the main group, and singled out Jack, his particular chum. He refused to explain either his hurry or his mirth further than to fling out a vague sentence about a race, and thereafter he ambled contentedly along beside Jack in the lead, and told how he had won a hundred and sixty dollars in a crap game the last time he was in Shoshone, and how he had kept on until he had "quit ten dollars in the hole." The rest of the boys, catching a few words here and there, crowded close, and left the two girls to themselves, while Good Indian recounted in detail the fluctuations of the game; how he had seesawed for an hour, winning and losing alternately; and how his luck had changed suddenly just when he had made up his mind to play a five-dollar gold piece he had in his hand and quit.

"I threw naturals three times in succession," he said, "and let my bets ride. Then I got Big Dick, made good, and threw another natural. I was seeing those Spanish spurs and that peach of a headstall in Fernando's by that time; seeing them on Keno and me—they're in the window yet, Jack, and I went in when I first hit town and looked them over and priced them; a hundred and fifty, just about what we guessed he'd hold them at. And say, those conchos—you remember the size of 'em, Jack?—they're solid silver, hammered out and engraved by hand. Those Mexicans sure do turn out some fine work on their silver fixings!" He felt in his pocket for a match.

"Pity I didn't let well enough alone," he went on. "I had the price of the outfit, and ten dollars over. But then I got hoggish. I thought I stood a good chance of making seven lucky passes straight—I did once, and I never got over it, I guess. I was going to pinch down to ten—but I didn't; I let her ride. And SHOT CRAPS!"

He drew the match along the stamped saddle-skirt behind the cantle, because that gave him a chance to steal a look behind him without being caught in the act. Good, wide hat-brims have more uses than to shield one's face from the sun. He saw that Evadna was riding in what looked like a sulky silence beside her friend, but he felt no compunction for what he had done; instead he was exhilarated as with some heady wine, and he did not want to do any thinking about it—yet. He did not even want to be near Evadna. He faced to the front, and lighted his cigarette while he listened to the sympathetic chorus from the boys.

"What did you do then?" asked Gene.

"Well, I'd lost the whole blamed chunk on a pair of measly aces," he said. "I was pretty sore by that time, I'm telling you! I was down to ten dollars, but I started right in to bring back that hundred and sixty. Funny, but I felt exactly as if somebody had stolen that headstall and spurs right out of my hand, and I just had to get it back pronto. I started in with a dollar, lost it on craps—sixes, that time—sent another one down the same trail trying to make Little Joe come again, third went on craps, fourth I doubled on nine, lost 'em both on craps—say, I never looked so many aces and sixes in the face in my life! It was sure kay bueno, the luck I had that night. I got up broke, and had to strike Riley for money to get out of town with."

So for a time he managed to avoid facing squarely this new and very important factor which must henceforth have its place in the problem of his life.

B. M. Bower

CHAPTER XII

"THEM DAMN SNAKE"

Three hundred yards up the river, in the shade of a huge bowlder, round an end of which the water hurried in a green swirl that it might the sooner lie quiet in the deep, dark pool below, Good Indian, picking his solitary way over the loose rocks, came unexpectedly upon Baumberger, his heavy pipe sagging a corner of his flabby mouth, while he painstakingly detached a fly from his leader, hooked it into the proper compartment of his fly-book, and hesitated over his selection of another to take its place. Absorption was writ deep on his gross countenance, and he recognized the intruder by the briefest of flickering glances and the slightest of nods.

"Keep back from that hole, will yuh?" he muttered, jerking his head toward the still pool. "I ain't tried it yet."

Good Indian was not particularly interested in his own fishing. The sight of Baumberger, bulking there in the shade with his sagging cheeks and sagging pipe, his flopping old hat and baggy canvas fishing-coat, with his battered basket slung over his slouching shoulder and sagging with the weight of his catch; the sloppy wrinkles of his high, rubber boots shining blackly from recent immersion in the stream, caught his errant attention, and stayed him for a few minutes to watch.

Loosely disreputable looked Lawyer Baumberger, from the snagged hole in his hat-crown where a wisp of graying hair fluttered through, to the toes of his ungainly, rubber-clad feet; loosely disreputable, but not commonplace and not incompetent. Though his speech might be a slovenly mumble, there was no purposeless fumbling of the fingers that chose a fly and knotted it fast upon the leader. There was no bungling movement of hand or foot when he laid his pipe upon the rock, tiptoed around the corner, sent a mechanical glance upward toward the swaying branches of an overhanging tree, pulled out his six feet of silk line with a sweep of his arm, and with a delicate fillip, sent the fly skittering over the glassy center of the pool.

Good Indian, looking at him, felt instinctively that a part, at least, of the man's nature was nakedly revealed to him then. It seemed scarcely fair to read the lust of him and the utter abandonment to the hazard of the game. Pitiless he looked, with clenched teeth just showing between the loose lips drawn back in a grin that was half-snarl, half-involuntary contraction of muscles sympathetically tense.

That was when a shimmering thing slithered up, snapped at the fly, and flashed away to the tune of singing reel and the dance of the swaying rod. The man grew suddenly cruel and crafty and full of lust; and Good Indian, watching him, was conscious of an inward shudder of repulsion. He had fished all his life—had Good Indian—and had found joy in the sport. And here was he inwardly condemning a sportsman who stood self-revealed, repelling, hateful; a man who gloated over the struggle of something alive and at his mercy; to whom sport meant power indulged with impunity. Good Indian did not try to put the thing in words, but he felt it nevertheless.

"Brute!" he muttered aloud, his face eloquent of cold disgust.

At that moment Baumberger drew the tired fish gently into the shallows, swung him deftly upon the rocks, and laid hold of him greedily.

"Ain't he a beaut?" he cried, in his wheezy chuckle. "Wait a minute while I weigh him. He'll go over a pound, I'll bet money on it." Gloatingly he held it in his hands, removed the hook, and inserted under the gills the larger one of the little scales he carried inside his basket.

"Pound and four ounces," he announced, and slid the fish into his basket. He was the ordinary, good-natured, gross Baumberger now. Ho reached for his pipe, placed it in his mouth, and held out a hand to Good Indian for a match.

"Say, young fella, have you got any stand-in with your noble red brothers?" he asked, after he had sucked life into the charred tobacco.

"Cousins twice or three times removed, you mean," said Good Indian coldly, too proud and too lately repelled to meet the man on friendly ground. "Why do you ask?"

Baumberger eyed him speculatively while he smoked, and chuckled to himself.

"One of 'em—never mind placing him on his own p'ticular limb of the family tree—has been doggin' me all morning," he said at last, and waved a fishy hand toward the bluff which towered high above them. "Saw him when I was comin' up, about sunrise, pokin' along behind me in the sagebrush. Didn't think anything of that—thought maybe he was hunting or going fishing—but he's been sneakin' around behind me ever since. I don't reckon he's after my scalp—not enough hair to pay—but I'd like to know what the dickens he does mean."

"Nothing probably," Good Indian told him shortly, his eyes nevertheless searching the rocks for a sight of the watcher.

"Well, I don't much like the idea," complained Baumberger, casting an eye aloft in fear of snagging his line when he made another cast. "He was right up there a few minutes ago." He pointed his rod toward a sun-ridden ridge above them. "I got a flicker of his green blanket when he raised up and scowled down at me. He ducked when he saw me turn my head—looked to me like the surly buck that blew in to the ranch the night I came; Jim something-or-other. By the great immortal Jehosaphat!" he swore humorously, "I'd like to tie him up in his dirty blanket and heave him into the river—only it would kill all the fish in the Malad."

Good Indian laughed.

"Oh, I know it's funny, young fella," Baumberger growled. "About as funny as being pestered by a mosquito buzzing under your nose when you're playing a fish that keeps cuttin' figure eights in a hole the size uh that one there."

"I'll go up and take a look," Good Indian offered carelessly.

"Well, I wish you would. I can't keep my mind on m' fishing—just wondering what the deuce he's after. And say! You tell him I'll stand him on his off ear if I catch him doggie' me ag'in. Folks come with yuh?" he remembered to ask as he prepared for another cast into the pool.

"They're down there getting a campfire built, ready to fry what fish they catch," Good Indian informed him, as he turned to climb the bluff. "They're going to eat dinner under that big ledge by the rapids. You better go on down."

He stood for a minute, and watched Baumberger make a dexterous cast, which proved fruitless, before he began climbing up the steep slope of jumbled bowlders upon which the bluff itself seemed to rest. He was not particularly interested in his quest, but he was in the mood for purposeless action; he still did not want to think.

He climbed negligently, scattering loose rocks down the hill behind him. He had no expectation of coming upon Peppajee—unless Peppajee deliberately put himself in his way—and so there was no need of caution. He stopped once,

B. M. Bower

and stood long minutes with his head turned to catch the faint sound of high-keyed laughter and talk which drifted up to him. If he went higher, he thought, he might get a glimpse of them—of her, to tell his thought honestly. Whereupon he forgot all about finding and expostulating with Peppajee, and thought only a point of the ridge which would give him a clear view downstream.

To be sure, he might as easily have retraced his steps and joined the group, and seen every changing look in her face. But he did not want to be near her when others were by; he wanted her to himself, or not at all. So he went on, while the sun beat hotly down upon him and the rocks sent up dry waves of heat like an oven.

A rattlesnake buzzed its strident warning between two rocks, but before he turned his attention to the business of killing it, the snake had crawled leisurely away into a cleft, where he could not reach it with the stones he threw. His thoughts, however, were brought back to his surroundings so that he remembered Peppajee. He stood still, and scanned carefully the jumble of rocks and bowlders which sloped steeply down to the river, looking for a betraying bit of color or dirty gray hat-crown.

"But I could look my eyes out and welcome, if he didn't want to be seen," he concluded, and sat down while he rolled a cigarette. "And I don't know as I want to see him, anyway." Still, he did not move immediately. He was in the shade, which was a matter for congratulation on such a day. He had a cigarette between his lips, which made for comfort; and he still felt the exhilarating effects of his unpremeditated boldness, without having come to the point of sober thinking. He sat there, and blew occasional mouthfuls of smoke into the quivering heat waves, and stared down at the river rushing over the impeding rocks as if its very existence depended upon reaching as soon as possible the broader sweep of the Snake.

He finished the first cigarette, and rolled another from sheer force of habit rather than because he really wanted one. He lifted one foot, and laid it across his knee, and was drawing a match along the sole of his boot when his eyes chanced to rest for a moment upon a flutter of green, which showed briefly around the corner of a great square rock poised insecurely upon one corner, as if it were about to hurl its great bulk down upon the river it had watched so long. He held the blazing match poised midway to its destination while he looked; then he put it to the use he had meant it for, pulled his hat-brim down over his right eye and ear to shield them from the burn of the sun, and went picking his way idly over to the place.

"HUL-lo!" he greeted, in the manner of one who refuses to acknowledge the seriousness of a situation which confronts him suddenly. "What's the excitement?"

There was no excitement whatever. There was Peppajee, hunched up against the rock in that uncomfortable attitude which permits a man to come at the most intimate relations with the outside of his own ankle, upon which he was scowling in seeming malignity. There was his hunting-knife lying upon a flat stone near to his hand, with a fresh red blotch upon the blade, and there was his little stone pipe clenched between his teeth and glowing red within the bowl. Also there was the ankle, purple and swollen from the ligature above it—for his legging was off and torn into strips which formed a bandage, and a splinter of rock was twisted ingeniously in the wrappings for added tightness. From a crisscross of gashes a sluggish, red stream trickled down to the ankle-bone, and from there drip-dropped into a tiny, red pool in the barren, yellow soil.

"Catchum rattlesnake bite?" queried Good Indian inanely, as is the habit of the onlooker when the scene shouts forth eloquently its explanation, and questions are almost insultingly superfluous.

"Huh!" grunted Peppajee, disdaining further speech upon the subject, and regarded sourly the red drip.

"Want me to suck it?" ventured Good Indian unenthusiastically, eying the wound.

"Huh!" Peppajee removed the pipe, his eyes still upon his ankle. "Plenty blood come, mebbyso." To make sure, however, he kneaded the swollen flesh about the wound, thus accelerating slightly the red drip.

Then deliberately he took another turn with the rock, sending the buckskin thongs deeper into the flesh, and held the burning pipe against the skin above the wound until Good Indian sickened and turned away his head. When he looked again, Peppajee was sucking hard at the pipe, and gazing impersonally at the place. He bent again, and hid the glow of his pipe against his ankle. His thin lips tightened while he held it there, but the lean, brown fingers were firm as splinters of the rock behind him. When the fire cooled, he fanned it to life again with his breath, and when it winked redly at him he laid it grimly against his flesh.

So, while Good Indian stood and looked on with lips as tightly drawn as the other's, he seared a circle around the wound—a circle which bit deep and drew apart the gashes like lips opened for protest. He regarded critically his handiwork, muttered a "Bueno" under his breath, knocked the ashes from his pipe, and returned it to some mysterious hiding-place beneath his blanket. Then he picked up his moccasin.

"Them damn' snake, him no speakum," he observed disgustedly. "Heap fool me; him biteum"—he made a stabbing gesture with thumb and finger in the air by way of illustration—"then him go quick." He began gingerly trying to force the moccasin upon his foot, his mouth drawn down with the look of one who considers that he has been hardly used.

"How you get home?" Good Indian's thoughts swung round to practical things. "You got horse?"

Peppajee shook his head, reached for his knife, and slit the moccasin till it was no more than a wrapping. "Mebbyso heap walk," he stated simply.

"Mebbyso you won't do anything of the kind," Good Indian retorted. "You come down and take a horse. What for you all time watchum Baumberger?" he added, remembering then what had brought them both upon the bluff. "Baumberger all time fish—no more." He waved his hand toward the Malad. "Baumberger bueno—catchum fish—no more."

Peppajee got slowly and painfully upon his feet—rather, upon one foot. When Good Indian held out a steadying arm, he accepted it, and leaned rather heavily.

"Yo' eyes sick," said Peppajee, and grinned sardonically. "Yo' eyes see all time Squaw-with-sun-hair. Fillum yo' eyes, yo' see notting. Yo' catchum squaw, bimeby mebbyso see plenty mo'. Me no catchum sick eye. Mebbyso me see heap plenty."

"What you see, you all time watchum Baumberger?"

But Peppajee, hobbling where he must walk, crawling where he might, sliding carefully where a slanting bowlder offered a few feet of smooth descent, and taking hold of Good Indian's offered arm when necessity impelled him, pressed his thin lips together, and refused to answer. So they came at last to the ledge beside the rapids, where a thin wisp of smoke waved lazily in the vagrant breeze which played with the ripples and swayed languidly the smaller branches of the nearby trees.

Only Donny was there, sitting disgruntled upon the most comfortable rock he could find, sulking because the others had taken all the fishing-tackle that was of any account, and had left him to make shift with one bent, dulled hook, a lump of fat pork, and a dozen feet of line.

"And I can catch more fish than anybody in the bunch!" he began complainingly and without preface, waving a dirty hand contemptuously at the despised tackle when the two came slowly up. "That's the way it goes when you take a lot of girls along! They've got to have the best rods and tackle, and all they'll do will be to snag lines and lose leaders and hooks, and giggle alla squeal. Aw—DARN girls!"

"And I'm going to pile it on still thicker, Donny!" Good Indian grinned down at him. "I'm going to swipe your Pirate Chief for a while, till I take Peppajee into camp. He's gentle, and Peppajee's got a snake-bite. I'll be back before you get ready to go home."

"I'm ready to go home right now," growled Donny, sinking his chin between his two palms. "But I guess the walkin' ain't all taken up."

Good Indian regarded him frowningly, gave a little snort, and turned away. Donny in that mood was not to be easily placated, and certainly not to be ignored. He went over to the little flat, and selected Jack's horse, saddled him, and discovered that it had certain well-defined race prejudices, and would not let Peppajee put foot to the stirrup. Keno he knew would be no more tractable, so that he finally slapped Jack's saddle on Huckleberry, and so got Peppajee mounted and headed toward camp.

"You tell Jack I borrowed his saddle and Huckleberry," he called out to the drooping little figure on the rock. "But I'll get back before they want to go home."

But Donny was glooming over his wrongs, and neither heard nor wanted to hear. Having for his legacy a temper cumulative in its heat, he was coming rapidly to the point where he, too, started home, and left no word or message behind; a trivial enough incident in itself, but one which opened the way for some misunderstanding and fruitless speculation upon the part of Evadna.

CHAPTER XIII

CLOUD-SIGN VERSUS CUPID

Few men are ever called upon by untoward circumstance to know the sensations caused by rattlesnake bite, knife gashes, impromptu cauterization, and, topping the whole, the peculiar torture of congested veins and swollen muscles which comes from a tourniquet. The feeling must be unpleasant in the extreme, and the most morbid of sensation-seekers would scarcely put himself in the way of that particular experience.

Peppajee Jim, therefore, had reason in plenty for glowering at the world as he saw it that day. He held Huckleberry rigidly down to his laziest amble that the jar of riding might be lessened, kept his injured foot free from the stirrup, and merely grunted when Good Indian asked him once how he felt.

When they reached the desolation of the old placer-pits, however, he turned his eyes from the trail where it showed just over Huckleberry's ears, and regarded sourly the deep gashes and dislodged bowlders which told where water and the greed of man for gold had raged fiercest. Then, for the first time during the whole ride, he spoke.

"All time, yo' sleepum," he said, in the sonorous, oracular tone which he usually employed when a subject held his serious thought. "Peaceful Hart, him all same sleepum. All same slee-pum 'longside snake. No seeum snake, no thinkum mebbyso catchum bite. " He glanced down at his own snake-bitten foot.

B. M. Bower

"Snake bite, make all time much hurt." His eyes turned, and dwelt sharply upon the face of Good Indian.

"Yo' all time thinkum Squaw-with-sun-hair. Me tell yo' for watchum, yo' no think for watchum. Baumberga, him all same snake. Yo' think him all time catchum fish. HUH! Yo' heap big fool, yo' thinkum cat. Rattlesnake, mebbyso sleepum in sun one time. Yo' no thinkum bueno, yo' seeum sleep in sun. Yo' heap sabe him all time kay bueno jus' same. Yo' heap sabe yo' come close, him biteum. Mebbyso biteum hard, for killum yo' all time." He paused, then drove home his point like the true orator. "Baumberga catchum fish. All same rattlesnake sleepum in sun. Kay bueno."

Good Indian jerked his mind back from delicious recollection of one sweet, swift-passing minute, and half opened his lips for reply. But he did not speak; he did not know what to say, and it is ill-spent time—that passed in purposeless speech with such as Peppajee. Peppajee roused himself from meditation brief as it seemed deep, lifted a lean, brown hand to push back from his eyes a fallen lock of hair, and pointed straight away to the west.

"Las' night, sun go sleepum. Clouds come all same blanket, sun wrappum in blanket. Cloud look heap mad—mebbyso make much storm. Bimeby much mens come in cloud, stand so—and so—and so." With pointing finger he indicated a half circle. "Otha man come, heap big man. Stoppum 'way off, all time makeum sign, for fight. Me watchum. Me set by fire, watchum cloud makeum sign. Fire smoke look up for say, 'What yo' do all time, mebbyso?' Cloud man shakeum hand, makeum much sign. Fire smoke heap sad, bend down far, lookum me, lookum where cloud look. All time lookum for Peaceful Hart ranch. Me lay down for sleepum, me dream all time much fight. All time bad sign come. Kay bueno." Peppajee shook his head slowly, his leathery face set in deep, somber lines.

"Much trouble come heap quick," he said gravely, hitching his blanket into place upon his shoulder. "Me no sabe—all same, heap trouble come. Much mens, mebbyso much fight, much shootum—mebbyso kill. Peaceful Hart him all time laugh me. All same, me sabe smoke sign, sabe cloud sign, sabe—Baumberga. Heap ka-a-ay bueno!"

Good Indian's memory dashed upon him a picture of bright moonlight and the broody silence of a night half gone, and of a figure forming sharply and suddenly from the black shadow of the stable and stealing away into the sage, and of Baumberger emerging warily from that same shadow and stopping to light his pipe before he strolled on to the house and to the armchair upon the porch.

There might be a sinister meaning in that picture, but it was so well hidden that he had little hope of ever finding it. Also, it occurred to him that Peppajee, usually given over to creature comforts and the idle gossip of camp and the ranches he visited, was proving the sincerity of his manifest uneasiness by a watchfulness wholly at variance with his natural laziness. On the other hand, Peppajee loved to play the oracle, and a waving wisp of smoke, or the changing shapes in a wind-riven cloud meant to him spirit-sent prophecies not to be ignored.

He turned the matter over in his mind, was the victim of uneasiness for five minutes, perhaps, and then drifted off into wondering what Evadna was doing at that particular moment, and to planning how he should manage to fall behind with her when they all rode home, and so make possible other delicious moments. He even took note of certain sharp bends in the trail, where a couple riding fifty yards, say, behind a group would be for the time being quite hidden from sight and to all intents and purposes alone in the world for two minutes, or three—perhaps the time might be stretched to five.

The ranch was quiet, with even the dogs asleep in the shade. Peppajee insisted in one sentence upon going straight on to camp, so they did not stop. Without speaking, they plodded through the dust up the grade, left it, and followed the dim trail through the sagebrush and rocks to the Indian camp which seemed asleep also, except where three squaws were squatting in the sharply defined, conical shadow of a wikiup, mumbling desultorily the gossip of their little world, while their fingers moved with mechanical industry—one shining black head bent over a half-finished, beaded moccasin, another stitching a crude gown of bright-flowered calico, and the third braiding her hair afresh with leisurely care for its perfect smoothness. Good Indian took note of the group before it stirred to activity, and murmured anxiety over the bandaged foot of Peppajee.

"Me no can watchum more, mebbyso six days. Yo' no sleepum all time yo' walk—no thinkum all time squaw. Mebbyso yo' think for man-snake. Mebbyso yo' watchum," Peppajee said, as he swung slowly down from Huckleberry's back.

"All right. I'll watchum plenty," Good Indian promised lightly, gave a glance of passing, masculine interest at the squaw who was braiding her hair, and who was young and fresh-cheeked and bright-eyed and slender, forgot her the instant his eyes left her, and made haste to return to the Malad and the girl who held all his thoughts and all his desire.

That girl was sitting upon the rock which Donny had occupied, and she looked very much as if she were sulking, much as Donny had sulked. She had her chin in a pink palm and was digging little holes in the sand with the tip of her rod, which was not at all beneficial to the rod and did not appear even to interest the digger; for her wonderfully blue eyes were staring at the green-and-white churn of the rapids, and her lips were pursed moodily, as if she did not even see what she was looking at so fixedly.

Good Indian's eyes were upon her while he was dismounting, but he did not go to her immediately. Instead, he busied himself with unsaddling, and explained to the boys just why he had left so unaccountably. Secretly he was hoping that Evadna heard the explanation, and he raised his voice purposely. But

Evadna was not listening, apparently; and, if she had been, the noise of the rapids would have prevented her hearing what he said.

Miss Georgie Howard was frying fish and consistently snubbing Baumberger, who hulked loosely near the campfire, and between puffs at his pipe praised heavily her skill, and professed to own a ravenous appetite. Good Indian heard him as he passed close by them, and heard also the keen thrust she gave in return; and he stopped and half turned, looking at her with involuntary appreciation. His glance took in Baumberger next, and he lifted a shoulder and went on. Without intentionally resorting to subterfuge, he felt an urge to wash his hands, and he chose for his ablutions that part of the river's edge which was nearest Evadna.

First he stooped and drank thirstily, his hat pushed back, while his lips met full the hurrying water, clear and cold, yet with the chill it had brought from the mountain springs which fed it, and as he lifted his head he looked full at her.

Evadna stared stonily over him to where the water boiled fastest. He might have been one of the rocks, for all the notice she took of him.

Good Indian frowned with genuine puzzlement, and began slowly to wash his hands, glancing at her often in hope that he might meet her eyes. When she did not seem to see him at all, the smile of a secret shared joyously with her died from his own eyes, and when he had dried his hands upon his handkerchief he cast aside his inward shyness in the presence of the Hart boys and Miss Georgie and Baumberger, and went boldly over to her.

"Aren't you feeling well?" he asked, with tender proprietorship in his tone.

"I'm feeling quite well, thank you," returned Evadna frigidly, neglecting to look at him.

"What is the matter, then? Aren't you having a good time?"

"I'm enjoying myself very much—except that your presence annoys me. I wish you'd go away."

Good Indian turned on his heel and went; he felt that at last Evadna was looking at him, though he would not turn to make sure. And his instinct told him withal that he must ignore her mood if he would win her from it. With a freakish impulse, he headed straight for the campfire and Miss Georgie, but when he came up to her the look she gave him of understanding, with sympathy to soften it, sent him away again without speaking.

He wandered back to the river's edge—this time some distance from where Evadna sat—and began throwing pebbles at the black nose of a wave-washed bowlder away toward the other side. Clark and Gene, loitered up, watched him lazily, and, picking up other pebbles, started to do the same thing. Soon all the boys were throwing at the bowlder, and were making a good deal of noise over the various hits and misses, and the spirit of rivalry waxed stronger and stronger until it was like any other game wherein full-blooded youths strive against one another for supremacy. They came to the point of making bets, at first extravagant and then growing more and more genuinely in earnest, for we're gamblers all, at heart.

Miss Georgie burned a frying-panful of fish until they sent up an acrid, blue smoke, while she ran over to try her luck with a stone or two. Even Baumberger heaved himself up from where he was lounging, and strolled over to watch. But Evadna could not have stuck closer to her rock if she had been glued there, and if she had been blind and deaf she would not have appeared more oblivious.

Good Indian grew anxious, and then angry. The savage stirred within him, and counseled immediate and complete mastery of her—his woman. But there was the white man of him who said the thought was brute] and unchivalrous, and reminded the savage that one must not look upon a woman as a chattel, to be beaten or caressed, as the humor seized the master. And, last of all, there was the surface of him laughing with the others, fleering at those who fell short of the mark, and striving his utmost to be first of them all in accuracy.

He even smiled upon Miss Georgie when she hit the bowlder fairly, and, when the stench of the burning fish drifted over to them, he gave his supply of pebbles into her two hands, and ran to the rescue. He caught Evadna in the act of regarding him sidelong, just as a horse sometimes will keep an eye on the man with the rope in a corral; so he knew she was thinking of him, at least, and was wondering what he meant to do next, and the savage in him laughed and lay down again, knowing himself the master.

What he did was to throw away the burnt fish, clean the frying-pan, and start more sizzling over the fire, which he kicked into just the right condition. He whistled softly to himself while he broke dry sticks across his knee for the fire, and when Miss Georgie cried out that she had made three hits in succession, he called back: "Good shot!" and took up the tune where he had left off. Never, for one instant, was he unconscious of Evadna's secret watchfulness, and never, for one instant, did he let her see that she was in his thoughts.

He finished frying the fish, set out the sandwiches and doughnuts, and pickled peaches and cheese, and pounded upon a tin plate to announce that dinner was ready. He poured the coffee into the cups held out to him, and got the flask of cream from a niche between two rocks at the water's edge. He said "Too bad," when it became generally known that the glare of the sun upon the water had given Evadna a headache, and he said it exactly as he would have spoken if Jack, for instance, had upset the sugar.

He held up the broken-handled butcher knife that was in the camp kit, and declaimed tragically: "Is this a dagger that I see before me?" and much more of the kind that was eery. He saw

B. M. Bower

the reluctant dimple which showed fleetingly in Evadna's cheek, and also the tears which swelled her eyelids immediately after, but she did not know that he saw them, though another did.

He was taken wholly by surprise when Miss Georgie, walking past him afterward on her way to an enticing pool, nipped his arm for attention and murmured:

"You're doing fine—only don't overdo it. She's had just about all she can stand right now. Give her a chance to forgive you— and let her think she came out ahead! Good luck!" Whereupon she finished whatever she pretended to have been doing to her fishing-tackle, and beckoned Wally and Jack to come along.

"We've just got to catch that big one," she laughed, "so Mr. Baumberger can go home and attend to his own business!" It took imagination to feel sure there had been a significant accent on the last of the sentence, and Baumberger must have been imaginative. He lowered his head like a bull meditating assault, and his leering eyes shot her a glance of inquiry and suspicion. But Miss Georgie Howard met his look with a smile that was nothing more than idle amusement.

"I'd like nothing better than to get that four-pounder on my line," she added. "It would be the joke of the season—if a woman caught him."

"Bet you couldn't land him," chuckled Baumberger, breathing a sigh which might have been relief, and ambled away contentedly."I may not see you folks again till supper," he bethought him to call back. "I'm going to catch a dozen more—and then I thought I'd take 'em up to Pete Hamilton; I'm using his horse, yuh see, and—" He flung out a hand to round off the sentence, turned, and went stumbling over a particularly rocky place.

Miss Georgie stood where she was, and watched him with her mouth twisted to one side and three perpendicular creases between her eyebrows. When he was out of sight, she glanced at Evadna—once more perched sulkily upon the rock.

"Head still bad, chicken?" she inquired cheerfully. "Better stay here in the shade—I won't be gone long."

"I'm going to fish," said Evadna, but she did not stir, not even when Miss Georgie went on, convoyed by all the Hart boys.

Good Indian had volunteered the information that he was going to fish downstream, but he was a long time in tying his leader and fussing with his reel. His preparations were finished just when the last straggler of the group was out of sight. Then he laid down his rod, went over to Evadna, took her by the arm, and drew her back to the farther shelter of the ledge.

"Now, what's the trouble?" he asked directly. "I hope you're not trying to make yourself think I was only— You know what I meant, don't you? And you said yes. You said it with your lips, and with your eyes. Did you want more words? Tell me what it is that bothers you."

There was a droop to Evadna's shoulders, and a tremble to her mouth. She would not look at him. She kept her eyes gazing downward, perhaps to hide tears. Good Indian waited for her to speak, and when it seemed plain that she did not mean to do so, he yielded to his instinct and took her in his arms.

"Sweetheart!" he murmured against her ear, and it was the first time he had ever spoken the word to any woman. "You love me, I know it. You won't say it, but I know you do. I should have felt it this morning if you hadn't cared. You—you let me kiss you. And—"

"And after that you—you rode off and left me—and you went away by yourself, just as if—just as if nothing had happened, and you've acted ever since as if—" She bit her lips, turned her face away from him, plucked at his hands to free herself from his clasping arms, and then she laid her face down against him,

B. M. Bower

and sobbed.

Good Indian tried his best to explain his mood and his actions that day, and if he did not make himself very clear—which could scarcely be expected, since he did not quite understand it himself—he at least succeeded in lifting from her the weight of doubt and of depression.

They were astonished when Wally and Jack and Miss Georgie suddenly confronted them and proved, by the number of fish which they carried, that they had been gone longer than ten minutes or so. They were red as to their faces, and embarrassed as to manner, and Good Indian went away hurriedly after the horses, without meeting the quizzical glances of the boys, or replying t to certain pointed remarks which they fired after him.

"And he's the buckaroo that's got no use for girls!" commented Wally, looking after him, and ran his tongue meditatively along the loose edge of his cigarette. "Kid, I wish you'd tell me how you done it. It worked quick, anyhow."

"And thorough," grinned Jack. "I was thinking some of falling in love with you myself, Vad. Soon as some of the shine wore off, and you got so you acted like a real person."

"I saw it coming, when it first heaved in sight," chirped Miss Georgie, in a more cheerful tone than she had used that day; in too cheerful a tone to be quite convincing, if any one there had been taking notice of mere tones.

CHAPTER XIV

THE CLAIM-JUMPERS

"Guess that bobcat was after my ducks again, last night," commented Phoebe Hart, when she handed Baumberger his cup of coffee. "The way the dogs barked all night—didn't they keep you awake?"

"Never slept better in my life," drawled Baumberger, his voice sliding upward from the first word to the last. His blood-shot eyes, however, rather gave the lie to his statement. "I'm going to make one more try, 'long about noon, for that big one—girls didn't get him, I guess, for all their threats, or I'd heard about it. And I reckon I'll take the evening train home. Shoulda gone yesterday, by rights. I'd like to get a basket uh fish to take up with me. Great coffee, Mrs. Hart, and such cream I never did see. I sure do hate to leave so many good things and go back to a boardin' house. Look at this honey, now!" He sighed gluttonously, leaning slightly over the table while he fed.

"Dogs were barking at something down in the orchard," Wally volunteered, passing over Baumberger's monologue. "I was going down there, but it was so dark—and I thought maybe it was Gene's ghost. That was before the moon came up. Got any more biscuits, mum?"

"My trap wasn't sprung behind the chicken-house," said Donny. "I looked, first thing."

B. M. Bower

"Dogs," drawled Baumberger, his enunciation muffled by the food in his mouth, "always bark. And cats fight on shed-roofs. Next door to where I board there's a dog that goes on shift as regular as a policeman. Every night at—"

"Oh, Aunt Phoebe!" Evadna, crisp and cool in a summery dress of some light-colored stuff, and looking more than ever like a Christmas angel set a-flutter upon the top of a holiday fir in a sudden gust of wind, threw open the door, rushed halfway into the room, and stopped beside the chair of her aunt. Her hands dropped to the plump shoulder of the sitter. "Aunt Phoebe, there's a man down at the farther end of the strawberry patch! He's got a gun, Aunt Phoebe, and he's camped there, and when he heard me he jumped up and pointed the gun straight at me!"

"Why, honey, that can't be—you must have seen an Indian prowling after windfalls off the apricot trees there. He wouldn't hurt you." Phoebe reached up, and caught the hands in a reassuring clasp.

Evadna's eyes strayed from one face to another around the table till they rested upon Good Indian, as having found sanctuary there.

"But, Aunt Phoebe, he was WASN'T. He was a white man. And he has a camp there, right by that tree the lightning peeled the bark off. I was close before I saw him, for he was sitting down and the currant bushes were between. But I went through to get round where Uncle Hart has been irrigating and it's all mud, and he jumped up and pointed the gun AT me. Just as if he was going to shoot me. And I turned and ran." Her fingers closed upon the hand of her aunt, but her eyes clung to Good Indian, as though it was to him she was speaking.

"Tramp," suggested Baumberger, in a tone of soothing finality, as when one hushes the fear of a child. "Sick the dogs on him. He'll go—never saw the hobo yet that wouldn't run from a dog." He smiled leeringly up at her, and reached for a second helping of honey.

Good Indian pulled his glance from Evadna, and tried to bore through the beefy mask which was Baumberger's face, but all he found there was a gross interest in his breakfast and a certain indulgent sympathy for Evadna's fear, and he frowned in a baffled way.

"Who ever heard of a tramp camped in our orchard!" flouted Phoebe. "They don't get down here once a year, and then they always come to the house. You couldn't know there WAS any strawberry patch behind that thick row of trees—or a garden, or anything else."

"He's got a row of stakes running clear across tho patch," Evadna recalled suddenly. "Just like they do for a new street, or a railroad, or something. And—"

Good Indian pushed back his chair with a harsh, scraping noise, and rose. He was staring hard at Baumberger, and his whole face had sharpened till it had the cold, unyielding look of an Indian. And suddenly Baumberger raised his head and met full that look. For two breaths their eyes held each other, and then Baumberger glanced casually at Peaceful.

"Sounds queer—must be some mistake, though. You must have seen something, girl, that reminded you of stakes. The stub off a sagebrush maybe?" He ogled her quite frankly. "When a little girl gets scared—Sick the dogs on him," he advised the family collectively, his manner changing to a blustering anxiety that her fright should be avenged.

Evadna seemed to take his tone as a direct challenge. "I was scared, but I know quite well what I saw. He wasn't a tramp. Hehad a regular camp, with a coffee-pot and frying-pan and blankets. And there a line of stakes across the strawberry patch."

B. M. Bower

Before, the breakfast had continued to seem an important incident temporarily suspended. Now Peaceful Hart laid hand to his beard, eyed his wife questioningly, let his glance flicker over the faces of his sons, and straightened his shoulders unconsciously. Good Indian was at the door, his mouth set in a thin, straight, fighting line. Wally and Jack were sliding their chairs back from the table preparing to follow him.

"I guess it ain't anything much," Peaceful opined optimistically. "They can't do anything but steal berries, and they're most gone, anyhow. Go ask him what he wants, down there." The last sentence was but feeble sort of fiction that his boys would await his commands; as a matter of fact, they were outside before he spoke.

"Take the dogs along," called out Baumberger, quite as futilely, for not one of the boys was within hearing.

Until they heard footsteps returning at a run, the four stayed where they were. Baumberger rumbled on in a desultory sort of way, which might have caused an observant person to wonder where was his lawyer training, and the deep cunning and skill with which he was credited, for his words were as profitless and inconsequential as an old woman's. He talked about tramps, and dogs that barked o' nights, and touched gallantly upon feminine timidity and the natural, protective instincts of men.

Peaceful Hart may have heard half of what he said—but more likely he heard none of it. He sat drawing his white beard through his hand, and his mild, blue eyes were turned often to Phoebe in mute question. Phoebe herself was listening, but not to Baumberger; she was permitting Evadna to tuck in stray locks of her soft, brown hair, but her face was turned to the door which opened upon the porch. At the first clatter of running footsteps on the porch, she and Peaceful pushed back their chairs instinctively.

The runner was Donny, and every freckle stood out distinctly upon his face.

"There's four of 'em, papa!" he shouted, all in one breath. "They're jumpin' the ranch for placer claims. They said so. Each one's got a claim, and they're campin' on the corners, so they'll be close together. They're goin' to wash gold. Good Injun—"

"Oh!" screamed Evadna suddenly. "Don't let him—don't let them hurt him, Uncle Hart!"

"Aw, they ain't fightin'," Donny assured her disgustedly. "They're chewin' the rag down there, is all. Good Injun knows one of 'em."

Peaceful Hart stood indecisively, and stared, one and gripping the back of his chair. His lips were working so that his beard bristled about his mouth.

"They can't do nothing—the ranch belongs to me," he said, his eyes turning rather helplessly to Baumberger. "I've got my patent."

"Jumping our ranch!—for placer claims!" Phoebe stood up, leaning hard upon the table with both hands. "And we've lived here ever since Clark was a baby!"

"Now, now, let's not get excited over this," soothed Baumberger, getting out of his chair slowly, like the overfed glutton he was. He picked up a crisp fragment of biscuit, crunched it between his teeth, and chewed it slowly. "Can't be anything serious—and if it is, why—I'm here. A lawyer right on the spot may save a lot of trouble. The main thing is, let's not get excited and do something rash. Those boys—"

"Not excited?—and somebody jumping—our—ranch?" Phoebe's soft eyes gleamed at him. She was pale, so that her face had a peculiar, ivory tint.

"Now, now!" Baumberger put out a puffy hand admonishingly. "Let's keep cool—that's half the battle won. Keep cool." He reached for his pipe, got out his twisted leather tobacco pouch, and opened it with a twirl of his thumb and finger.

"You're a lawyer, Mr. Baumberger," Peaceful turned to him, still helpless in his manner. "What's the best thing to be done?"

"Don't—get—excited." Baumberger nodded his head for every word. "That's what I always say when a client comes to me all worked up. We'll go down there and see just how much there is to this, and—order 'em off. Calmly, calmly! No violence— no threats—just tell 'em firmly and quietly to leave." He stuffed his pipe carefully, pressing down the tobacco with the tip of a finger. "Then," he added with slow emphasis, "if they don't go, after—say twenty-four hours' notice—why, we'll proceed to serve an injunction." He drew a match along the back of his chair, and lighted his pipe.

"I reckon we'd better go and look after those boys of yours," he suggested, moving toward the door rather quickly, for all his apparent deliberation. "They're inclined to be hot-headed, and we must have no violence, above all things. Keep it a civil matter right through. Much easier to handle in court, if there's no violence to complicate the case."

"They're looking for it," Phoebe reminded him bluntly. "The man had a gun, and threw down on Vadnie."

"He only pointed it at me, auntie," Evadna corrected, ignorant of the Western phrase.

The two women followed the men outside and into the shady yard, where the trees hid completely what lay across the road and beyond the double row of poplars. Donny, leaning far forward and digging his bare toes into the loose soil for more speed, raced on ahead, anxious to see and hear all that took place.

"If the boys don't stir up a lot of antagonism," Baumberger kept urging Peaceful and Phoebe, as they hurried into the garden, "the matter ought to be settled without much trouble. You can get an injunction, and—"

"The idea of anybody trying to hold our place for mineral land!" Phoebe's indignation was cumulative always, and was now bubbling into wrath. "Why, my grief! Thomas spent one whole summer washing every likely spot around here. He never got anything better than colors on this ranch—and you can get them anywhere in Idaho, almost. And to come right into our garden, in the right—and stake a placer claim!" Her anger seemed beyond further utterance. "The idea!" she finished weakly.

"Well—but we mustn't let ourselves get excited," soothed Baumberger, the shadow of him falling darkly upon Peaceful and Phoebe as he strode along, upon the side next the sun. Peppajee would have called that an evil thing, portending much trouble and black treachery.

"That's where people always blunder in a thing like this. A little cool-headedness goes farther than hard words or lead. And," he added cheeringly, "it may be a false alarm, remember. We won't borrow trouble. We'll just make sure of our ground, first thing we do."

"It's always easy enough to be calm over the other fellow's trouble," said Phoebe sharply, irritated in an indefinable way by the oily optimism of the other. "It ain't your ox that's gored, Mr. Baumberger."

They skirted the double row of grapevines, picked their way over a spot lately flooded from the ditch, which they crossed upon two planks laid side by side, went through an end of the currant patch, made a detour around a small jungle of gooseberry bushes, and so came in sight of the strawberry

B. M. Bower

patch and what was taking place near the lightning-scarred apricot tree. Baumberger lengthened his stride, and so reached the spot first.

The boys were grouped belligerently in the strawberry patch, just outside a line of new stakes, freshly driven in the ground. Beyond that line stood a man facing them with a .45-.70 balanced in the hollow of his arm. In the background stood three other men in open spaces in the shrubbery, at intervals of ten rods or so, and they also had rifles rather conspicuously displayed. They were grinning, all three. The man just over the line was listening while Good Indian spoke; the voice of Good Indian was even and quiet, as if he were indulging in casual small talk of the country, but that particular claim-jumper was not smiling. Even from a distance they could see that he was fidgeting uncomfortably while he listened, and that his breath was beginning to come jerkily.

"Now, roll your blankets and GIT!" Good Indian finished sharply, and with the toe of his boot kicked the nearest stake clear of the loose soil. He stooped, picked it up, and cast it contemptuously from him. It landed three feet in front of the man who had planted it, and he jumped and shifted the rifle significantly upon his arm, so that the butt of it caressed his right shoulder-joint.

"Now, now, we don't want any overt acts of violence here," wheezed Baumberger, laying hand upon Good Indian's shoulder from behind. Good Indian shook off the touch as if it were a tarantula upon him.

"You go to the devil," he advised chillingly.

"Tut, tut!" Baumberger reproved gently. "The ladies are within hearing, my boy. Let's get at this thing sensibly and calmly. Violence only makes things worse. See how quiet Wally and Jack and Clark and Gene are! THEY realize how childishly spiteful it would be for them to follow your example. They know better. They don't want—"

Jack grinned, and hitched his gun into plainer view. "When we start in, it won't be STICKS we're sending to His Nibs," he observed placidly. "We're just waiting for him to ante."

"This," said Baumberger, a peculiar gleam coming into his leering, puffy-lidded eyes, and a certain hardness creeping into his voice, "this is a matter for your father and me to settle. It's just-a-bide-beyond you youngsters. This is a civil case. Don't foolishly make it come under the criminal code. But there!" His voice purred at them again. "You won't. You're all too clear-headed and sensible."

"Oh, sure!" Wally gave his characteristic little snort."We're only just standing around to see how fast the cabbages grow!"

Baumberger advanced boldly across the dead line.

"Stanley, put down that gun, and explain your presence here and your object," he rumbled. "Let's get at this thing right end to. First, what are you doing here?"

The man across the line did not put down his rifle, except that he let the butt of it drop slightly away from his shoulder so that the sights were in alignment with an irrigating shovel thrust upright into the ground ten feet to one side of the group. His manner lost little of its watchfulness, and his voice was surly with defiance when he spoke. But Good Indian, regarding him suspiciously through half-closed lids, would have sworn that a look of intelligence flashed between those two. There was nothing more than a quiver of his nostrils to betray him as he moved over beside Evadna—for the pure pleasure of being near her, one would think; in reality, while the pleasure was there, that he might see both Baumberger's face and Stanley's without turning more than his eyes.

"All there is to it," Stanley began blustering, "you see before yuh. I've located twenty acres here as a placer claim. That there's the northwest corner—ap-prox'm'tley—close as I could come by sightin'. Your fences are straight with yer land, and I

B. M. Bower

happen to sabe all yer corners. I've got a right here. I believe this ground is worth more for the gold that's in it than for the turnips you can make grow on top—and that there makes mineral land of it, and as such, open to entry. That's accordin' to law. I ain't goin' to build no trouble—but I sure do aim to defend my prope'ty rights if I have to. I realize yuh may think diffrunt from me. You've got a right to prove, if yuh can, that all this ain't mineral land. I've got jest as much right to prove it is."

He took a breath so deep it expanded visibly his chest—a broad, muscular chest it was—and let his eyes wander deliberately over his audience.

"That there's where *I* stand," he stated, with arrogant self-assurance. His mouth drew down at the corners in a smile which asked plainly what they were going to do about it, and intimated quite as plainly that he did not care what they did, though he might feel a certain curiosity as an onlooker.

"I happen to know—" Peaceful began, suddenly for him. But Baumberger waved him into silence.

"You'll have to prove there's gold in paying quantities here," he stated pompously.

"That's what I aim to do," Stanley told him imperturbably.

"*I* proved, over fifteen years ago, that there WASN'T," Peaceful drawled laconically, and sucked so hard upon his pipe that his cheeks held deep hollows.

Stanley grinned at him. "Sorry I can't let it go at that," he said ironically. "I reckon I'll have to do some washin' myself, though, before I feel satisfied there ain't."

"Then you haven't panned out anything yet?" Phoebe caught him up.

Stanley's eyes flickered a questioning glance at Baumberger, and Baumberger puffed out his chest and said:

"The law won't permit you to despoil this man's property without good reason. We can serve an injunction—"

"You can serve and be darned." Stanley's grin returned, wider than before.

"As Mr. Hart's legal adviser," Baumberger began, in the tone he employed in the courtroom—a tone which held no hint of his wheezy chuckle or his oily reassurance—"I hereby demand that you leave this claim which you have staked out upon Thomas Hart's ranch, and protest that your continued presence here, after twenty-four hours have expired, will be looked upon as malicious trespass, and treated as such."

Stanley still grinned. "As my own legal adviser," he returned calmly, "I hereby declare that you can go plumb to HEL-ena." Stanley evidently felt impelled to adapt his vocabulary to feminine ears, for he glanced at them deprecatingly and as if he wished them elsewhere.

If either Stanley or Baumberger had chanced to look toward Good Indian, he might have wondered why that young man had come, of a sudden, to resemble so strongly his mother's people. He had that stoniness of expression which betrays strong emotion held rigidly in check, with which his quivering nostrils and the light in his half-shut eyes contrasted strangely. He had missed no fleeting glance, no guarded tone, and he was thinking and weighing and measuring every impression as it came to him. Of some things he felt sure; of others he was half convinced; and there was more which he only suspected. And all the while he stood there quietly beside Evadna, his attitude almost that of boredom.

"I think, since you have been properly notified to leave," said Baumberger, with the indefinable air of a lawyer who gathers up his papers relating to one case, thrusts them into his pocket, and turns his attention to the needs of his next client, "we'll just have it out with these other fellows, though I look upon Stanley," he added half humorously, "as a test case. If he goes, they'll all go."

"Better say he's a TOUGH case," blurted Wally, and turned on his heel. "What the devil are they standing around on one foot for, making medicine?" he demanded angrily of Good Indian, who unceremoniously left Evadna and came up with him. "I'D run him off the ranch first, and do my talking about it afterward. That hunk uh pork is kicking up a lot uh dust, but he ain't GETTING anywhere!"

"Exactly." Good Indian thrust both hands deep into his trousers pockets, and stared at the ground before him.

Wally gave another snort. "I don't know how it hits you, Grant—but there's something fishy about it."

"Ex-actly." Good Indian took one long step over the ditch, and went on steadily.

Wally, coming again alongside, turned his head, and regarded him attentively.

"Injun's on top," he diagnosed sententiously after a minute. "Looks like he's putting on a good, thick layer uh war-paint, too." He waited expectantly. "You might hand me the brush when you're through," he hinted grimly. "I might like to get out after some scalps myself."

"That so?" Good Indian asked inattentively, and went on without waiting for any reply. They left the garden, and went down the road to the stable, Wally passively following Grant's lead. Someone came hurrying after them, and they turned to see Jack. The others had evidently stayed to hear the legal harangue to a close.

"Say, Stanley says there's four beside the fellows we saw," Jack announced, rather breathlessly, for he had been running through the loose, heavy soil of the garden to overtake them. "They've located twenty acres apiece, he says—staked 'em out in the night and stuck up their notices—and everyone's going to STICK. They're all going to put in grizzlies and mine the whole thing, he told dad. He just the same as accused dad right out of covering up valuable mineral land on purpose. And he says the law's all on their side." He leaned hard against the stable, and drew his fingers across his forehead, white as a girl's when he pushed back his hat. "Baumberger," he said cheerlessly, "was still talking injunction when I left, but—" He flung out his hand contemptuously.

"I wish dad wasn't so—" began Wally moodily, and let it go at that.

Good Indian threw up his head with that peculiar tightening of lips which meant much in the way of emotion.

"He'll listen to Baumberger, and he'll lose the ranch listening," he stated distinctly. "If there's anything to do, we've got to do it."

"We can run 'em off—maybe," suggested Jack, his fighting instincts steadied by the vivid memory of four rifles held by four men, who looked thoroughly capable of using them.

"This isn't a case of apple-stealing," Good Indian quelled sharply, and got his rope from his saddle with the manner of a man who has definitely made up his mind.

"What CAN we do, then?" Wally demanded impatiently.

"Not a thing at present." Good Indian started for the little pasture, where Keno was feeding and switching methodically at the flies. "You fellows can do more by doing nothing to-day than if you killed off the whole bunch."

He came back in a few minutes with his horse, and found the

B. M. Bower

two still moodily discussing the thing. He glanced at them casually, and went about the business of saddling.

"Where you going?" asked Wally abruptly, when Grant was looping up the end of his latigo.

"Just scouting around a little," was the unsatisfactory reply he got, and he scowled as Good Indian rode away.

CHAPTER XV

SQUAW-TALK-FAR-OFF HEAP SMART

Good Indian spoke briefly with the good-looking young squaw, who had a shy glance for him when he came up; afterward he took hold of his hat by the brim, and ducked through the low opening of a wikiup which she smilingly pointed out to him.

"Howdy, Peppajee? How you foot?" he asked, when his unaccustomed eyes discerned the old fellow lying back against the farther wall.

"Huh! Him heap sick all time." Having his injury thus brought afresh to his notice, Peppajee reached down with his hands, and moved the foot carefully to a new position.

"Last night," Good Indian began without that ceremony of long waiting which is a part of Indian etiquette, "much men come to Hart ranch. Eight." He held up his two outspread hands, with the thumbs tucked inside his palms. "Come in dark, no seeum till sun come back. Makeum camp. One man put sticks in ground, say that part belong him. Twenty acres." He flung up his hands, lowered them, and immediately raised them again. "Eight men do that all same. Have guns, grub, blankets—stop there all time. Say they wash gold. Say that ranch have much gold, stake placer claims. Baumberger"—he saw Peppajee's eyelids draw together—"tell men to go away. Tell Peaceful he fight those men—in court. You sabe Ask

Great Father to tell those men they go away, no wash gold on ranch." He waited.

There is no hurrying the speech of an Indian. Peppajee smoked stolidly, his eyes half closed and blinking sleepily. The veneer of white men's ways dropped from him when he entered his own wikiup, and he would not speak quickly.

"Las' night—mebbyso yo' watchum?" he asked, as one who holds his judgment in abeyance.

"I heap fool. I no watch. I let those men come while I think of—a girl. My eyes sleep." Good Indian was too proud to parry, too bitter with himself to deny. He had not said the thing before, even to himself, but it was in his heart to hate his love, because it had cost this catastrophe to his friends.

"Kay bueno." Peppajee's voice was harsh. But after a time he spoke more sympathetically. "Yo' no watchum. Yo' let heap trouble come. This day yo' heart bad, mebbyso. This day yo' no thinkum squaw all time. Mebbyso yo' thinkum fight, no sabe how yo' fight."

Grant nodded silently. It would seem that Peppajee understood, even though his speech was halting. At that moment much of the unfounded prejudice, which had been for a few days set aside because of bigger things, died within him. He had disliked Peppajee as a pompous egotist among his kind. His latent antagonism against all Indians because they were unwelcomely his blood relatives had crystallized here and there against; certain individuals of the tribe. Old Hagar he hated coldly. Peppajee's staginess irritated him. In his youthful arrogance he had not troubled to see the real man of mettle under that dingy green blanket. Now he looked at Peppajee with a startled sense that he had never known him at all, and that Peppajee was not only a grimy Indian—he was also a man.

"Me no sabe one thing. One otha thing me sabe. Yo' no b'lieve

Baumberga one frien'. Him all same snake. Them mens come, Baumberga tellum come all time. All time him try for foolum Peaceful. Yo' look out. Yo' no sleepum mo'. All time yo' watchum."

"I come here," said Good Indian; "I think you mebbyso hear talk, you tell me. My heart heap sad, I let this trouble come. I want to kill that trouble. Mebbyso make my friends laugh, be heap glad those men no stealum ranch. You hear talk, mebbyso you tell me now."

Peppajee smoked imperturbably what time his dignity demanded. At length he took the pipe from his mouth, stretched out his arm toward Hartley, and spoke in his sonorous tone, calculated to add weight to his words.

"Yo' go speakum Squaw-talk-far-off," he commanded. "All time makum talk—talk—" He drummed with his fingers upon his left forearm. "Mebbyso heap sabe. Heap sabe Baumberga kay bueno. He thinkum sabe stealum ranch. All time heap talk come Man-that-coughs, come all same Baumberga. Heap smart, dat squaw." A smile laid its faint light upon his grim old lips, and was gone. "Thinkum yo' heap bueno, dat squaw. All time glad for talkum yo'. Yo' go."

Good Indian stood up, his head bent to avoid scraping his hat against the sloping roof of the wikiup.

"You no hear more talk all time you watch?" he asked, passing over Miss Georgie's possible aid or interest in the affair.

"Much talkum—no can hear. All time them damn' Baumberga shut door—no talkum loud. All time Baumberga walkum in dark. Walkum where apples grow, walkum grass, walkum all dat ranch all time. All time me heap watchum. Snake come, bitum foot—no can watchum mo'. Dat time, much mens come. Yo' sabe. Baumberga all time talkum, him heap frien' Peacefu'—heap snake all time. Speakum two tongue Yo' no b'lievum. All time heap big liar, him. Yo' go, speakum Squaw-talk-far-off. Bueno, dat squaw. Heap smart, all same mans. Yo' go. Pikeway." He settled back with a gesture of finality, and so Good Indian left him.

Old Hagar shrilled maledictions after him when he passed through the littered camp on his way back to where he had left his horse, but for once he was deaf to her upbraidings. Indeed, he never heard her—or if he did, her clamor was to him as the yelping of the dogs which filled his ears, but did not enter his thoughts.

The young squaw smiled at him shy-eyed as he went by her, and though his physical eyes saw her standing demurely there in the shade of her wikiup, ready to shrink coyly away from too bold a glance, the man-mind of him was blind and took no notice. He neither heard the baffled screaming of vile epithets when old Hagar knew that her venom could not strike through the armor of his preoccupation, nor saw the hurt look creep into the soft eyes of the young squaw when his face did not turn toward her after the first inattentive glance.

Good Indian was thinking how barren had been his talk with Peppajee, and was realizing keenly how much he had expected from the interview. It is frequently by the depth of our disappointment only that we can rightly measure the height of our hope. He had come to Peppajee for something tangible, some thing that might be called real evidence of the conspiracy he suspected. He had got nothing but suspicion to match his own. As for Miss Georgie Howard—

"What can she do?" he thought resentfully, feeling as if he had been offered a willow switch with which to fight off a grizzly. It seemed to him that he might as sensibly go to Evadna herself for assistance, and that, even his infatuation was obliged to admit, would be idiotic. Peppajee, he told himself when he reached his horse, was particularly foolish sometimes.

With that in his mind, he mounted—and turned Keno's head toward Hartley. The distance was not great—little more than half a mile—but when he swung from the saddle in the square blotch of shade east by the little, red station house upon the parched sand and cinders, Keno's flanks were heaving like the silent sobbing of a woman with the pace his master's spurred heels had required of him.

Miss Georgie gave her hair a hasty pat or two, pushed a novel out of sight under a Boise newspaper, and turned toward him with a breezily careless smile when he stepped up to the open door and stopped as if he were not quite certain of his own mind, or of his welcome.

He was secretly thinking of Peppajee's information that Miss Georgie thought he was "bueno," and he was wondering if it were true. Not that he wanted it to be true! But he was man enough to look at her with a keener interest than he had felt before. And Miss Georgie, if one might judge by her manner, was woman enough to detect that interest and to draw back her skirts, mentally, ready for instant flight into unapproachableness.

"Howdy, Mr. Imsen?" she greeted him lightly. "In what official capacity am I to receive you, please? Do YOU want to send a telegram?" The accent upon the pronoun was very faint, but it was there for him to notice if he liked. So much she helped him. She was a bright young woman indeed, that she saw he wanted help.

"I don't believe I came to see you officially at all," he said, and his eyes lighted a little as he looked at her. "Peppajee Jim told me to come. He said you're a 'heap smart squaw, all same mans.'"

"Item: One pound of red-and-white candy for Peppajee Jim next time I see him." Miss Georgie laughed—but she also sat down so that her face was turned to the window. "Are you in urgent need of a heap smart squaw?" she asked. "I thought"— she caught herself up, and then went recklessly on—"I thought yesterday that you had found one!"

"It's brains I need just now." After the words were out, Good Indian wanted to swear at himself for seeming to belittle Evadna. "I mean," he corrected quickly—"do you know what I mean? I'll tell you what has happened, and if you don't know then, and can't help me, I'll just have to apologize for coming, and get out."

"Yes, I think you had better tell me why you need me particularly. I know the chicken's perfect, and doesn't lack brains, and you didn't mean that she does. You're all stirred up over something. What's wrong?" Miss Georgie would have spoken in just that tone if she had been a man or if Grant had been a woman.

So Good Indian told her.

"And you imagine that it's partly your fault, and that it wouldn't have happened if you had spent more time keeping your weather eye open, and not so much making love?" Miss Georgie could be very blunt, as well as keen. "Well, I don't see how you could prevent it, or what you could have done— unless you had kicked old Baumberger into the Snake. He's the god in this machine. I'd swear to that."

Good Indian had been fiddling with his hat and staring hard at a pile of old ties just outside the window. He raised his head, and regarded her steadily. It was beginning to occur to him that there was a good deal to this Miss Georgie, under that offhand, breezy exterior. He felt himself drawn to her as a person whom he could trust implicitly.

"You're right as far as I'm concerned," he owned, with his queer, inscrutable smile. "I think you're also right about him. What makes you think so, anyway?"

Miss Georgie twirled a ring upon her middle finger for a moment before she looked up at him.

"Do you know anything about mining laws?" she asked, and

when he swung his head slightly to one side in a tacit negative, she went on: "You say there are eight jumpers. Concerted action, that. Premeditated. My daddy was a lawyer," she threw in by way of explanation. "I used to help him in the office a good deal. When he—died, I didn't know enough to go on and be a lawyer myself, so I took to this." She waved her hand impatiently toward the telegraph instrument.

"So it's like this: Eight men can take placer claims—can hold them, you know—for one man. That's the limit, a hundred and sixty acres. Those eight men aren't jumping that ranch as eight individuals; they're in the employ of a principal who is engineering the affair. If I were going to shy a pebble at the head mogul, I'd sure try hard to hit our corpulent friend with the fishy eye. And that," she added, "is what all these cipher messages for Saunders mean, very likely. Baumberger had to have someone here to spy around for him and perhaps help him choose—or at least get together—those eight men. They must have come in on the night train, for I didn't see them. I'll bet they're tough customers, every mother's son of them! Fighters down to the ground, aren't they?"

"I only saw four. They were heeled, and ready for business, all right," he told her. "Soon as I saw what the game was, and that Baumberger was only playing for time and a free hand, I pulled out. I thought Peppajee might give me something definite to go on. He couldn't, though."

"Baumberger's going to steal that ranch according to law, you see," Miss Georgie stated with conviction. "They've got to pan out a sample of gold to prove there's pay dirt there, before they can file their claims. And they've got to do their filing in Shoshone. I suppose their notices are up O.K. I wonder, now, how they intend to manage that? I believe," she mused, "they'll have to go in person—I don't believe Baumberger can do that all himself legally. I've got some of daddy's law-books over in my trunk, and maybe I can look it up and make sure. But I know they haven't filed their claims yet. They've GOT to take possession first, and they've got to show a sample of ore, or

B. M. Bower

dust, it would be in this case. The best thing to do—" She drew her eyebrows together, and she pinched her under lip between her thumb and forefinger, and she stared abstractedly at Good Indian. "Oh, hurry up, Grant!" she cried unguardedly. "Think—think HARD, what's best to do!"

"The only thing I can think of," he scowled, "is to kill that—"

"And that won't do, under the circumstances," she cut in airily." There'd still be the eight. I'D like," she declared viciously, "to put rough-on-rats in his dinner, but I intend to refrain from doing as I'd like, and stick to what's best."

Good Indian gave her a glance of grateful understanding. "This thing has hit me hard," he confided suddenly. "I've been holding myself in all day. The Harts are like my own folks. They're all I've had, and she's been—they've all been—" Then the instinct of repression walled in his emotion, and he let the rest go in a long breath which told Miss Georgie all she needed to know. So much of Good Indian would never find expression in speech; all that was best of him would not, one might be tempted to think.

"By the way, is there any pay dirt on that ranch?" Miss Georgie kept herself rigidly to the main subject.

"No, there isn't. Not," he added dryly, "unless it has grown gold in the last few years. There are colors, of course. All this country practically can show colors, but pay dirt? No!"

"Look out," she advised him slowly, "that pay dirt doesn't grow over night! Sabe?"

Good Indian's eyes spoke admiration of her shrewdness.

"I must be getting stupid, not to have thought of that," he said.

"Can't give me credit for being 'heap smart'?" she bantered.

"Can't even let me believe I thought of something beyond the ken of the average person? Not," she amended ironically, "that I consider YOU an average person! Would you mind"—she became suddenly matter of fact—"waiting here while I go and rummage for a book I want? I'm almost sure I have one on mining laws. Daddy had a good deal of that in his business, being in a mining country. We've got to know just where we stand, it seems to me, because Baumberger's going to use the laws himself, and it's with the law we've got to fight him."

She had to go first and put a stop to the hysterical chattering of the sounder by answering the summons. It proved to be a message for Baumberger, and she wrote it down in a spiteful scribble which left it barely legible.

"Betraying professional secrets, but I don't care," she exclaimed, turning swiftly toward him. "Listen to this:

"How's fishing? Landed the big one yet? Ready for fry?"

She threw it down upon the table with a pettish gesture that was wholly feminine. "Sounds perfectly innocent, doesn't it? Too perfectly innocent, if you ask me." She stared out of the window abstractedly, her brows pinched together and her lips pursed with a corner between her teeth, much as she had stared after Baumberger the day before; and when she spoke she seemed to have swung her memory back to him then.

"He came up yesterday—with fish for Pete, he SAID, and of course he really did have some—and sent a wire to Shoshone. I found it on file when I came back. That was perfectly innocent, too. It was:

"Expect to land big one to-night. Plenty of small fry. Smooth trail."

"I've an excellent memory, you see." She laughed shortly. "Well, I'll go and hunt up that book, and we'll proceed to glean the wisdom of the serpent, so that we won't be compelled to remain as harmless as the dove! You won't mind waiting here?"

He assured her that he would not mind in the least, and she ran out bareheaded into the hot sunlight. Good Indian leaned forward a little in his chair so that he could watch her running across to the shack where she had a room or two, and he paid her the compliment of keeping her in his thoughts all the time she was gone. He felt, as he had done with Peppajee, that he had not known Miss Georgie at all until to-day, and he was a bit startled at what he was finding her to be.

"Of course," she laughed, when she rustled in again like a whiff of fresh air, "I had to go clear to the bottom of the last trunk I looked in. Lucky I only have three to my name, for it would have been in the last one just the same, if I'd had two dozen and had ransacked them all. But I found it, thank Heaven!"

She came eagerly up to him—he was sitting in the beribboned rocker dedicated to friendly callers, and had the rug badly rumpled with his spurs, which he had forgotten to remove—and with a sweep of her forearm she cleared the little table of novel, newspaper, and a magazine and deck of cards, and barely saved her box of chocolates from going bottom up on the floor.

"Like candy? Help yourself, if you do," she said, and tucked a piece into her mouth absent-mindedly before she laid the leather-bound book open on the table. "Now, we'll see what information Mr. Copp can give us. He's a high authority—General Land Office Commissioner, if you please. He's a few years old—several years old, for that matter—but I don't think he's out of date; I believe what he says still goes. M-m-m!-'Liens on Mines'—'Clause Inserted in Patents'—'Affidavits Taken Without Notice to Opposing'—oh, it must be here—it's GOT to be here!"

She was running a somewhat sticky forefinger slowly down the index pages. "It isn't alphabetically arranged, which I consider sloppy of Mr. Copp. Ah-h! 'Minerals Discovered After Patent Has Issued to Agricultural Claimant'—two hundred and eight. We'll just take a look at that first. That's what they're claiming, you know." She hitched her chair closer, and flipped the leaves eagerly. When she found the page, they touched heads over it, though Miss Georgie read aloud.

"Oh, it's a letter—but it's a decision, and as such has weight. U-m!

"SIR: In reply to your letter of inquiry . . . I have to state that all mineral deposits discovered on land after United States Patent therefor has issued to a party claiming under the laws regulating the disposal of agricultural lands, pass with the patent, and this office has no further jurisdiction in the premise. Very respectfully,"

"PASS WITH THE PATENT!" Miss Georgie turned her face so that she could look into Grant's eyes, so close to her own. "Old Peaceful must surely have his patent—Baumberger can't be much of a lawyer, do you think? Because that's a flat statement. There's no chance for any legal quibbling in that— IS there?"

"That's about as straight as he could put it," Good Indian agreed, his face losing a little of its anxiety.

"Well, we'll just browse along for more of the same," she suggested cheerfully, and went back to the index. But first she drew a lead pencil from where it had been stabbed through her hair, and marked the letter with heavy brackets, wetting the lead on her tongue for emphasis.

"Agricultural Claimants Entitled to Full Protection," she read hearteningly from the index, and turned hastily to see what was to be said about it. It happened to be another decision rendered in a letter, and they jubilated together over the sentiment conveyed therein.

"Now, here is what I was telling you, Grant," she said suddenly, after another long minute of studying silently the index. "'Eight Locaters of Placer Ground May Convey to One Party'—and Baumberger's certainly that party!—'Who Can Secure Patent for One Hundred and Sixty Acres.' We'll just read up on that, and find out for sure what the conditions are. Now, here"—she had found the page quickly—listen to this:

"I have to state that if eight bona-fide locaters"

("Whether they're that remains to be proven, Mr. Baumberger!")

"each having located twenty acres, in accordance with the congressional rules and regulations, should convey all their right, title, and interest in said locations to one person, such person might apply for a patent—"

"And so on into tiresomeness. Really, I'm beginning to think Baumberger's awfully stupid, to even attempt such a silly thing. He hasn't a legal leg to stand on. 'Goes with the patent'—that sounds nice to me. They're not locating in good faith—those eight jumpers down there." She fortified herself with another piece of candy. "All you need," she declared briskly, "is a good lawyer to take this up and see it through."

"You seem to be doing pretty well," he remarked, his eyes dwelling rather intently upon her face, and smiling as they did so.

"I can read what's in the book," she remarked lightly, her eyes upon its pages as if she were consciously holding them from meeting his look. "But it will take a lawyer to see the case through the courts. And let me tell you one thing very emphatically." She looked at him brightly. "Many a case as strong as this has been lost, just by legal quibbling and ignorance of how to handle it properly. Many a case without a leg to stand on has been won, by smooth work on the part of some lawyer. Now, I'll just jot down what they'll have to do, and prove, if they get that land—and look here, Mr. Man, here's another thing to consider. Maybe Baumberger doesn't expect to get a patent. Maybe he means to make old Peaceful so deucedly sick of the thing that he'll sell out cheap rather than fight the thing to a finish. Because this can be appealed, and taken up and up, and reopened because of some technical error—oh, as Jenny Wren says in—in—"

"Our Mutual Friend?" Good Indian suggested unexpectedly.

"Oh, you've read it!—where she always says: '*I* know their tricks and their manners!' And I do, from being so much with daddy in the office and hearing him talk shop. I know that, without a single bit of justice on their side, they could carry this case along till the very expense of it would eat up the ranch and leave the Harts flat broke. And if they didn't fight and keep on fighting, they could lose it—so there you are."

She shut the book with a slam. "But," she added more brightly when she saw the cloud of gloom settle blacker than before on his face, and remembered that he felt himself at least partly to blame, "it helps a lot to have the law all on our side, and—" She had to go then, because the dispatcher was calling, and she knew it must be a train order. "We'll read up a little more, and see just what are the requirements of placer mining laws—and maybe we can make it a trifle difficult for those eight to comply!" she told him over her shoulder, while her fingers chittered a reply to the call, and then turned her attention wholly to receiving the message.

Good Indian, knowing well the easy custom of the country which makes smoking always permissible, rolled himself a cigarette while he waited for her to come back to his side of the room. He was just holding the match up and waiting for a clear blaze before setting his tobacco afire, when came a tap-tap of feet on the platform, and Evadna appeared in the half-open doorway.

"Oh!" she exclaimed, and widened her indigo eyes at him

sitting there and looking so much at home.

"Come right in, chicken," Miss Georgie invited cordially. "Don't stand there in the hot sun. Mr. Imsen is going to turn the seat of honor over to you this instant. Awfully glad you came. Have some candy."

Evadna sat down in the rocker, thrust her two little feet out so that the toe, of her shoes showed close together beyond the hem of her riding-skirt, laid her gauntleted palms upon the arms of the chair and rocked methodically, and looked at Grant and then at Miss Georgie, and afterward tilted up her chin and smiled superciliously at an insurance company's latest offering to the public in the way of a calendar two feet long.

"When did you come up?" Good Indian asked her, trying so hard to keep a placating note out of his voice that he made himself sound apologetic.

"Oh—about an hour ago, I think," Evadna drawled sweetly— the sweet tones which always mean trouble, when employed by a woman.

Good Indian bit his lip, got up, and threw his cigarette out of the window, and looked at her reproachfully, and felt vaguely that he was misunderstood and most unjustly placed upon the defensive.

"I only came over," Evadna went on, as sweetly as before, "to say that there's a package at the store which I can't very well carry, and I thought perhaps you wouldn't mind taking it— when you go."

"I'm going now, if you're ready," he told her shortly, and reached for his hat.

Evadna rocked a moment longer, making him wait for her reply. She glanced at Miss Georgie still busy at the telegraph table, gave a little sigh of resignation, and rose with evident reluctance.

"Oh—if you're really going," she drawled, and followed him outside.

B. M. Bower

CHAPTER XVI

"DON'T GET EXCITED!"

Lovers, it would seem, require much less material for a quarrel than persons in a less exalted frame of mind.

Good Indian believed himself very much in love with his Christmas angel, and was very much inclined to let her know it, but at the same time he saw no reason why he should not sit down in Miss Georgie's rocking-chair, if he liked, and he could not quite bring himself to explain even to Evadna his reason for doing so. It humiliated him even to think of apologizing or explaining, and he was the type of man who resents humiliation more keenly than a direct injury.

As to Evadna, her atmosphere was that of conscious and magnanimous superiority to any feeling so humanly petty as jealousy—which is extremely irritating to anyone who is at all sensitive to atmospheric conditions.

She stopped outside the window long enough to chirp a commonplace sentence or two to Miss Georgie, and to explain just why she couldn't stay a minute longer. "I told Aunt Phoebe I'd be back to lunch—dinner, I mean—and she's so upset over those horrible men planted in the orchard—did Grant tell you about it?—that I feel I ought to be with her. And Marie has the toothache again. So I really must go. Good-by—come down whenever you can, won't you?" She smiled, and she waved a hand, and she held up her riding-skirt daintily as she turned away. "You didn't say goodby to Georgie," she reminded Grant, still making use of the chirpy tone. "I hope I am not in any way responsible."

"I don't see how you could be," said Good Indian calmly; and that, for some reason, seemed to intensify the atmosphere with which Evadna chose to surround herself.

She led Huckleberry up beside the store platform without giving Grant a chance to help, mounted, and started on while he was in after the package—a roll not more than eight inches long, and weighing at least four ounces, which brought an ironical smile to his lips. But she could not hope to outrun him on Huckleberry, even when Huckleberry's nose was turned toward home, and he therefore came clattering up before she had passed the straggling outpost of rusty tin cans which marked, by implication, the boundary line between Hartley and the sagebrush waste surrounding it.

"You seem to be in a good deal of a hurry," Good Indian observed.

"Not particularly," she replied, still chirpy as to tone and supercilious as to her manner.

It would be foolish to repeat all that was said during that ride home, because so much meaning was conveyed in tones and glances and in staring straight ahead and saying nothing. They were sparring politely before they were over the brow of the hill behind the town; they were indulging in veiled sarcasm—which came rapidly out from behind the veil and grew sharp and bitter—before they started down the dusty grade; they were not saying anything at all when they rounded the Point o' Rocks and held their horses rigidly back from racing home, as was their habit, and when they dismounted at the stable, they refused to look at each other upon any pretext whatsoever.

Baumberger, in his shirt-sleeves and smoking his big pipe, lounged up from the pasture gate where he had been indolently rubbing the nose of a buckskin two-year-old with an affectionate disposition, and wheezed out the information that it was warm. He got the chance to admire a very stiff pair of shoulders and a neck to match for his answer.

"I wasn't referring to your manner, m' son," he chuckled, after he had watched Good Indian jerk the latigo loose and pull off the saddle, showing the wet imprint of it on Keno's hide. "I wish the weather was as cool!"

Good Indian half turned with the saddle in his hands, and slapped it down upon its side so close to Baumberger that he took a hasty step backward, seized Keno's dragging bridle-reins, and started for the stable. Baumberger happened to be in the way, and he backed again, more hastily than before, to avoid being run over.

"Snow blind?" he interrogated, forcing a chuckle which had more the sound of a growl.

Good Indian stopped in the doorway, slipped off the bridle, gave Keno a hint by slapping him lightly on the rump, and when the horse had gone on into the cool shade of the stable, and taking his place in his stall, began hungrily nosing the hay in his manger, he came back to unsaddle Huckleberry, who was nodding sleepily with his under lip sagging much like Baumberger's while he waited. That gentleman seemed to be once more obstructing the path of Good Indian. He dodged back as Grant brushed past him.

"By the great immortal Jehosaphat!" swore Baumberger, with an ugly leer in his eyes, "I never knew before that I was so small I couldn't be seen with the naked eye!"

"You're so small in my estimation that a molecule would look like a hay-stack alongside you!" Good Indian lifted the skirt of Evadna's side-saddle, and proceeded calmly to loosen the cinch. His forehead smoothed a trifle, as if that one sentence had relieved him of some of his bottled bitterness.

"YOU ain't shrunk up none—in your estimation," Baumberger forgot his pose of tolerant good nature to say. His heavy jaw trembled as if he had been overtaken with a brief attack of palsy; so also did the hand which replaced his pipe between his loosely quivering lips. "That little yellow-haired witch must have given yuh the cold shoulder; but you needn't take it out on me. Had a quarrel?" He painstakingly brushed some ashes from his sleeve, once more the wheezing, chuckling fat man who never takes anything very seriously.

"Did you ever try minding your own business?" Grant inquired with much politeness of tone.

"We-e-ell, yuh see, m' son, it's my business to mind other people's business!" He chuckled at what he evidently considered a witty retort. "I've been pouring oil on the troubled waters all forenoon—maybe I've kinda got the habit."

"Only you're pouring it on a fire this time."

"That dangerous, yuh mean?"

"You're liable to start a conflagration you can't stop, and that may consume yourself, is all."

"Say, they sure do teach pretty talk in them colleges!" he purred, grinning loosely, his own speech purposely uncouth.

Good Indian turned upon him, stopped as quickly, and let his anger vent itself in a sneer. It had occurred to him that Baumberger was not goading him without purpose—because Baumberger was not that kind of man. Oddly enough, he had a short, vivid, mental picture of him and the look on his face when he was playing the trout; it seemed to him that there was something of that same cruel craftiness now in his eyes and around his mouth. Good Indian felt for one instant as if he were that trout, and Baumberger was playing him skillfully. "He's trying to make me let go all holds and tip my hand," he thought, keenly reading him, and he steadied himself.

B. M. Bower

"What d'yuh mean by me pouring oil on fire!" Baumberger urged banteringly. "Sounds like the hero talking to the villain in one of these here save-him-he's-my-sweetheart plays."

"You go to the devil," said Good Indian shortly.

"Don't repeat yourself, m' son; it's a sign uh failing powers. You said that to me this morning, remember? And—don't—get—excited!" His right arm raised slightly when he said that, as if he expected a blow for his answer.

Good Indian saw that involuntary arm movement, but he saw it from the tail of his eye, and he drew his lips a little tighter. Clearly Baumberger was deliberately trying to force him into a rage that would spend some of its force in threats, perhaps. He therefore grew cunningly calm, and said absolutely nothing. He led Huckleberry into the stable, came out, and shut the door, and walked past Baumberger as if he were not there at all. And Baumberger stood with his head lowered so that his flabby jaw was resting upon his chest, and stared frowningly after him until the yard gate swung shut behind his tall, stiffly erect figure.

"I gotta WATCH that jasper," he mumbled over his pipe, as a sort of summing up, and started slowly to the house. Halfway there he spoke again in the same mumbling undertone. "He's got the Injun look in his eyes t'-day. I gotta WATCH him."

He did watch him. It is astonishing how a family can live for months together, and not realize how little real privacy there is for anyone until something especial comes up for secret discussion. It struck Good Indian forcibly that afternoon, because he was anxious for a word in private with Peaceful, or with Phoebe, and also with Evadna—if it was only to continue their quarrel.

At dinner he could not speak without being heard by all. After dinner, the family showed an unconscious disposition to "bunch." Peaceful and Baumberger sat and smoked upon that part of the porch which was coolest, and the boys stayed close by so that they could hear what might be said about the amazing state of affairs down in the orchard.

Evadna, it is true, strolled rather self-consciously off to the head of the pond, carefully refraining, as she passed, from glancing toward Good Indian. He felt that she expected him to follow, but he wanted first to ask Peaceful a few questions, and to warn him not to trust Baumberger, so he stayed where he was, sprawled upon his back with a much-abused cushion under his head and his hat tilted over his face, so that he could see Baumberger's face without the scrutiny attracting notice.

He did not gain anything by staying, for Peaceful had little to say, seeming to be occupied mostly with dreamy meditations. He nodded, now and then, in response to Baumberger's rumbling monologues, and occasionally he removed his pipe from his mouth long enough to reply with a sentence where the nod was not sufficient. Baumberger droned on, mostly relating the details of cases he had won against long odds— cases for the most part similar to this claim-jumping business.

Nothing had been done that day, Grant gathered, beyond giving the eight claimants due notice to leave. The boys were evidently dissatisfied about something, though they said nothing. They shifted their positions with pettish frequency, and threw away cigarettes only half smoked, and scowled at dancing leaf-shadows on the ground.

When he could no longer endure the inaction, he rose, stretched his arms high above his head, settled his hat into place, gave Jack a glance of meaning, and went through the kitchen to the milk-house. He felt sure that Baumberger's ears were pricked toward the sound of his footsteps, and he made them purposely audible.

"Hello, Mother Hart," he called out cheerfully to Phoebe, pottering down in the coolness. "Any cream going to waste, or buttermilk, or cake?" He went down to her, and laid his hand upon her shoulder with a caressing touch which brought tears into her eyes. "Don't you worry a bit, little mother," he said softly. "I think we can beat them at their own game. They've stacked the deck, but we'll beat it, anyhow." His hand slid down to her arm, and gave it a little, reassuring squeeze.

"Oh, Grant, Grant!" She laid her forehead against him for a moment, then looked up at him with a certain whimsical solicitude. "Never mind our trouble now. What's this about you and Vadnie? The boys seem to think you two are going to make a match of it. And HAVE you been quarreling, you two? I only want," she added, deprecatingly, "to see my biggest boy happy, and if I can do anything in any way to help—"

"You can't, except just don't worry when we get to scrapping." His eyes smiled down at her with their old, quizzical humor, which she had not seen in them for some days. "I foresee that we're due to scrap a good deal of the time," he predicted. "We're both pretty peppery. But we'll make out, all right. You didn't"—he blushed consciously—"you didn't think I was going to—to fall dead in love—"

"Didn't I?" Phoebe laughed at him openly. "I'd have been more surprised if you hadn't. Why, my grief! I know enough about human nature, I hope, to expect—"

"Churning?" The voice of Baumberger purred down to them. There he stood bulkily at the top of the steps, good-naturedly regarding them. "Mr. Hart and I are goin' to take a ride up to the station—gotta send a telegram or two about this little affair"—he made a motion with his pipe toward the orchard— "and I just thought a good, cold drink of buttermilk before we start wouldn't be bad." His glance just grazed Good Indian, and passed him over as being of no consequence.

"If you don't happen to have any handy, it don't matter in the least," he added, and turned to go when Phoebe shook her head. "Anything we can get for yuh at the store, Mrs. Hart? Won't be any trouble at all—Oh, all right." He had caught another shake of the head.

"We may be gone till supper-time," he explained further, "and I trust to your good sense, Mrs. Hart, to see that the boys keep away from those fellows down there." The pipe, and also his head, again indicated the men in the orchard. "We don't want any ill feeling stirred up, you understand, and so they'd better just keep away from 'em. They're good boys—they'll do as you say." He leered at her ingratiatingly, shot a keen, questioning look at Good Indian, and went his lumbering way.

Grant went to the top of the steps, and made sure that he had really gone before he said a word. Even then he sat down upon the edge of the stairway with his back to the pond, so that he could keep watch of the approaches to the spring-house; he had become an exceedingly suspicious young man overnight.

"Mother Hart, on the square, what do you think of Baumberger?" he asked her abruptly. "Come and sit down; I want to talk with you—if I can without having the whole of Idaho listening."

"Oh, Grant—I don't know what to think! He seems all right, and I don't know why he shouldn't be just what he seems; he's got the name of being a good lawyer. But something—well, I get notions about things sometimes. And I can't, somehow, feel just right about him taking up this jumping business. I don't know why. I guess it's just a feeling, because I can see you don't like him. And the boys don't seem to, either, for some reason. I guess it's because he won't let 'em get right after those fellows and drive 'em off the ranch. They've been uneasy as they could be all day." She sat down upon a rough stool just inside the door, and looked up at him with troubled eyes. "And I'm getting it, too—seems like I'd go all to pieces if I can't do SOMETHING!" She sighed, and tried to cover the sigh with a laugh—which was not, however, a great success. "I wish I could be as cool-headed as Thomas," she said, with a tinge of petulance. "It don't seem to worry him none!"

"What does he think of Baumberger? Is he going to let him take the case and handle it to please himself?" Good Indian was tapping his boot-toe thoughtfully upon the bottom step, and glancing up now and then as a precaution against being overheard.

"I guess so," she admitted, answering the last question first. "I haven't had a real good chance to talk to Thomas all day. Baumberger has been with him most of the time. But I guess he is; anyway, Baumberger seems to take it for granted he's got the case. Thomas hates to hurt anybody's feelings, and, even if he didn't want him, he'd hate to say so. But he's as good a lawyer as any, I guess. And Thomas seems to like him well enough. Thomas," she reminded Good Indian unnecessarily, "never does say much about anything."

"I'd like to get a chance to talk to him," Good Indian observed. "I'll have to just lead him off somewhere by main strength, I guess. Baumberger sticks to him like a bur to a dog's tail. What are those fellows doing down there now ? Does anybody know?"

"You heard what he said to me just now," Phoebe said, impatiently. "He don't want anybody to go near. It's terribly aggravating," she confessed dispiritedly, "to have a lot of ruffians camped down, cool as you please, on your own ranch, and not be allowed to drive 'em off. I don't wonder the boys are all sulky. If Baumberger wasn't here at all, I guess we'd have got rid of 'em before now. I don't know as I think very much of lawyers, anyhow. I believe I'd a good deal rather fight first and go,to law about it afterward if I had to. But Thomas is so—CALM!"

"I think I'll go down and have a look," said Good Indian suddenly. "I'm not under Baumberger's orders, if the rest of the bunch is. And I wish you'd tell Peaceful I want to talk to him, Mother Hart—will you? Tell him to ditch his guardian angel somehow. I'd like to see him on the quiet if I can, but if I can't—"

"Can't be nice, and forgiving, and repentant, and—a dear?"
Evadna had crept over to him by way of the rocks behind the
pond, and at every pause in her questioning she pushed him
forward by his two shoulders. "I'm so furious I could beat you!
What do you mean, savage, by letting a lady stay all afternoon
by herself, waiting for you to come and coax her into being
nice to you? Don't you know I H-A-ATE you?" She had him
by the ears, then, pulling his head erratically from side to side,
and she finished by giving each ear a little slap and laid her
arms around his neck. "Please don't look at me that way, Aunt
Phoebe," she said, when she discovered her there inside the
door. "Here's a horrible young villain who doesn't know how
to behave, and makes me do all the making up. I don't like
him one bit, and I just came to tell him so and be done. And I
don't suppose," she added, holding her two hands tightly over
his mouth, "he has a word to say for himself."

Since he was effectually gagged, Grant had not a word to say.
Even when he had pulled her hands away and held them
prisoners in his own, he said nothing. This was Evadna in a
new and unaccountable mood, it seemed to him. She had
certainly been very angry with him at noon. She had accused
him, in that roundabout way which seems to be a woman's
favorite method of reaching a real grievance, of being fickle
and neglectful and inconsiderate and a brute.

The things she had said to him on the way down the grade had
rankled in his mind, and stirred all the sullen pride in his
nature to life, and he could not forget them as easily as she
appeared to have done. Good Indian was not in the habit of
saying things, even in anger, which he did not mean, and he
could not understand how anyone else could do so. And the
things she had said!

But here she was, nevertheless, laughing at him and blushing
adorably because he still held her fast, and making the blood of
him race most unreasonably.

"Don't scold me, Aunt Phoebe," she begged, perhaps because

there was something in Phoebe's face which she did not quite understand, and so mistook for disapproval of her behavior. "I should have told you last night that we're—well, I SUPPOSE we're supposed to be engaged!" She twisted her hands away from him, and came down the steps to her aunt. "It all happened so unexpectedly—really, I never dreamed I cared anything for him, Aunt Phoebe, until he made me care. And last night I couldn't tell you, and this morning I was going to, but all this horrible trouble came up—and, anyway," she finished with a flash of pretty indignation, "I think Grant might have told you himself! I don't think it's a bit nice of him to leave everything like that for me. He might have told you before he went chasing off to—to Hartley." She put her arms around her aunt's neck. "You aren't angry, are you, Aunt Phoebe?" she coaxed. "You—you know you said you wanted me to be par-TIC-ularly nice to Grant!"

"Great grief, child! You needn't choke me to death. Of course I'm not angry." But Phoebe's eyes did not brighten.

"You look angry," Evadna pouted, and kissed her placatingly.

"I've got plenty to be worked up over, without worrying over your love affairs, Vadnie." Phoebe's eyes sought Grant's anxiously. "I don't doubt but what it's more important to you than anything else on earth, but I'm thinking some of the home I'm likely to lose."

Evadna drew back, and made a movement to go.

"Oh, I'm sorry I interrupted you then, Aunt Phoebe. I suppose you and Grant were busy discussing those men in the orchard—"

"Don't be silly, child. You aren't interrupting anybody, and there's no call for you to run off like that. We aren't talking secrets that I know of."

In some respects the mind of Good Indian was extremely

simple and direct. His knowledge of women was rudimentary and based largely upon his instincts rather than any experience he had had with them. He had been extremely uncomfortable in the knowledge that Evadna was angry, and strongly impelled, in spite of his hurt pride, to make overtures for peace. He was puzzled, as well as surprised, when she seized him by the shoulders and herself made peace so bewitchingly that he could scarcely realize it at first. But since fate was kind, and his lady love no longer frowned upon him, he made the mistake of taking it for granted she neither asked nor expected him to explain his seeming neglect of her and his visit to Miss Georgie at Hartley.

She was not angry with him. Therefore, he was free to turn his whole attention to this trouble which had come upon his closest friends. He reached out, caught Evadna by the hand, pulled her close to him, and smiled upon her in a way to make her catch her breath in a most unaccountable manner.

But he did not say anything to her; he was a young man unused to dalliance when there were serious things at hand.

"I'm going down there and see what they're up to," he told Phoebe, giving Evadna's hand a squeeze and letting it go. "I suspect there's something more than keeping the peace behind Baumberger's anxiety to have them left strictly alone. The boys had better keep away, though."

"Are you going down in the orchard?" Evadna rounded her unbelievably blue eyes at him. "Then I'm going along."

"You'll do nothing of the kind, little Miss Muffit," he declared from the top step.

"Why not?"

"I might want to do some swearing." He grinned down at her, and started off.

"Now, Grant, don't you do anything rash!" Phoebe called after him sharply.

"Don't—get—excited!" he retorted, mimicking Baumberger.

"I'm going a little way, whether you want me to or not," Evadna threatened, pouting more than ever.

She did go as far as the porch with him, and was kissed and sent back like a child. She did not, however, go back to her aunt, but ran into her own room, where she could look out through the grove toward the orchard—and to the stable as well, though that view did not interest her particularly at first. It was pure accident that made her witness what took place at the gate.

CHAPTER XVII

A LITTLE TARGET-PRACTICE

A grimy buck with no hat of any sort and with his hair straggling unbraided over one side of his face to conceal a tumor which grew just over his left eye like a large, ripe plum, stood outside the gate, in doubt whether to enter or remain where he was. When he saw Good Indian he grunted, fumbled in his blanket, and held out a yellowish envelope.

"Ketchum Squaw-talk-far-off," he explained gutturally.

Good Indian took the envelope, thinking it must be a telegram, though he could not imagine who would be sending him one. His name was written plainly upon the outside, and within was a short note scrawled upon a telegraph form:

"Come up as soon as you possibly can. I've something to tell you."

That was what she had written. He read it twice before he looked up.

"What time you ketchum this?" he asked, tapping the message with his finger.

"Mebbyso one hour." The buck pulled a brass watch ostentatiously from under his blanket, held it to his ear a moment, as if he needed auricular assurance that it was

B. M. Bower

running properly, and pointed to the hour of three. "Ketchum one dolla, mebbyso pikeway quick. No stoppum," he said virtuously.

"You see Peaceful in Hartley?" Good Indian asked the question from an idle impulse; in reality, he was wondering what it was that Miss Georgie had to tell him.

"Peacefu', him go far off. On train. All same heap fat man go 'long. Mebbyso Shoshone, mebbyso Pocatello."

Good Indian looked down at the note, and frowned; that, probably, was what she had meant to tell him, though he could not see where the knowledge was going to help him any. If Peaceful had gone to Shoshone, he was gone, and that settled it. Undoubtedly he would return the next day—perhaps that night, even. He was beginning to feel the need of a quiet hour in which to study the tangle, but he had a suspicion that Baumberger had some reason other than a desire for peace in wanting the jumpers left to themselves, and he started toward the orchard, as he had at first intended.

"Mebbyso ketchum one dolla, yo'," hinted Charlie, the buck.

But Good Indian went on without paying any attention to him. At the road he met Jack and Wally, just returning from the orchard.

"No use going down there," Jack informed him sulkily. "They're just laying in the shade with their guns handy, doing nothing. They won't let anybody cross their line, and they won't say anything—not even when you cuss 'em. Wally and I got black in the face trying to make them come alive. Baumberger got back yet? Wally and I have got a scheme—"

"He and your dad took the train for Shoshone. Say, does anyone know what that bunch over in the meadow is up to?" Good Indian leaned his back against a tree, and eyed the two morosely.

"Clark and Gene are over there," said Wally. "But I'd gamble they aren't doing any more than these fellows are. They haven't started to pan out any dirt—they haven't done a thing, it looks like, but lay around in the shade. I must say I don't sabe their play. And the worst of it is," he added desperately, "a fellow can't do anything."

"I'm going to break out pretty darned sudden," Jack observed calmly. "I feel it coming on." He smiled, but there was a look of steel in his eyes.

Good Indian glanced at him sharply.

"Now, you fellows' listen to me," he said. "This thing is partly my fault. I could have prevented it, maybe, if I hadn't been so taken up with my own affairs. Old Peppajee told me Baumberger was up to some devilment when he first came down here. He heard him talking to Saunders in Pete Hamilton's stable. And the first night he was here, Peppajee and I saw him down at the stable at midnight, talking to someone. Peppajee kept on his trail till he got that snake bite, and he warned me a plenty. But I didn't take much stock in it—or if I did—" He lifted his shoulders expressively.

"So," he went on, after a minute of bitter thinking, "I want you to keep out of this. You know how your mother would feel—You don't want to get foolish. You can keep an eye on them—to-night especially. I've an idea they're waiting for dark; and if I knew why, I'd be a lot to the good. And if I knew why old Baumberger took your father off so suddenly, why—I'd be wiser than I am now." He lifted his hat, brushed the moisture from his forehead, and gave a grunt of disapproval when his eyes rested on Jack.

"What yuh loaded down like that for?" he demanded. "You fellows better put those guns in cold storage. I'm like Baumberger in one respect—we don't want any violence!" He grinned without any feeling of mirth.

"Something else is liable to be put in cold storage first," Wally hinted, significantly. "I must say I like this standing around and looking dangerous, without making a pass! I wish something would break loose somewhere."

"I notice you're packing yours, large as life," Jack pointed out. "Maybe you're just wearing it for an ornament, though."

"Sure!" Good Indian, feeling all at once the utter futility of standing there talking, left them grumbling over their forced inaction, without explaining where he was going, or what he meant to do. Indeed, he scarcely knew himself. He was in that uncomfortable state of mind where one feels that one must do something, without having the faintest idea of what that something is, or how it is to be done. It seemed to him that they were all in the same mental befuddlement, and it seemed impossible to stay on the ranch another hour without making a hostile move of some sort—and he knew that, when he did make a move, he at least ought to know why he did it.

The note in his pocket gave him an excuse for action of some sort, even though he felt sure that nothing would come of it; at least, he thought, he would have a chance to discuss the thing with Miss Georgie again—and while he was not a man who must have everything put into words, he had found comfort and a certain clarity of thought in talking with her.

"Why don't you invite me to go along?" Evadna challenged from the gate, when he was ready to start. She laughed when she said it, but there was something beneath the laughter, if he had only been close enough to read it.

"I didn't think you'd want to ride through all that dust and heat again to-day," he called back. "You're better off in the shade."

"Going to call on 'Squaw-talk-far-off'—AGAIN?" She was still laughing, with something else beneath the laugh.

He glanced at her quickly, wondering where she had gotten the name, and in his wonder neglected to make audible reply. Also he passed over the change to ride back to the gate and tell her good-by—with a hasty kiss, perhaps, from the saddle—as a lover should have done.

He was not used to love-making. For him, it was settled that they loved each other, and would marry some day—he hoped the day would be soon. It did not occur to him that a girl wants to be told over and over that she is the only woman in the whole world worth a second thought or glance; nor that he should stop and say just where he was going, and what he meant to do, and how reluctant he was to be away from her. Trouble sat upon his mind like a dead weight, and dulled his perception, perhaps. He waved his hand to her from the stable, and galloped down the trail to the Point o' Rocks, and his mind, so far as Evadna was concerned, was at ease.

Evadna, however, was crying, with her arms folded upon the top of the gate, before the cloud which marked his passing had begun to sprinkle the gaunt, gray sagebushes along the trail with a fresh layer of choking dust. Jack and Wally came up, scowling at the world and finding no words to match their gloom. Wally gave her a glance, and went on to the blacksmith shop, but Jack went straight up to her, for he liked her well.

"What's the matter?" he asked dully. "Mad because you can't smoke up the ranch?"

Evadna fumbled blindly for her handkerchief, scoured her eyes well when she found it, and put up the other hand to further shield her face.

"Oh, the whole place is like a GRAVEYARD," she complained. "Nobody will talk, or do anything but just wander around! I just can't STAND it!" Which was not frank of her.

"It's too hot to do much of anything," he said apologetically.

"We might take a ride, if you don't mind the heat."

"You don't want to ride," she objected petulantly. "Why didn't you go with Good Indian?" he countered.

"Because I didn't want to. And I do wish you'd quit calling him that; he has a real name, I believe."

"If you're looking for a scrap," grinned Jack, "I'll stake you to my six gun, and you can go down and kill off a few of those claim-jumpers. You seem to be in just about the proper frame uh mind to murder the whole bunch. Fly at it!"

"It begins to look as if we women would have to do something," she retorted cruelly. "There doesn't seem to be a man on the ranch with spirit enough to stop them from digging up the whole—"

"I guess that'll be about enough," Jack interrupted her, coldly. "Why didn't you say that to Good Indian?"

"I told you not to call him that. I don't see why everybody is so mean to-day. There isn't a person—"

When Jack laughed, he shut his eyes until he looked through narrow slits under heavy lashes, and showed some very nice teeth, and two deep dimples besides the one which always stood in his chin. He laughed then, for the first time that day, and if Evadna had been in a less vixenish temper she would have laughed with him just as everyone else always did. But instead of that, she began to cry again, which made Jack feel very much a brute.

"Oh, come on and be good," he urged remorsefully. But Evadna turned and ran back into the house and into her room, and cried luxuriously into her pillow. Jack, peeping in at the window which opened upon the porch, saw her there, huddled upon the bed.

In the spring-house his mother sat crying silently over her helplessness, and failed to respond to his comforting pats upon the shoulder. Donny struck at him viciously when Jack asked him an idle question, and Charlie, the Indian with the tumor over his eye, scowled from the corner of the house where he was squatting until someone offered him fruit, or food, or tobacco. He was of an acquisitive nature, was Charlie—and the road to his favor must be paved with gifts.

"This is what I call hell," Jack stated aloud, and went straight away to the strawberry patch, took up his stand with his toes against Stanley's corner stake, cursed him methodically until he had quite exhausted his vocabulary, and put a period to his forceful remarks by shooting a neat, round hole through Stanley's coffee-pot. And Jack was the mild one of the family.

By the time he had succeeded in puncturing recklessly the frying-pan, and also the battered pan in which Stanley no doubt meant to wash his samples of soil, his good humor returned. So also did the other boys, running in long leaps through the garden and arriving at the spot very belligerent and very much out of breath.

"Got to do something to pass away the time," Jack grinned, bringing his front sight once more to bear upon the coffee—pot, already badly dented and showing three black holes. "And I ain't offering any violence to anybody. You can't hang a man, Mr. Stanley, for shooting up a frying-pan. And I wouldn't—hurt—you—for—anything!" He had just reloaded, so that his bullets saw him to the end of the sentence.

Stanley watched his coffee-pot dance and roll like a thing in pain, and swore when all was done. But he did not shoot, though one could see how his fingers must itch for the feel of the trigger.

"Your old dad will sweat blood for this—and you'll be packing your blanket on your back and looking for work before snow flies," was his way of summing up.

Still, he did not shoot.

It was like throwing pebbles at the bowlder in the Malad, the day before.

When Phoebe came running in terror toward the fusillade, with Marie and her swollen face, and Evadna and her red eyes following in great trepidation far behind, they found four claim-jumpers purple from long swearing, and the boys gleefully indulging in revolver practice with various camp utensils for the targets.

They stopped when their belts were empty as well as their guns, and they went back to the house with the women, feeling much better. Afterward they searched the house for more "shells," clattering from room to room, and looking into cigar boxes and upon out-of-the-way shelves, while Phoebe expostulated in the immediate background.

"Your father would put a stop to it pretty quick if he was here," she declared over and over. "Just because they didn't shoot back this time is no sign they won't next time you boys go to hectoring them." All the while she knew she was wasting her breath, and she had a secret fear that her manner and her tones were unconvincing. If she had been a man, she would have been their leader, perhaps. So she retreated at last to her favorite refuge, the milk-house, and tried to cover her secret approval with grumbling to herself.

There was a lull in the house. The boys, it transpired, had gone in a body to Hartley after more cartridges, and the cloud of dust which hovered long over the trail testified to their haste. They returned surprisingly soon, and they would scarcely wait for their supper before they hurried back through the garden. One would think that they were on their way to a dance, so eager they were.

They dug themselves trenches in various parts of the garden, laid themselves gleefully upon their stomachs, and proceeded to exchange, at the top of their strong, young voices, ideas upon the subject of claim-jumping, and to punctuate their remarks with leaden periods planted neatly and with precision in the immediate vicinity of one of the four.

They had some trouble with Donny, because he was always jumping up that he might yell the louder when one of the enemy was seen to step about uneasily whenever a bullet pinged closer than usual, and the rifles began to bark viciously now and then. It really was unsafe for one to dance a clog, with flapping arms and taunting laughter, within range of those rises, and they told Donny so.

They ordered him back to the house; they threw clods of earth at his bare legs; they threatened and they swore, but it was not until Wally got him by the collar and shook him with brotherly thoroughness that Donny retreated in great indignation to the house.

They were just giving themselves wholly up to the sport of sending little spurts of loose earth into the air as close as was safe to Stanley, and still much too close for his peace of mind or that of his fellows, when Donny returned unexpectedly with the shotgun and an enthusiasm for real bloodshed.

He fired once from the thicket of currant bushes, and, from the remarks which Stanley barked out in yelping staccato, he punctured that gentleman's person in several places with the fine shot of which the charge consisted. He would have fired again if the recoil had not thrown him quite off his balance, and it is possible that someone would have been killed as a result. For Stanley began firing with murderous intent, and only the dusk and Good Indian's opportune arrival prevented serious trouble.

Good Indian had talked long with Miss Georgie, and had agreed with her that, for the present at least, there must be no violence. He had promised her flatly that he would do all in his power to keep the peace, and he had gone again to the

Indian camp to see if Peppajee or some of his fellows could give him any information about Saunders.

Saunders had disappeared unaccountably, after a surreptitious conference with Baumberger the day before, and it was that which Miss Georgie had to tell him. Saunders was in the habit of sleeping late, so that she did not know until noon that he was gone. Pete was worried, and garrulously feared the worst. The worst, according to Pete Hamilton, was sudden death of a hemorrhage.

Miss Georgie asserted unfeelingly that Saunders was more in danger of dying from sheer laziness than of consumption, and she even went so far as to hint cynically, that even his laziness was largely hypocritical.

"I don't believe there's a single honest thing about the fellow," she said to Good Indian. "When he coughs, it sounds as if he just did it for effect. When he lies in the shade asleep, I've seen him watching people from under his lids. When he reads, his ears seem always pricked up to hear everything that's going on, and he gives those nasty little slanty looks at everybody within sight. I don't believe he's really gone—because I can't imagine him being really anything. But I do believe he's up to something mean and sneaky, and, since Peppajee has taken this matter to heart, maybe he can find out something. I think you ought to go and see him, anyway, Mr. Imsen."

So Good Indian had gone to the Indian camp, and had afterward ridden along the rim of the bluff, because Sleeping Turtle had seen someone walking through the sagebrush in that direction. From the rim-rock above the ranch, Good Indian had heard the shooting, though the trees hid from his sight what was taking place, and he had given over his search for Saunders and made haste to reach home.

He might have gone straight down the bluff afoot, through a rift in the rim-rock where it was possible to climb down into the fissure and squeeze out through a narrow opening to the bowlder-piled bluff. But that took almost as much time as he would consume in riding around, and so he galloped back to the grade and went down at a pace to break his neck and that of Keno as well if his horse stumbled.

He reached home in time to see Donny run across the road with the shotgun, and the orchard in time to prevent a general rush upon Stanley and his fellows—which was fortunate. He got them all out of the garden and into the house by sheer determination and biting sarcasm, and bore with surprising patience their angry upbraidings. He sat stoically silent while they called him a coward and various other things which were unpleasant in the extreme, and he even smiled when they finally desisted and trailed off sullenly to bed.

But when they were gone he sat alone upon the porch, brooding over the day and all it had held of trouble and perplexity. Evadna appeared tentatively in the open door, stood there for a minute or two waiting for some overture upon his part, gave him a chilly good-night when she realized he was not even thinking of her, and left him. So great was his absorption that he let her go, and it never occurred to him that she might possibly consider herself ill-used. He would have been distressed if he could have known how she cried herself to sleep but, manlike, he would also have been puzzled.

CHAPTER XVIII

A SHOT FROM THE RIM-ROCK

Good Indian was going to the stable to feed the horses next morning, when something whined past him and spatted viciously against the side of the chicken-house. Immediately afterward he thought he heard the sharp crack which a rifle makes, but the wind was blowing strongly up the valley, and he could not be sure.

He went over to the chicken-house, probed with his knife-blade into the plank where was the splintered hole, and located a bullet. He was turning it curiously in his fingers when another one plunked into the boards, three feet to one side of him; this time he was sure of the gun-sound, and he also saw a puff of blue smoke rise up on the rim-rock above him. He marked the place instinctively with his eyes, and went on to the stable, stepping rather more quickly than was his habit.

Inside, he sat down upon the oats-box, and meditated upon what he should do. He could not even guess at his assailant, much less reach him. A dozen men could be picked off by a rifle in the hands of one at the top, while they were climbing that bluff.

Even if one succeeded in reaching the foot of the rim-rock, there was a forty-foot wall of unscalable rock, with just the one narrow fissure where it was possible to climb up to the level above, by using both hands to cling to certain sharp projections while the feet sought a niche here and there in the wall. Easy enough—if one were but left to climb in peace, but absolutely suicidal if an enemy stood above.

He scowled through the little paneless window at what he could see of the bluff, and thought of the mile-long grade to be climbed and the rough stretch of lava rock, sage, and scattered bowlders to be gone over before one could reach the place upon a horse. Whoever was up there, he would have more than enough time to get completely away from the spot before it would be possible to gain so much as a glimpse of him.

And who could he be? And why was he shooting at Good Indian, so far a non-combatant, guiltless of even firing a single shot since the trouble began?

Wally came in, his hat far back on his head, a cigarette in the corner of his mouth, and his manner an odd mixture of conciliation and defiance, ready to assume either whole-heartedly at the first word from the man he had cursed so unstintingly before he slept. He looked at Good Indian, caught sight of the leaden pellet he was thoughtfully turning round and round in his fingers, and chose to ignore for the moment any unpleasantness in their immediate past.

"Where you ketchum?" he asked, coming a bit closer.

"In the side of the chicken-house." Good Indian's tone was laconic.

Wally reached out, and took the bullet from him that he might juggle it curiously in his own fingers. "I don't think!" he scouted.

"There's another one there to match this," Good Indian stated calmly, "and if I should walk over there after it, I'll gamble there'd be more."

Wally dropped the flattened bullet, stooped, and groped for it in the litter on the floor, and when he had found it he eyed it more curiously than before. But he would have died in his tracks rather than ask a question.

"Didn't anybody take a shot at you, as you came from the house?" Good Indian asked when he saw the mood of the other.

"If he did, he was careful not to let me find it out." Wally's expression hardened.

"He was more careless a while ago," said Good Indian. "Some fellow up on the bluff sent me a little morning salute. But," he added slowly, and with some satisfaction, "he's a mighty poor shot."

Jack sauntered in much as Wally had done, saw Good Indian sitting there, and wrinkled his eyes shut in a smile.

"Please, sir, I never meant a word I said!" he began, with exaggerated trepidation. "Why the dickens didn't you murder the whole yapping bunch of us, Grant?" He clapped his hand affectionately upon the other's shoulder. "We kinda run amuck yesterday afternoon," he confessed cheerfully, "but it sure was fun while it lasted!"

"There's liable to be some more fun of the same kind," Wally informed him shortly. "Good Injun says someone on the bluff took a shot at him when he was coming to the stable. If any of them jumpers—"

"It's easy to find out if it was one of them," Grant cut in, as if the idea had just come to him. We can very soon see if they're all on their little patch of soil. Let's go take a look."

They went out guardedly, their eyes upon the rim-rock. Good Indian led the way through the corral, into the little pasture, and across that to where the long wall of giant poplars shut off the view.

"I admire courage," he grinned, "but I sure do hate a fool."
Which was all the explanation he made for the detour that hid
them from sight of anyone stationed upon the bluff, except
while they were passing from the stable-door to the corral; and
that, Jack said afterward, didn't take all day.

Coming up from the rear, they surprised Stanley and one other
peacefully boiling coffee in a lard pail which they must have
stolen in the night from the ranch junk heap behind the
blacksmith shop. The three peered out at them from a distant
ambush, made sure that there were only two men there, and
went on to the disputed part of the meadows. There the four
were pottering about, craning necks now and then toward the
ranch buildings as if they half feared an assault of some kind.
Good Indian led the way back to the stable.

"If there was any way of getting around up there without being
seen," he began thoughtfully, "but there isn't. And while I
think of it," he added, "we don't want to let the women know
about this."

"They're liable to suspect something," Wally reminded dryly,
"if one of us gets laid out cold."

Good Indian laughed. "It doesn't look as if he could hit
anything smaller than a haystack. And anyway, I think I'm the
boy he's after, though I don't see why. I haven't done a
thing—yet."

"Let's feed the horses and then pace along to the house, one at
a time, and find out," was Jack's reckless suggestion. "Anybody
that knows us at all can easy tell which is who. And I guess it
would be tolerably safe."

Foolhardy as the thing looked to be, they did it, each after his
own manner of facing a known danger. Jack went first because,
as he said, it was his idea, and he was willing to show his heart
was in the right place. He rolled and lighted a cigarette,
wrinkled his eyes shut in a laugh, and strolled nonchalantly out

B. M. Bower

of the stable.

"Keep an eye on the rim-rock, boys," he called back, without turning his head. A third of the way he went, stopped dead still, and made believe inspect something upon the ground at his feet.

"Ah, go ON!" bawled Wally, his nerves all on edge.

Jack dug his heel into the dust, blew the ashes from his cigarette, and went on slowly to the gate, passed through, and stood well back, out of sight under the trees, to watch.

Wally snorted disdain of any proceeding so spectacular, but he was as he was made, and he could not keep his dare-devil spirit quite in abeyance. He twitched his hat farther back on his head, stuck his hands deep into his pockets, and walked deliberately out into the open, his neck as stiff as a newly elected politician on parade. He did not stop, as Jack had done, but he facetiously whistled "Tramp, tramp, tramp, the boys are marching," and he went at a pace which permitted him to finish the tune before he reached the gate. He joined Jack in the shade, and his face, when he looked back to the stable, was anxious.

"It must be Grant he wants, all right," he muttered, resting one hand on Jack's shoulder and speaking so he could not be overheard from the house. "And I wish to the Lord he'd stay where he's at."

But Good Indian was already two paces from the door, coming steadily up the path, neither faster nor slower than usual, with his eyes taking in every object within sight as he went, and his thumb hooked inside his belt, near where his gun swung at his hip. It was not until his free hand was upon the gate that lack and Wally knew they had been holding their breath.

"Well—here I am," said Good Indian, after a minute, smiling down at them with the sunny look in his eyes. "I'm beginning to think I had a dream. Only"—he dipped his fingers into the pocket of his shirt and brought up the flattened bullet—"that is pretty blamed realistic—for a dream." His eyes searched involuntarily the rim-rock with a certain incredulity, as if he could not bring himself to believe in that bullet, after all.

"But two of the jumpers are gone," said Wally. "I reckon we stirred 'em up some yesterday, and they're trying to get back at us."

"They've picked a dandy place," Good Indian observed. "I think maybe it would be a good idea to hold that fort ourselves. We should have thought of that; only I never thought—"

Phoebe, heavy-eyed and pale from wakefulness and worry, came then, and called them in to breakfast. Gene and Clark came in, sulky still, and inclined to snappishness when they did speak. Donny announced that he had been in the garden, and that Stanley told him he would blow the top of his head off if he saw him there again. "And I never done a thing to him!" he declared virtuously.

Phoebe set down the coffee-pot with an air of decision.

"I want you boys to remember one thing," she said firmly, "and that is that there must be no more shooting going on around here. It isn't only what Baumberger thinks—I don't know as ho's got anything to say about it—it's what I think. I know I'm only a woman, and you all consider yourselves men, whether you are or not, and it's beneath your dignity, maybe, to listen to your mother.

"But your mother has seen the day when she was counted on as much, almost, as if she'd been a man. Why, great grief! I've stood for hours peeking out a knot-hole in the wall, with that same old shotgun Donny got hold of, ready to shoot the first Injun that stuck his nose from behind a rock."

B. M. Bower

The color came into her cheeks at the memory, and a sparkle into her eyes. "I've seen real fighting, when it was a life-and-death matter. I've tended to the men that were shot before my eyes, and I've sung hymns over them that died. You boys have grown up on some of the stories about the things I've been through.

"And here last night," she reproached irritatedly, I heard someone say: 'Oh, come on—we're scaring Mum to death!' The idea! 'scaring Mum!' I can tell you young jackanapes one thing: If I thought there was anything to be gained by it, or if it would save trouble instead of MAKING trouble,'MUM' could go down there right now, old as she is, and SCARED as she is, and clean out the whole, measly outfit!" She stared sternly at the row of faces bent over their plates.

"Oh, you can laugh—it's only your mother!" she exclaimed indignantly, when she saw Jack's eyes go shut and Gene's mouth pucker into a tight knot. "But I'll have you to know I'm boss of this ranch when your father's gone, and if there's any more of that kid foolishness to-day—laying behind a currant bush and shooting COFFEE-POTS!—I'll thrash the fellow that starts it! It isn't the kind of fighting I'VE been used to. I may be away behind the times—I guess I am!—but I've always been used to the idea that guns weren't to be used unless you meant business. This thing of getting out and PLAYING gun-fight is kinda sickening to a person that's seen the real thing.

"Scaring Mum to death!" She seemed to find it very hard to forget that, or to forgive it. "'SCARING MUM'—and Jack, there, was born in the time of an Indian uprising, and I laid with your father's revolver on the pillow where I could put my hand on it, day or night! YOU scare Mum! MUM will scare YOU, if there's any more of that let's-play-Injun business going on around this ranch. Why, I'd lead you down there by the ear, every mother's son of you, and tell that man Stanley to SPANK you!"

"Mum can whip her weight in wildcats any old time," Wally announced after a heavy silence, and glared aggressively from one foolish-looking face to another.

As was frequently the case, the wave of Phoebe's wrath ebbed harmlessly away in laughter as the humorous aspect of her tirade was brought to her attention.

"Just the same, I want you should mind what I tell you," she said, in her old motherly tone, "and keep away from those ruffians down there. You can't do anything but make 'em mad, and give 'em an excuse for killing someone. When your father gets back, we'll see what's to be done."

"All right, Mum. We won't look toward the garden to-day," Wally promised largely, and held out his cup to her to be refilled." You can keep my gun, if you want to make dead sure."

"No, I can trust my boys, I hope," and she glowed with real pride in them when she said it.

Good Indian lingered on the porch for half an hour or so, waiting for Evadna to appear. She may have seen him through the window—at any rate she slipped out very quietly, and had her breakfast half eaten before he suspected that she was up; and when he went into the kitchen, she was talking animatedly with Marie about Mexican drawn-work, and was drawing intricate little diagrams of certain patterns with her fork upon the tablecloth.

She looked up, and gave him a careless greeting, and went back to discussing certain "wheels" in the corner of an imaginary lunch-cloth and just how one went about making them. He made a tentative remark or two, trying to win her attention to himself, but she pushed her cup and saucer aside to make room for further fork drawings, and glanced at him with her most exaggerated Christmas-angel look.

"Don't interrupt, please," she said mincingly. "This is IMPORTANT. And," she troubled to explain, "I'm really in a hurry, because I'm going to help Aunt Phoebe make strawberry jam."

If she thought that would fix his determination to remain and have her to himself for a few minutes, she was mistaken in her man. Good Indian turned on his heel, and went out with his chin in the air, and found that Gene and Clark had gone off to the meadow, with Donny an unwelcome attendant, and that Wally and Jack were keeping the dust moving between the gate and the stable, trying to tempt a shot from the bluff. They were much inclined to be skeptical regarding the bullet which Good Indian carried in his breast-pocket.

"WE can't raise anybody," Wally told him disgustedly, "and I've made three round trips myself. I'm going to quit fooling around, and go to work."

Whether he did or not, Good Indian did not wait to prove. He did not say anything, either, about his own plans. He was hurt most unreasonably because of Evadna's behavior, and he felt as if he were groping about blindfolded so far as the Hart trouble was concerned. There must be something to do, but he could not see what it was. It reminded him oddly of when he sat down with his algebra open before him, and scowled at a problem where the x y z's seemed to be sprinkled through it with a diabolical frequency, and there was no visible means of discovering what the unknown quantities could possibly be.

He saddled Keno, and rode away in that silent preoccupation which the boys called the sulks for want of a better understanding of it. As a matter of fact, he was trying to put Evadna out of his mind for the present, so that he could think clearly of what he ought to do. He glanced often up at the rim-rock as he rode slowly to the Point o' Rocks, and when he was halfway to the turn he thought he saw something moving up there.

He pulled up to make sure, and a little blue ball puffed out like a child's balloon, burst, and dissipated itself in a thin, trailing ribbon, which the wind caught and swept to nothing. At the same time something spatted into the trail ahead of him, sending up a little spurt of fine sand.

Keno started, perked up his ears toward the place, and went on, stepping gingerly. Good Indian's lips drew back, showing his teeth set tightly together. "Still at it, eh?" he muttered aloud, pricked Keno's flanks with his rowels, and galloped around the Point.

There, for the time being, he was safe. Unless the shooter upon the rim-rock was mounted, he must travel swiftly indeed to reach again a point within range of the grade road before Good Indian would pass out of sight again. For the trail wound in and out, looping back upon itself where the hill was oversleep, hidden part of the time from the receding wall of rock by huge bowlders and giant sage.

Grant knew that he was safe from that quarter, and was wondering whether he ought to ride up along the top of the bluff before going to Hartley, as he had intended.

He had almost reached the level, and was passing a steep, narrow, little gully choked with rocks, when something started up so close beside him that Keno ducked away and squatted almost upon his haunches. His gun was in his hand, and his finger crooked upon the trigger, when a voice he faintly recognized called to him softly:

"Yo' no shoot—no shoot—me no hurtum. All time yo' frien'." She stood trembling beside the trail, a gay, plaid shawl about her shoulders in place of the usual blanket, her hair braided smoothly with bright, red ribbons entwined through it. Her dress was a plain slip of bright calico, which had four-inch roses, very briery and each with a gaudy butterfly poised upon the topmost petals running over it in an inextricable tangle. Beaded moccasins were on her feet, and her eyes were

B. M. Bower

frightened eyes, with the wistfulness of a timid animal. Yet she did not seem to be afraid of Good Indian.

"I sorry I scare yo' horse," she said hesitatingly, speaking better English than before. "I heap hurry to get here. I speak with yo'."

"Well, what is it?" Good Indian's tone was not as brusque as his words; indeed, he spoke very gently, for him. This was the good-looking young squaw he had seen at the Indian camp. "What's your name?" he asked, remembering suddenly that he had never heard it.

"Rachel. Peppajee, he my uncle." She glanced up at him shyly, then down to where the pliant toe of her moccasin was patting a tiny depression into the dust. "Bad mans like for shoot yo'," she said, not looking directly at him again. "Him up there, all time walk where him can look down, mebbyso see you, mebbyso shootum."

"I know—I'm going to ride around that way and round him up." Unconsciously his manner had the arrogance of strength and power to do as he wished, which belongs to healthy young males.

"N-o, no-o!" She drew a sharp breath " o' no good there! Dim shoot yo'. Yo' no go! Ah-h—I sorry I tellum yo' now. Bad mans, him. I watch, I take care him no shoot. Him shoot, mebbyso *I* shoot!"

With a little laugh that was more a plea for gentle judgment than anything else, she raised the plaid shawl, and gave him a glimpse of a rather battered revolver, cheap when it was new and obviously well past its prime.

"I want yo'—" she hesitated; "I want yo'—be heap careful. I want yo' no ride close by hill. Ride far out!" She made a sweeping gesture toward the valley. "All time I watch."

He was staring at her in a puzzled way. She was handsome, after her wild, half-civilized type, and her anxiety for his welfare touched him and besought his interest.

"Indians go far down—" She swept her arm down the narrowing river valley. "Catch fish. Peppajee stay—no can walk far. I stay. All go, mebbyso stay five days." Her hand lifted involuntarily to mark the number.

He did not know why she told him all that, and he could not learn from her anything about his assailant. She had been walking along the bluff, he gathered—though why, she failed to make clear to him. She had, from a distance, caught a glimpse of a man watching the valley beneath him. She had seen him raise a rifle, take long aim, and shoot—and she had known that he was shooting at Good Indian.

When he asked her the second time what was her errand up there—whether she was following the man, or had suspected that he would be there—she shook her head vaguely and took refuge behind the stolidity of her race.

In spite of her pleading, he put his horse to scrambling up the first slope which it was possible to climb, and spent an hour riding, gun in hand, along the rim of the bluff, much as he had searched it the evening before.

But there was nothing alive that he could discover, except a hawk which lifted itself languorously off a high, sharp rock, and flapped lazily out across the valley when he drew near. The man with the rifle had disappeared as completely as if he had never been there, and there was not one chance in a hundred of hunting him out, in all that rough jumble.

When he was turning back at last toward Hartley, he saw Rachel for a moment standing out against the deep blue of the sky, upon the very rim of the bluff. He waved a hand to her, but she gave no sign; only, for some reason, he felt that she was watching him ride away, and he had a brief, vagrant memory of the wistfulness he had seen in her eyes.

On the heels of that came a vision of Evadna swinging in the hammock which hung between the two locust trees, and he longed unutterably to be with her there. He would be, he promised himself, within the next hour or so, and set his pace in accordance with his desire, resolved to make short work of his investigations in Hartley and his discussion of late events with Miss Georgie.

He had not, it seemed to him, had more than two minutes with Evadna since that evening of rapturous memory when they rode home together from the Malad, and afterward sat upon the stone bench at the head of the pond, whispering together so softly that they did not even disturb the frogs among the lily-pads within ten feet of them. It was not so long ago, that evening. The time that had passed since might be reckoned easily in hours, but to Good Indian it seemed a month, at the very least.

CHAPTER XIX

EVADNA GOES CALLING

"I have every reason to believe that your two missing jumpers took the train for Shoshone last night," Miss Georgie made answer to Good Indian's account of what had happened since he saw her." Two furtive-eyed individuals answering your description bought round-trip tickets and had me flag sixteen for them. They got on, all right. I saw them. And if they got off before the next station they must have landed on their heads, because Sixteen was making up time and Shorty pulled the throttle wide open at the first yank, I should judge, from the way he jumped out of town. I've been expecting some of them to go and do their filing stunt—and if the boys have begun to devil them any, the chances are good that they'd take turns at it, anyway. They'd leave someone always on the ground, that's a cinch.

"And Saunders," she went on rapidly, "returned safe enough. He sneaked in just before I closed the office last night, and asked for a telegram. There wasn't any, and he sneaked out again and went to bed—so Pete told me this morning. And most of the Indians have pulled out—squaws, dogs, papooses, and all—on some fishing or hunting expedition. I don't know that it has anything to do with your affairs, or would even interest you, though. And there has been no word from Peaceful, and they can't possibly get back now till the four-thirty—five.

"And that's all I can tell you, Mr. Imsen," she finished crisply, and took up a novel with a significance which not even the dullest man could have ignored.

Good Indian stared, flushed hotly, and made for the door.

"Thank you for the information. I'm afraid this has been a lot of bother for you," he said stiffly, gave her a ceremonious little bow, and went his way stiff-necked and frowning.

Miss Georgie leaned forward so that she could see him through the window. She watched him cross to the store, go up the three rough steps to the platform, and disappear into the yawning blackness beyond the wide-open door.

She did not open the novel and begin reading, even then. She dabbed her handkerchief at her eyes, muttered: "My Heavens, what a fool!" apropos of nothing tangible, and stared dully out at the forlorn waste of cinders with rows of shining rails running straight across it upon ties half sunken in the black desolation, and at the red abomination which was the pump-house squatting beside the dripping tank, the pump breathing asthmatically as it labored to keep the sliding water gauge from standing at the figure which meant reproach for the grimy attendant.

"What a fool—what a fool!" she repeated at the end of ten moody minutes. Then she threw the novel into a corner of the room, set her lower jaw into the square lines of stubbornness, went over to the sleeping telegraph instrument which now and then clicked and twittered in its sleep, called up Shoshone, and commanded the agent there to send down a quart freezer of ice cream, a banana cake, and all the late magazines he could find, including—especially including—the alleged "funny" ones.

"You certainly—are—the prize—fool!" she said, when she switched off the current, and she said it with vicious emphasis. Whereupon she recovered the novel, seated herself determinedly in the beribboned rocker, flipped the leaves of the book spitefully until she found one which had a corner turned down, and read a garden-party chapter much as she used to study her multiplication table when she was ten and hated arithmetic.

A freight was announced over the wire, arrived with a great wheezing and snorting, which finally settled to a rhythmic gasping of the air pump, while a few boxes of store supplies were being dumped unceremoniously upon the platform. Miss Georgie was freight agent as well as many other things, and she went out and stood bareheaded in the sun to watch the unloading.

She performed, with the unthinking precision which comes of long practice, the many little duties pertaining to her several offices, and when the wheels began once more to clank, and she had waved her hand to the fireman, the brakeman, and the conductor, and had seen the dirty flags at the rear of the swaying caboose flap out of sight around the low, sage-covered hill, she turned rather dismally to the parlor end of the office, and took up the book with her former air of grim determination. So for an hour, perhaps.

"Is Miss Georgie Howard at home?" It was Evadna standing in the doorway, her indigo eyes fixed with innocent gayety—which her mouth somehow failed to meet halfway in mirth—upon the reader.

"She is, chicken, and overjoyed at the sight of you!" Miss Georgie rose just as enthusiastically as if she had not seen Evadna slip from Huckleberry's back, fuddle the tie-rope into what looked like a knot, and step lightly upon the platform. She had kept her head down—had Miss Georgie—until the last possible second, because she was still being a fool and had permitted a page of her book to fog before her eyes. There was no fog when she pushed Evadna into the seat of honor, however, and her mouth abetted her eyes in smiling.

"Everything at tho ranch is perfectly horrid," Evadna

complained pathetically, leaning back in the rocking-chair. "I'd just as soon be shut up in a graveyard. You can't IMAGINE what it's like, Georgie, since those horrible men came and camped around all over the place! All yesterday afternoon and till dark, mind you, the boys were down there shooting at everything but the men, and they began to shoot back, and Aunt Phoebe was afraid the boys would be hit, and so we all went down and—oh, it was awful! If Grant hadn't come home and stopped them, everybody would have been murdered. And you should have heard how they swore at Grant afterward! They just called him everything they could think of for making them stop. I had to sit around on the other side of the house—and even then I couldn't help hearing most of it.

"And to-day it is worse, because they just go around like a lot of dummies and won't do anything but look mean. Aunt Phoebe was so cross—CROSS, mind you!—because I burnt the jam. And some of the jumpers are missing, and nobody knows where they went— and Marie has got the toothache worse than ever, and won't go and have it pulled because it will HURT! I don't see how it can hurt much worse than it does now—she just goes around with tears running down into the flannel around her face till I could SHAKE her!" Evadna laughed—a self-pitying laugh, and rocked her small person violently. "I wish I could have an office and live in it and telegraph things to people," she sighed, and laughed again most adorably at her own childishness. "But really and truly, it's enough to drive a person CRAZY, down at the ranch!"

"For a girl with a brand-new sweetheart—" Miss Georgie reproved quizzically, and reached for the inevitable candy box.

"A lot of good that does, when he's never there!" flashed Evadna, unintentionally revealing her real grievance. "He just eats and goes—and he isn't even there to eat, half the time. And when he's there, he's grumpy, like all the rest." She was saying the things she had told herself, on the way up, that she would DIE rather than say; to Miss Georgie, of all people.

"I expect he's pretty worried, chicken, over that land business." Miss Georgie offered her candy, and Evadna waved the box from her impatiently, as if her spirits were altogether too low for sweets.

"Well, I'm very sure I'M not to blame for those men being there," she retorted petulantly. "He"— she hesitated, and then plunged heedlessly on—"he acts just as if I weren't anybody at all. I'm sure, if he expects me to be a doll to be played with and then dumped into a corner where I'm to smile and smile until he comes and picks me up again—"

"Now, chicken, what's the use of being silly?" Miss Georgie turned her head slightly away, and stared out of the window. "He's worried, I tell you, and instead of sulking because he doesn't stay and make love—"

"Well, upon my word! Just as if I wanted—"

"You really ought to help him by being kind and showing a little sympathy, instead—"

"It appears that the supply of sympathy—"

"Instead of making it harder for him by feeling neglected and letting him see that you do. My Heavens above!" Miss Georgie faced her suddenly with pink cheeks. "When a man is up against a problem—and carries his life in his hand—"

"You don't know a thing about it!" Evadna stopped rocking, and sat up very straight in the chair. "And even if that were true, is that any reason why he should AVOID me? I'M not threatening his life!"

"He doesn't avoid you. And you're acting sillier than I ever supposed you could. He can't be in two places at once, can he? Now, let's be sensible, chicken. Grant—"

"Oh—h!" There was a peculiar, sliding inflection upon that

word, which made Miss Georgie's hand shut into a fist.

"Grant"—Miss Georgie put a defiant emphasis upon it—"is doing all he can to get to the bottom of that jumping business. There's something crooked about it, and he knows it, and is trying to—"

a"I know all that." Evadna interrupted without apology.

"Well, of course, if you DO—then I needn't tell you how silly it is for you to complain of being neglected, when you know his time is all taken up with trying to ferret out a way to block their little game. He feels in a certain sense responsible—"

"Yes, I know. He thinks he should have been watching somebody or something instead of—of being with me. He took the trouble to make that clear to me, at least!" Evadna's eyes were very blue and very bright, but there was no look of an angel in her face.

Miss Georgie pressed her lips together tightly for a minute. When she spoke, she was cheerfully impersonal as to tone and manner.

"Chicken, you're a little goose. The man is simply crazy about you, and harassed to death with this ranch business. Once that's settled—well, you'll see what sort of a lover he can be!"

"Thank you so much for holding out a little hope and encouragement, my dear!" Evadna, by the way, looked anything but thankful; indeed, she seemed to resent the hope and the encouragement as a bit of unwarranted impertinence. She glanced toward the door as if she meditated an immediate departure, but ended by settling back in the chair and beginning to rock again.

"It's a nasty, underhand business from start to finish," said Miss Georgie, ignoring the remark. "It has upset everybody— me included, and I'm sure it isn't my affair. It's just one of those tricky cases that you know is rotten to the core, and yet you can't seem to get hold of anything definite. My dad had one or two experiences with old Baumberger—and if ever there was a sly old mole of a man, he's one.

"Did you ever take after a mole, chicken? They used to get in our garden at home. They burrow underneath the surface, you know, and one never sees them. You can tell by the ridge of loose earth that they're there, and if you think you've located Mr. Mole, and jab a stick down, why—he's somewhere else, nine times in ten. I used to call them Baumbergers, even then. Dad," she finished reminiscently, "was always jabbing his law stick down where the earth seemed to move—but he never located old Baumberger, to my knowledge."

She stopped, because Evadna, without a shadow of doubt, was looking bored. Miss Georgie regarded her with the frown she used when she was applying her mental measuring-stick. She began to suspect that Evadna was, after all, an extremely self-centered little person; she was sorry for the suspicion, and she was also conscious of a certain disappointment which was not altogether for herself.

"Ah, well"—she dismissed analysis and the whole subject with a laugh that was partly yawn—"away with dull care. Away with dull everything. It's too hot to think or feel. A real emotion is as superfluous and oppressive as a—a 'camel petticoat!" This time her laugh was real and infectiously carefree. "Take off your hat, chicken. I'll go beg a hunk of ice from my dear friend Peter, and make some lemonade as is lemonade; or claret punch, if you aren't a blue ribboner, or white-ribboner, or some other kind of a good-ribboner." Miss Georgie hated herself for sliding into sheer flippancy, but she preferred that extreme to the other, and she could not hold her ground just then at the "happy medium."

Evadna, however, seemed to disapprove of the flippancy. She did not take off her hat, and she stated evenly that she must go, and that she really did not care for lemonade, or claret punch, either.

"What, in Heaven's name, DO you care for—besides yourself?" flared Miss Georgie, quite humanly exasperated. "There, chicken—the heat always turns me snappy," she repented instantly. "Please pinch me." She held out a beautiful, tapering forearm, and smiled.

"I'm the snappy one," said Evadna, but she did not smile as she began drawing on her gauntlets slowly and deliberately.

If she were waiting for Miss Georgie to come back to the subject of Grant, she was disappointed, for Miss Georgie did not come to any subject whatever. A handcar breezed past the station, the four section-men pumping like demons because of the slight down grade and their haste for their dinner.

Huckleberry gave one snort and one tug backward upon the tie rope and then a coltish kick into the air when he discovered that he was free. After that, he took off through the sagebrush at a lope, too worldly-wise to follow the trail past the store, where someone might rush out and grab him before he could dodge away. He was a wise little pinto—Huckleberry.

"And now, I suppose I'll have the pleasure of walking home," grumbled Evadna, standing upon the platform and gazing, with much self-pity, after her runaway.

"It's noon—stay and eat dinner with me, chicken. Some of the boys will bring him back after you the minute he gets to the ranch. It's too hot to walk." Miss Georgie laid a hand coaxingly upon her arm.

But Evadna was in her mood of perversity. She wouldn't stay to dinner, because Aunt Phoebe would be expecting her. She wouldn't wait for Huckleberry to be brought back to her, because she would never hear the last of it. She didn't mind the heat the least bit, and she would walk. And no, she wouldn't borrow Miss Georgie's parasol; she hated parasols, and she always had and always would. She gathered up her riding-skirt, and went slowly down the steps.

Miss Georgie could be rather perverse herself upon occasion. She waited until Evadna was crunching cinders under her feet before she spoke another word, and then she only called out a flippant, "Adios, senorita!"

Evadna knew no Spanish at all. She lifted her shoulders in what might be disdain, and made no reply whatever.

"Little idiot!" gritted Miss Georgie—and this time she was not speaking of herself.

B. M. Bower

CHAPTER XX

MISS GEORGIE ALSO MAKES A CALL

Saunders, limp and apathetic and colorless, shuffled over to the station with a wheelbarrow which had a decrepit wheel, that left an undulating imprint of its drunken progress in the dust as it went. He loaded the boxes of freight with the abused air of one who feels that Fate has used him hardly, and then sidled up to the station door with the furtive air which Miss Georgie always inwardly resented.

She took the shipping bill from him with her fingertips, reckoned the charges, and received the money without a word, pushing a few pieces of silver toward him upon the table. As he bent to pick them up clawing unpleasantly with vile finger-nails—she glanced at him contemptuously, looked again more attentively, pursed her lips with one corner between her teeth, and when he had clawed the last dime off the smooth surface of the table, she spoke to him as if he were not the reptile she considered him, but a live human.

"Horribly hot, isn't it? I wish *I* could sleep till noon. It would make the days shorter, anyway."

"I opened up the store, and then I went back to bed," Saunders replied limply. "Just got up when the freight pulled in. Made so blamed much noise it woke me. I seem to need a good deal of sleep." He coughed behind his hand, and lingered inside the door. It was so unusual for Miss Georgie to make conversation with him that Saunders was almost pitifully eager to be agreeable.

"If it didn't sound cruel, this weather," said Miss Georgie lightly, still looking at him—or, more particularly, at the crumpled, soiled collar of his coarse blue shirt—"I'd advise you to get out of Hartley once a day, if it was no more than to take a walk. Though to be sure," she smiled, "the prospect is not inviting, to say the least. Put it would be a change; I'd run up and down the track, if I didn't have to stick here in this office all day."

"I can't stand walking," Saunders whined. "It makes me cough." To illustrate, he gave another little hack behind his hand. "I went up to the stable yesterday with a book, and laid down in the hay. And I went to sleep, and Pete thought I was lost, I guess." He grinned, which was not pleasant, for he chewed tobacco and had ugly, discolored teeth into the bargain.

"I like to lay in the hay," he added lifelessly. "I guess I'll take my bed up there; that lean-to is awful hot."

"Well, you're lucky that you can do exactly as you please, and sleep whenever you please." Miss Georgie turned to her telegraph instrument, and began talking in little staccato sparks of electricity to the agent at Shoshone, merely as a hint to Saunders to take himself away.

"Ain't been anything for me?" he asked, still lingering.

Miss Georgie shook her head. He waited a minute longer, and then sidled out, and when he was heard crunching over the cinders with his barrow-load of boxes, she switched off the current abruptly, and went over to the window to watch him.

"Item," she began aloud, when he was quite gone, her eyes staring vacantly down the scintillating rails to where they seemed to meet in one glittering point far away in the desert."

Item—" But whatever the item was, she jotted it down silently in that mental memorandum book which was one of her whims. "Once I put a thing in that little blue book of mine," she used to tell her father, "it's there for keeps. And there's the advantage that I never leave it lying around to be lost, or for other people to pick up and read to my everlasting undoing. It's better than cipher—for I don't talk in my sleep."

The four- thirty- five train came in its own time, and brought the two missing placer miners. But it did not bring Baumberger, nor Peaceful Hart, nor any word of either. Miss Georgie spent a good deal of time staring out of the window toward the store that day, and when she was not doing that she was moving restlessly about the little office, picking things up without knowing why she did so, and laying them down again when she discovered them in her hands and had no use for them. The ice cream came, and the cake, and the magazines; and she left the whole pile just inside the door without undoing a wrapping.

At five o'clock she rose abruptly from the rocker, in which she had just deposited herself with irritated emphasis, and wired her chief for leave of absence until seven.

"It's important, Mr. Gray. Business which can't wait," she clicked urgently. "I'll be back before Eight is due. Please." Miss Georgie did not often send that last word of her own volition. All up and down the line she was said to be "Independent as a hog on ice"—a simile not pretty, perhaps, nor even exact, but frequently applied, nevertheless, to self-reliant souls like the Hartley operator.

Be that as it may, she received gracious permission to lock the office door from the outside, and she was not long in doing so, and heaved a great sigh of relief when it was done. She went straight to the store, and straight back to where Pete Hamilton was leaning over a barrel redolent of pickled pork. He came up with dripping hands and a treasure-trove of flabby meat, and while he was dangling it over the barrel until the superfluous brine dripped away, she asked him for a horse.

"I dunno where Saunders is again," he said, letting his consent be taken for granted. "But I'll go myself and saddle up, if you'll mind the store. Soon as I finish waitin' on this customer," he added, casting a glance toward a man who sat upon the counter and dangled his legs while he apathetically munched stale pretzels and waited for his purchases.

"Oh, I can saddle, all right, Pete. I've got two hours off, and I want to ride down to see how the Harts are getting along. Exciting times down there, from all accounts."

"Maybe I can round up Saunders. He must be somewheres around," Pete suggested languidly, wrapping the pork in a piece of brown paper and reaching for the string which dangled from the ball hung over his head.

"Saunders is asleep, very likely. If he isn't in his room, never mind hunting him. The horse is in the stable, I suppose. I can saddle better than Saunders."

Pete tied the package, wiped his hands, and went heavily out. He returned immediately, said that Saunders must be up at the stable, and turned his attention to weighing out five pounds of white beans.

Miss Georgie helped herself to a large bag of mixed candy, and put the money in the drawer, laid her key upon the desk for safe-keeping, repinned her white sailor hat so that the hot wind which blew should not take it off her head, and went cheerfully away to the stable.

She did not saddle the horse at once. She first searched the pile of sweet-smelling clover in the far end, made sure that no man was there, assured herself in the same manner of the fact that she was absolutely alone in the stable so far as humans were concerned, and continued her search; not for Saunders now, but for sagebrush. She went outside, and looked carefully at her immediate surroundings.

"There's hardly a root of it anywhere around close," she said to herself. "Nor around the store, either—nor any place where one would be apt to go ordinarily."

She stood there meditatively for a few minutes, remembered that two hours do not last long, and saddled hurriedly. Then, mounting awkwardly because of the large, lumpy bag of candy which she must carry in her hands for want of a pocket large enough to hold it, she rode away to the Indian camp.

The camp was merely a litter of refuse and the ashes of various campfires, with one wikiup standing forlorn in the midst. Miss Georgie never wasted precious time on empty ceremony, and she would have gone into that tent unannounced and stated her errand without any compunction whatever. Put Peppajee was lying outside, smoking in the shade, with his foot bandaged and disposed comfortably upon a folded blanket. She tossed him the bag of candy, and stayed upon her horse.

"Howdy, Peppajee? How your foot? Pretty well, mebbyso?"

"Mebbyso bueno. Sun come two time, mebbyso walk all same no snake biteum." Peppajee's eyes gloated over the gift as he laid it down beside him.

"That's good. Say, Peppajee," Miss Georgie reached up to feel her hatpins and to pat her hair, "I wish you'd watch Saunders. Him no good. I think him bad. I can't keep an eye on him. Can you?"

"No can walk far." Peppajee looked meaningly at his bandages. "No can watchum."

"Well, but you could tell somebody else to watch him. I think he do bad thing to the Harts. You like Harts. You tell somebody to watch Saunders."

"Indians pikeway—ketchum fish. Come back, mebbyso tellum watchum."

Miss Georgie drew in her breath for further argument, decided that it was not worth while, and touched up her horse with the whip. "Good-by," she called back, and saw that Peppajee was looking after her with his eyes, while his face was turned impassively to the front.

"You're just about as satisfying to talk to as a stump," she paid tribute to his unassailable calm. "There's four bits wasted," she sighed, "to say nothing of the trouble I had packing that candy to you—you ungrateful old devil." With which unladylike remark she dismissed him from her mind as a possible ally.

At the ranch, the boys were enthusiastically blistering palms and stiffening the muscles of their backs, turning the water away from the ditches that crossed the disputed tracts so that the trespassers there should have none in which to pan gold— or to pretend that they were panning gold. Since the whole ranch was irrigated by springs running out here and there from under the bluff, and all the ditches ran to meadow and orchard and patches of small fruit, and since the springs could not well be stopped from flowing, the thing was not to be done in a minute.

And since there were four boys with decided ideas upon the subject—ideas which harmonized only in the fundamental desire to harry the interlopers, the thing was not to be done without much time being wasted in fruitless argument.

Wally insisted upon running the water all into a sandy hollow where much of it would seep away and a lake would do no harm, the main objection to that being that it required digging at least a hundred yards of new ditch, mostly through rocky soil.

Jack wanted to close all the headgates and just let the water go where it wanted to—which was easy enough, but ineffective,

B. M. Bower

because most of it found its way into the ditches farther down the slope.

Gene and Clark did not much care how the thing was done—so long as it was done their way. At least, that is what they said.

It was Good Indian who at length settled the matter. There were five springs altogether; he proposed that each one make himself responsible for a certain spring, and see to it that no water reached the jumpers.

"And I don't care a tinker's dam how you do it," he said. "Drink it all, if you want to. I'll take the biggest—that one under the milk-house." Whereat they jeered at him for wanting to be close to Evadna.

"Well, who has a better right?" he challenged, and then inconsiderately left them before they could think of a sufficiently biting retort.

So they went to work, each in his own way, agreeing mostly in untiring industry. That is how Miss Georgie found them occupied—except that Good Indian had stopped long enough to soothe Evadna and her aunt, and to explain that the water would really not rise much higher in the milk-house, and that he didn't believe Evadna's pet bench at the head of the pond would be inaccessible because of his efforts.

Phoebe was sloshing around upon the flooded floor of her milk-house, with her skirts tucked up and her indignation growing greater as she gave it utterance, rescuing her pans of milk and her jars of cream. Evadna, upon the top step, sat with her feet tucked up under her as if she feared an instant inundation. She, also, was giving utterance to her feminine irritation at the discomfort—of her aunt presumably, since she herself was high and dry.

"And it won't do a BIT of good. They'll just knock that dam

business all to pieces to-night—" She was scolding Grant.

"Swearing, chicken? Things must be in a great state!"

Grant grinned at Miss Georgie, forgetting for the moment his rebuff that morning. "She did swear, didn't she?" he confirmed wickedly. "And she's been working overtime, trying to reform me. Wanted to pin me down to 'my goodness!' and 'oh, dear!'—with all this excitement taking place on the ranch!"

"I wasn't swearing at all. Grant has been shoveling sand all afternoon, building a dam over by the fence, and the water has been rising and rising till—" She waved her hand gloomily at her bedraggled Aunt Phoebe working like a motherly sort of gnome in its shadowy grotto. "Oh, if I were Aunt Phoebe, I should just shake you, Grant Imsen!"

"Try it," he invited, his eyes worshiping her in her pretty petulance. "I wish you would."

As Miss Georgie went past them down the steps, her face had the set look of one who is consciously and deliberately cheerful under trying conditions.

"Don't quarrel, children," she advised lightly. "Howdy, Mrs. Hart? What are they trying to do—drown you?"

"Oh, these boys of mine! They'll be the death of me, what with the things they won't do, and the things they WILL do. They're trying now to create a water famine for the jumpers, and they're making their own mother swim for the good of the cause." Phoebe held out a plump hand, moist and cold from lifting cool crocks of milk, and laughed at her own predicament.

"The water won't rise any more, Mother Hart," Grant called down to her from the top step, where he was sitting unblushingly beside Evadna. "I told you six inches would be the limit, and then it would run off in the new ditch. You know I explained just why—"

"Oh, yes, I know you explained just WHY," Phoebe cut in disconsolately and yet humorously, "but explanations don't seem to help my poor milk-house any. And what about the garden, and the fruit, if you turn tho water all down into the pasture? And what about the poor horses getting their feet wet and catching their death of cold? And what's to hinder that man Stanley and his gang from packing water in buckets from the lake you're going to have in the pasture?"

She looked at Miss Georgie whimsically. "I'm an ungrateful, bad-tempered old woman, I guess, for they're doing it because it's the only thing they can do, since I put my foot down on all this bombarding and burning good powder just to ease their minds. They've got to do something, I suppose, or they'd all burst. And I don't know but what it's a good thing for 'em to work off their energy digging ditches, even if it don't do a mite of good."

Good Indian was leaning forward with his elbows on his knees, murmuring lover's confidences behind the shield of his tilted hat, which hid from all but Evadna his smiling lips and his telltale, glowing eyes. He looked up at that last sentence, though it is doubtful if he had heard much of what she had been saying.

"It's bound to do good if it does anything," he said. with an optimism which was largely the outgrowth of his beatific mood, which in its turn was born of his nearness to Evadna and her gracious manner toward him. "We promised not to molest them on their claims. But if they get over the line to meddle with our water system, or carry any in buckets—which they can't, because they all leak like the deuce"—he grinned as he thought of the bullet holes in them—"why, I don't know but what someone might object to that, and send them back on their own side of the line."

He picked up a floating ribbon-end which was a part of

Evadna's belt, and ran it caressingly through his fingers in a way which set Miss Georgie's teeth together. "I'm afraid," he added dryly, his eyes once more seeking Evadna's face with pure love hunger, "they aren't going to make much of a stagger at placer mining, if they haven't any water." He rolled the ribbon up tightly, and then tossed it lightly toward her face. "ARE they, Goldilocks?"

"Are they what? I've told you a dozen times to stop calling me that. I had a doll once that I named Goldilocks, and I melted her nose off—she was wax—and you always remind me of the horrible expression it gave to her face. I'd go every day and take her out of the bureau-drawer and look at her, and then cry my eyes out. Won't you come and sit down, Georgie? There's room. Now, what was the discussion, and how far had we got? Aunt Phoebe, I don't believe it has raised a bit lately. I've been watching that black rock with the crack in it." Evadna moved nearer to Good Indian, and pulled her skirts close upon the other side, thereby making a space at least eight inches wide for Miss Georgie's accommodation.

"I can't sit anywhere," said Miss Georgie, looking at her watch. "By the way, chicken, did you have to walk all the way home?"

Evadna looked sidelong at Good Indian, as if a secret had been betrayed." No," she said, "I didn't. I just got to the top of the grade when a squaw came along, and she was leading Huckleberry. A gaudy young squaw, all red and purple and yellow. She was awfully curious about you, Grant. She wanted to know where you were and what you were doing. I hope you aren't a flirtatious young man. She seemed to know you pretty well, I thought."

She had to explain to her Aunt Phoebe and Grant just how she came to be walking, and she laughed at the squaw's vivid costume, and declared she would have one like it, because Grant must certainly admire colors. She managed, innocently enough, to waste upon such trivialities many of Miss Georgie's precious minutes.

At last that young woman, after glancing many times at her watch, and declining an urgent invitation to stay to supper, declared that she must go, and tried to give Good Indian a significant look without being detected in the act by Evadna. But Good Indian, for the time being wholly absorbed by the smiles of his lady, had no eyes for her, and seemed to attach no especial meaning to her visit. So that Miss Georgie, feminine to her finger-tips and oversensitive perhaps where those two were concerned, suddenly abandoned her real object in going to the ranch, and rode away without saying a word of what she had come to say.

She was a direct young woman who was not in the habit of mincing matters with herself, or of dodging an issue, and she bluntly called herself a fool many times that evening, because she had not said plainly that she would like to talk with Grant "and taken him off to one side—by the ear, if necessary—and talked to him, and told him what I went down there to tell him," she said to herself angrily. "And if Evadna didn't like it, she could do the other thing. It does seem as if girls like that are always having the trail smoothed down for them to dance their way through life, while other people climb over rocks— mostly with packs on their shoulders that don't rightly belong to them." She sighed impatiently. "It must be lovely to be absolutely selfish—when you're pretty enough and young enough to make it stick!" Miss Georgie was, without doubt, in a nasty temper that night.

CHAPTER XXI

SOMEBODY SHOT SAUNDERS

The hot days dropped, one by one, into the past like fiery beads upon a velvety black cord. Miss Georgie told them silently in the meager little office, and sighed as they slipped from under her white, nervous fingers. One—nothing happened that could be said to bear upon the one big subject in her mind, the routine work of passing trains and dribbling business in the express and freight departments, and a long afternoon of heat and silence save for the asthmatic pump, fifty yards down the main track. Two—this exactly like the first, except that those inseparables, Hagar, Viney, and Lucy, whom Miss Georgie had inelegantly dubbed "the Three Greases," appeared, silent, blanket-enshrouded, and perspiring, at the office door in mid-afternoon. Half a box of soggy chocolates which the heat had rendered a dismally sticky mass won from them smiles and half-intelligible speech. Fishing was poor—no ketchum. Three—not even the diversion of the squaws to make her forget the dragging hours. Nothing—nothing—nothing, she told herself apathetically when that third day had slipped upon the black cord of a soft, warm night, star-sprinkled and unutterably lonely as it brooded over the desert.

On the morning of the fourth day, Miss Georgie woke with the vague sense that something had gone wrong. True railroader as she had come to be, she thought first that there had been a wreck, and that she was wanted at the telegraph instrument. She was up and partly dressed before the steps and

214   B. M. Bower

the voices which had broken her sleep had reached her door.

Pete Hamilton's voice, trembling with excitement, called to her.

"What is it? What has happened?" she cried from within, beset by a hundred wild conjectures.

"Saunders—somebody shot Saunders. Wire for a doctor, quick as yuh can. He ain't dead yet—but he's goin' t' die, sure. Hurry up and wire—" Somebody at the store called to him, and he broke off to run lumberingly in answer to the summons. Miss Georgie made haste to follow him.

Saunders was lying upon a blanket on the store platform, and Miss Georgie shuddered as she looked at him.

He was pasty white, and his eyes looked glassy under his half-closed lids. He had been shot in the side— at the stable, he had gasped out when Pete found him lying in the trail just back of the store. Now he seemed beyond speech, and the little group of section-hands, the Chinese cook at the section-house, and the Swede foreman, and Pete seemed quite at a loss what to do.

"Take him in and put him to bed," Miss Georgie commanded, turning away. "See if he's bleeding yet, and—well, I should put a cold compress on the wound, I think. I'll send for a doctor—but he can't get here till nine o'clock unless you want to stand the expense of a special. And by that time—"

Saunders moved his head a trifle, and lifted his heavy lids to look at her, which so unnerved Miss Georgie that she turned and ran to the office. When she had sent the message she sat drumming upon the table while she waited for an answer.

"G-r-a-n-" her fingers had spelled when she became conscious of the fact, flushed hotly, and folded her hands tightly together in her lap.

"The doctor will come—Hawkinson, I sent for," she announced later to Pete, holding out the telegram. She glanced reluctantly at the wrinkled blanket where Saunders had lain, caught a corner of her under lip between her teeth, and, bareheaded though she was, went down the steps and along the trail to the stable.

"I've nearly an hour before I need open the office," she said to herself, looking at her watch. She did not say what she meant to do with that hour, but she spent a quarter of it examining the stable and everything in it. Especially did she search the loose, sandy soil in its vicinity for tracks.

Finally she lifted her skirts as a woman instinctively does at a street crossing, and struck off through the sagebrush, her eyes upon a line of uncertain footsteps as of a drunken man reeling that way. They were not easy to follow—or they would not have been if she had not felt certain of the general direction which they must take. More than once she lost sight of them for several rods, but she always picked them up farther along. At one place she stopped, and stood perfectly still, her skirts held back tightly with both hands, while she stared fascinatedly at a red smear upon a broken branch of sage and the smooth-packed hollow in the sand where he must have lain.

"He's got nerve—I'll say that much for him," she observed aloud, and went on.

The footprints were plain where he crossed the grade road near the edge of the bluff, but from there on it was harder to follow them because of the great patches of black lava rock lying even with the surface of the ground, where a dozen men might walk abreast and leave no sign that the untrained eye, at least, could detect.

"This is a case for Indians," she mused, frowning over an open space where all was rock. "Injun Charlie would hunt tracks all day for a dollar or two; only he'd make tracks just to prove himself the real goods." She sighed, stood upon her tiptoes, and peered out over the sage to get her bearings, then started on at a hazard. She went a few rods, found herself in a thick tangle of brush through which she could not force her way, started to back out, and caught her hair on a scraggly scrub which seemed to have as many prongs as there are briers on a rosebush. She was struggling there with her hands fumbling unavailingly at the back of her bowed head, when she was pounced upon by someone or something through the sage. She screamed.

"The—deuce!" Good Indian brought out the milder expletive with the flat intonation which the unexpected presence of a lady frequently gives to a man's speech. "Lucky I didn't take a shot at you through the bushes. I did, almost, when I saw somebody moving here. Is this your favorite place for a morning ramble?" He had one hand still upon her arm, and he was laughing openly at her plight. But he sobered when he stooped a little so that he could see her face, for there were tears in her eyes, and Miss Georgie was not the sort of young woman whom one expects to shed tears for slight cause.

"If you did it—and you must have—I don't see how you can laugh about it, even if he is a crawling reptile of a man that ought to be hung!" The tears were in her voice as well as her eyes, and there were reproach and disappointment also.

"Did what—to whom—to where, to why?" Good Indian let go her arm, and began helpfully striving with the scraggly scrub and its prongs. "Say, I'll just about have to scalp you to get you loose. Would you mind very much, Squaw-talk-far-off?" He ducked and peered into her face again, and again his face sobered. "What's the matter?" he asked, in an entirely different tone—which Miss Georgie, in spite of her mood, found less satisfying than his banter.

"Saunders—OUCH; I'd as soon be scalped and done with, as to have you pull out a hair at a time—Saunders crawled home with a bullet in his ribs. And I thought—"

"Saunders!" Good Indian stared down at her, his hands dropped upon her head.

Miss Georgie reached up, caught him by the wrists, and held him so while she tilted her head that she might look up at him.

"Grant!" she cried softly. "He deserved it. You couldn't help it—he would have shot you down like a dog, just because he was hired to do it, or because of some hold over him. Don't think I blame you—or that anyone would if they knew the truth. I came out to see—I just HAD to make sure—but you must get away from here. You shouldn't have stayed so long—" Miss Georgie gave a most unexpected sob, and stopped that she might grit her teeth in anger over it.

"You think I shot him." As Good Indian said it, the sentence was merely a statement, rather than an accusation or a reproach.

"I don't blame you. I suspected he was the man up here with the rifle. That day—that first day, when you told me about someone shooting at you—he came over to the station. And I saw two or three scraps of sage sticking under his shirt-collar, as if he had been out in the brush; you know how it breaks off and sticks, when you go through it. And he said he had been asleep. And there isn't any sage where a man would have to go through it unless he got right out in it, away from the trails. I thought then that he was the man—"

"You didn't tell me." And this time he spoke reproachfully.

"It was after you had left that I saw it. And I did go down to the ranch to tell you. But I—you were so—occupied—in other directions—" She let go his wrists, and began fumbling at her hair, and she bowed her head again so that her face was hidden from him.

"You could have told me, anyway," Good Indian said constrainedly.

"You didn't want her to know. I couldn't, before her. And I didn't want to—hurt her by—" Miss Georgie fumbled more with her words than with her hair.

"Well, there's no use arguing about that." Good Indian also found that subject a difficult one. "You say he was shot. Did he say—"

"He wasn't able to talk when I saw him. Pete said Saunders claimed he was shot at the stable, but I know that to be a lie." Miss Georgie spoke with unfeeling exactness. "That was to save himself in case he got well, I suppose. I believe the man is going to die, if he hasn't already; he had the look—I've seen them in wrecks, and I know. He won't talk; he can't. But there'll be an investigation—and Baumberger, I suspect, will be just as willing to get you in this way as in any other. More so, maybe. Because a murder is always awkward to handle."

"I can't see why he should want to murder me." Good Indian took her hands away from her hair, and set himself again to the work of freeing her. "You've been fudging around till you've got about ten million more hairs wound up," he grumbled.

"Wow! ARE you deliberately torturing me?" she complained, winking with the pain of his good intentions. "I don't believe he does want to murder you. I think that was just Saunders trying to make a dandy good job of it. He doesn't like you, anyway—witness the way you bawled him out that day you roped—ow-w!—roped the dog. Baumberger may have wanted him to keep an eye on you—My Heavens, man! Do you think you're plucking a goose?"

"I wouldn't be surprised," he retorted, grinning a little. "Honest! I'm trying to go easy, but this infernal bush has sure got a strangle hold on you—and your hair is so fluffy it's a deuce of a job. You keep wriggling and getting it caught in new places. If you could only manage to stand still—but I suppose you can't.

"By the way," he remarked casually, after a short silence, save for an occasional squeal from Miss Georgie, "speaking of Saunders—I didn't shoot him."

Miss Georgie looked up at him, to the further entanglement of her hair. "You DIDN'T? Then who did?"

"Search ME," he offered figuratively and briefly.

"Well, I will." Miss Georgie spoke with a certain decisiveness, and reaching out a sage-soiled hand, took his gun from the holster at his hip. He shrank away with a man's instinctive dislike of having anyone make free with his weapons, but it was a single movement, which he controlled instantly.

"Stand still, can't you?" he admonished, and kept at work while she examined the gun with a dexterity and ease of every motion which betrayed her perfect familiarity with firearms. She snapped the cylinder into place, sniffed daintily at the end of the barrel, and slipped the gun back into its scabbard.

"Don't think I doubted your word," she said, casting a slanting glance up at him without moving her head. "But I wanted to be able to swear positively, if I should happen to be dragged into the witness-box—I hope it won't be by the hair of the head!—that your gun has not been fired this morning. Unless you carry a cleaning rod with you," she added, "which would hardly be likely."

"You may search me if you like," Good Indian suggested, and for an engaged young man, and one deeply in love withal, he displayed a contentment with the situation which was almost reprehensible.

"No use. If you did pack one with you, you'd be a fool not to throw it away after you had used it. No, I'll swear to the gun as it is now. Are you ever going to get my hair loose? I'm due at the office right this minute, I'll bet a molasses cooky." She looked at her watch, and groaned. "I'd have to telegraph myself back to get there on time now," she said. "Twenty-four—that fast freight—is due in eighteen minutes exactly. I've got to be there. Take your jackknife and cut what won't come loose. Really, I mean it, Mr. Imsen."

"I was under the impression that my name is Grant—to friends."

"My name is 'Dennis,' if I don't beat that freight," she retorted curtly. "Take your knife and give me a hair cut—quick! I can do it a different way, and cover up the place."

"Oh, all right—but it's a shame to leave a nice bunch of hair like this hanging on a bush."

"Tell me, what were you doing up here, Grant? And what are you going to do now? We haven't much time, and we've been fooling when we should have been discussing 'ways and means.'"

"Well, I got up early, and someone took a shot at me again. This time he clipped my hat-brim." He took off his hat, and showed her where the brim had a jagged tear half an inch deep. "I ducked, and made up my mind I'd get him this time, or know the reason why. So I rode up the other way and back behind the orchard, and struck the grade below the Point o' Rocks, and so came up here hunting him. I kept pretty well out of sight—we've done that before; Jack and I took sneak yesterday, and came up here at sunrise, but we couldn't find anything. I was beginning to think he had given it up. So I was just scouting around here when I heard you rustling the bushes over here. I was going to shoot, but I changed my mind, and thought I'd land on you and trust to the lessons I got in football and the gun. And the rest," he declaimed whimsically, "you know.

"Now, duck away down—oh, wait a minute." He gave a jerk at the knot of his neckerchief, flipped out the folds, spread it carefully over her head, and tied it under her chin, patting it into place and tucking stray locks under as if he rather enjoyed doing it." Better wear it till you're out of the brush," he advised, "if you don't want to get hung up somewhere again."

She stood up straight, with a long, deep sigh of relief.

"Now, pikeway," he smiled. "And don't run bareheaded through the bushes again. You've still got time to beat that train. And—about Saunders—don't worry. I can get to the ranch without being seen, and no one will know I was up here, unless you tell them."

"Oh, I shall of course!" Miss Georgie chose to be very sarcastic. "I think I shall wire the information to the sheriff. Don't come with me—and leave tracks all over the country. Keep on the lava rock. Haven't you got any sense at all?"

"You made tracks yourself, madam, and you've left a fine lot of incriminating evidence on that bush. I'll have to waste an hour picking off the hair, so they won't accuse you of shooting Saunders." Good Indian spoke lightly, but they both stopped, nevertheless, and eyed the offending bush anxiously.

"You haven't time," Miss Georgie decided. "I can easily get around that, if it's put up to me. You go on back. Really, you must!" her eyes implored him.

"Oh, vey-ree well. We haven't met this morning. Good-by, Squaw-talk-far-off. I'll see you later, perhaps."

Miss Georgie still had that freight heavy on her conscience, but she stood and watched him stoop under an overhanging branch and turn his head to smile reassuringly back at her; then, with a pungent stirring of sage odors, the bushes closed in behind him, and it was as if he had never been there at all. Whereupon Miss Georgie once more gathered her skirts together and ran to the trail, and down that to the station.

She met a group of squaws, who eyed her curiously, but she

B. M. Bower

was looking once more at her watch, and paid no attention, although they stood huddled in the trail staring after her. She remembered that she had left the office unlocked and she rushed in, and sank panting into the chair before her telegraph table just as the smoke of the fast freight swirled around the nose of the low, sage-covered hill to the west.

CHAPTER XXII

A BIT OF PAPER

Good Indian came out upon the rim-rock, looked down upon the ranch beneath him, and knew, by various little movements about the place, that breakfast was not yet ready. Gene was carrying two pails of milk to the house, and Wally and Jack were watering the horses that had been stabled overnight. He was on the point of shouting down to them when his arm was caught tightly from behind. He wheeled about and confronted Rachel. Clothed all in dull gray she was, like a savage young Quakeress. Even the red ribbons were gone from her hair, which was covered by the gray blanket wrapped tightly around her slim body. She drew him back from the rim of the bluff.

"You no shout," she murmured gravely. "No lettum see you here. You go quick. Ketchum you cayuse, go to ranch. You no tellum you be this place."

Good Indian stood still, and looked at her. She stood with her arms folded in her blanket, regarding him with a certain yearning steadfastness.

"You all time think why," she said, shrewdly reading his thoughts, "I no take shame. I glad." She flushed, and looked away to the far side of the Snake. "Bad mans no more try for shoot you, mebbyso. I heap—"

Good Indian reached out, and caught her by both shoulders.

B. M. Bower

"Rachel—if you did that, don't tell me about it. Don't tell me anything. I don't ask you—I don't want to know." He spoke rapidly, in the grip of his first impulse to shield her from what she had done. But he felt her begin to tremble under his fingers, and he stopped as suddenly as he had begun.

"You no glad? You think shame for me? You think I—all time—very—bad!" Tragedy was in her voice, and in her great, dark eyes. Good Indian gulped.

"No, Rachel. I don't think that. I want to help you out of this, if I can, and I meant that if you didn't tell me anything about it, why—I wouldn't know anything about it. You sabe."

"I sabe." Her lips curved into a pathetic little smile. "I sabe you know all what I do. You know for why, me thinkum. You think shame. I no take shame. I do for you no get kill-dead. All time Man-that-coughs try for shootum you. All time I try for—" She broke off to stare questioningly up into his face. "I no tell, you no like for tell," she said quietly. "All same, you go. You ketchum you hoss, you go ranch. I think sheriff mans mebbyso come pretty quick. No find out you be here. I no like you be here this time."

Good Indian turned, yielding to the pleading of her eyes. The heart of him ached dully with the weight of what she had done, and with an uneasy comprehension of her reason for doing it. He walked as quickly as the rough ground would permit, along the bluff toward the grade; and she, with the instinctive deference to the male which is the heritage of primitive woman, followed soft-footedly two paces behind him. Once where the way was clear he stopped, and waited for her to come alongside, but Rachel stopped and waited also, her eyes hungrily searching his face with the look a dog has for his master. Good Indian read the meaning of that look, and went on, and turned no more toward her until he reached his horse.

"You'd better go on to camp, and stay there, Rachel," he said, as casually as he could. "No trouble will come to you." He hesitated, biting his lip and plucking absently the tangles from the forelock of his horse. "You sabe grateful?" he asked finally. And when she gave a quick little nod, he went on: "Well, I'm grateful to you. You did what a man would do for his friend. I sabe. I'm heap grateful, and I'll not forget it. All time I'll be your friend. Good—by." He mounted, and rode away. He felt, just then, that it was the kindest thing he could do.

He looked back once, just as he was turning into the grade road. She was standing, her arms folded in her gray blanket, where he had left her. His fingers tightened involuntarily the reins, so that Keno stopped and eyed his master inquiringly. But there was nothing that he might say to her. It was not words that she wanted. He swung his heels against Keno's flanks, and rode home.

Evadna rallied him upon his moodiness at breakfast, pouted a little because he remained preoccupied under her teasing, and later was deeply offended because he would not tell her where he had been, or what was worrying him.

"I guess you better send word to the doctor he needn't come," the pump man put his head in at the office door to say, just as the freight was pulling away from the water-tank. "Saunders died a few minutes ago. Pete says you better notify the coroner—and I reckon the sheriff, too. Pretty tough to be shot down like that in broad daylight."

"I think I'd rather be shot in daylight than in the dark," Miss Georgie snapped unreasonably because her nerves were all a-jangle, and sent the messages as requested.

Saunders was neither a popular nor a prominent citizen, and there was none to mourn beside him. Peter Hamilton, as his employer and a man whose emotions were easily stirred, was shocked a shade lighter as to his complexion and a tone lower as to his voice perhaps, and was heard to remark frequently that it was "a turrible thing," but the chief emotion which the tragedy roused was curiosity, and that fluttering excitement which attends death in any form.

A dozen Indians hung about the store, the squaws peering inquisitively in at the uncurtained window of the lean-to—where the bed held a long immovable burden with a rumpled sheet over it—and the bucks listening stolidly to the futile gossip on the store porch.

Pete Hamilton, anxious that the passing of his unprofitable servant should be marked by decorum if not by grief, mentally classed the event with election day, in that he refused to sell any liquor until the sheriff and coroner arrived. He also, after his first bewilderment had passed, conceived the idea that Saunders had committed suicide, and explained to everyone who would listen just why he believed it. Saunders was sickly, for one thing. For another, Saunders never seemed to get any good out of living. He had read everything he could get his hands on—and though Pete did not say that Saunders chose to die when the stock of paper novels was exhausted, he left that impression upon his auditors.

The sheriff and the coroner came at nine. All the Hart boys, including Donny, were there before noon, and the group of Indians remained all day wherever the store cast its shadow. Squaws and bucks passed and repassed upon the footpath between Hartley and their camp, chattering together of the big event until they came under the eye of strange white men, whereupon they. were stricken deaf and dumb, as is the way of our nation's wards.

When the sheriff inspected the stable and its vicinity, looking for clews, not a blanket was in sight, though a dozen eyes watched every movement suspiciously. When at the inquest that afternoon, he laid upon the table a battered old revolver of cheap workmanship and long past its prime, and testified that he had found it ten feet from the stable-door, in a due line southeast from the hay-corral, and that one shot had been fired from it, there were Indians in plenty to glance furtively at the weapon and give no sign.

The coroner showed the bullet which he had extracted from the body of Saunders, and fitted it into the empty cartridge which had been under the hammer in the revolver, and thereby proved to the satisfaction of everyone that the gun was intimately connected with the death of the man. So the jury arrived speedily, and without further fussing over evidence, at the verdict of suicide.

Good Indian drew a long breath, put on his hat, and went over to tell Miss Georgie. The Hart boys lingered for a few minutes at the store, and then rode on to the ranch without him, and the Indians stole away over the hill to their camp. The coroner and the sheriff accepted Pete's invitation into the back part of the store, refreshed themselves after the ordeal, and caught the next train for Shoshone. So closed the incident of Saunders' passing, so far as the law was concerned.

"Well," Miss Georgie summed up the situation, "Baumberger hasn't made any sign of taking up the matter. I don't believe, now, that he will. I wired the news to the papers in Shoshone, so he must know. I think perhaps he's glad to get Saunders out of the way—for he certainly must have known enough to put Baumberger behind the bars.

"But I don't see," she said, in a puzzled way, "how that gun came onto the scene. I looked all around the stable this morning, and I could swear there wasn't any gun."

"Well, he did pick it up—fortunately," Good Indian returned grimly. "I'm glad the thing was settled so easily."

She looked up at him sharply for a moment, opened her lips to ask a question, and then thought better of it.

"Oh, here's your handkerchief," she said quietly, taking it from the bottom of her wastebasket. "As you say, the thing is settled. I'm going to turn you out now. The four-thirty-five is due pretty soon—and I have oodles of work."

He looked at her strangely, and went away, wondering why Miss Georgie hated so to have him in the office lately.

On the next day, at ten o'clock, they buried Saunders on a certain little knoll among the sagebrush; buried him without much ceremony, it is true, but with more respect than he had received when he was alive and shambling sneakily among them. Good Indian was there, saying little and listening attentively to the comments made upon the subject, and when the last bit of yellow gravel had been spatted into place he rode down through the Indian camp on his way home, thankful that everyone seemed to accept the verdict of suicide as being final, and anxious that Rachel should know it. He felt rather queer about Rachel; sorry for her, in an impersonal way; curious over her attitude toward life in general and toward himself in particular, and ready to do her a good turn because of her interest.

But Rachel, when he reached the camp, was not visible. Peppajee Jim was sitting peacefully in the shade of his wikiup when Grant rode up, and he merely grunted in reply to a question or two. Good Indian resolved to be patient. He dismounted, and squatted upon his heels beside Peppajee, offered him tobacco, and dipped a shiny, new nickel toward a bright-eyed papoose in scanty raiment, who stopped to regard him inquisitively.

"I just saw them bury Saunders," Good Indian remarked, by way of opening a conversation. "You believe he shot himself?"

Peppajee took his little stone pipe from his lips, blew a thin wreath of smoke, and replaced the stem between his teeth, stared stolidly straight ahead of him, and said nothing.

"All the white men say that," Good Indian persisted, after he had waited a minute. Peppajee did not seem to hear.

"Sheriff say that, too. Sheriff found the gun."

"Mebbyso sheriff mans heap damfool. Mebbyso heap smart. No sabe."

Good Indian studied him silently. Reticence was not a general characteristic of Peppajee; it seemed to indicate a thorough understanding of the whole affair. He wondered if Rachel had told her uncle the truth.

"Where's Rachel?" he asked suddenly, the words following involuntarily his thought.

Peppajee sucked hard upon his pipe, took it away from his mouth, and knocked out the ashes upon a pole of the wikiup frame.

"Yo' no speakum Rachel no more," he said gravely. "Yo' ketchum 'Vadnah; no ketchum otha squaw. Bad medicine come. Heap much troubles come. Me no likeum. My heart heap bad."

"I'm Rachel's friend, Peppajee." Good Indian spoke softly so that others might not hear. "I sabe what Rachel do. Rachel good girl. I don't want to bring trouble. I want to help."

Peppajee snorted.

"Yo' make heap bad heart for Rachel," he said sourly. "Yo' like for be friend, yo' no come no more, mebbyso. No speakum. Bimeby mebbyso no have bad heart no more. Kay bueno. Yo' white mans. Rachel mebbyso thinkum all time yo' Indian. Mebbyso thinkum be yo' squaw. Kay bueno. Yo' all time white mans. No speakum Rachel no more, yo' be friend.

Yo' speakum, me like to kill yo', mebbyso." He spoke calmly, but none the less his words carried conviction of his sincerity.

Within the wikiup Good Indian heard a smothered sob. He listened, heard it again, and looked challengingly at Peppajee. But Peppajee gave no sign that he either heard the sound or saw the challenge in Good Indian's eyes.

"I Rachel's friend," he said, speaking distinctly with his face half turned toward the wall of deerskin. "I want to tell Rachel what the sheriff said. I want to thank Rachel, and tell her I'm her friend. I don't want to bring trouble." He stopped and listened, but there was no sound within.

Peppajee eyed him comprehendingly, but there was no yielding in his brown, wrinkled face.

"Yo' Rachel's frien', yo' pikeway," he insisted doggedly.

From under the wall of the wikiup close to Good Indian on the side farthest from Peppajee, a small, leafless branch of sage was thrust out, and waggled cautiously, scraping gently his hand. Good Indian's fingers closed upon it instinctively, and felt it slowly withdrawn until his hand was pressed against the hide wall. Then soft fingers touched his own, fluttered there timidly, and left in his palm a bit of paper, tightly folded. Good Indian closed his hand upon it, and stood up.

"All right, I go," he said calmly to Peppajee, and mounted.

Peppajee looked at him stolidly, and said nothing.

"One thing I would like to know." Good Indian spoke again. "You don't care any more about the men taking Peaceful's ranch. Before they came, you watch all the time, you heap care. Why you no care any more? Why you no help?"

Peppajee's mouth straightened in a grin of pure irony.

"All time Baumberga try for ketchum ranch, me try for stoppum," he retorted. "Yo' no b'lievum, Peacefu' no b'lievum. Me tellum yo' cloud sign, tellum yo' smoke sign, tellum yo' hear much bad talk for ketchum ranch. Yo' all time think for ketchum 'Vadnah squaw. No think for stoppum mens. Yo' all time let mens come, ketchum ranch. Yo' say fightum in co't. Cloud sign say me do notting. Yo' lettum come. Yo' mebbyso makum go. Me no care."

"I see. Well, maybe you're right." He tightened the reins, and rode away, the tight little wad of paper still hidden in his palm. When he was quite out of sight from the camp and jogging leisurely down the hot trail, he unfolded it carefully and looked at it long.

His face was grave and thoughtful when at last he tore it into tiny bits and gave it to the hot, desert wind. It was a pitiful little message, printed laboriously upon a scrap of brown wrapping—paper. It said simply:

"God by i lov yo."

CHAPTER XXIII

THE MALICE OF A SQUAW

Good Indian looked in the hammock, but Evadna was not there. He went to the little stone bench at the head of the pond, and when he still did not see her he followed the bank around to the milk-house, where was a mumble of voices. And, standing in the doorway with her arm thrown around her Aunt Phoebe's shoulders in a pretty protective manner, he saw her, and his eyes gladdened. She did not see him at once. She was facing courageously the three inseparables, Hagar, Viney, and Lucy, squatted at the top of the steps, and she was speaking her mind rapidly and angrily. Good Indian knew that tone of old, and he grinned. Also he stopped by the corner of the house, and listened shamelessly.

"That is not true," she was saying very clearly. "You're a bad old squaw and you tell lies. You ought to be put in jail for talking that way." She pressed her aunt's shoulder affectionately. "Don't you mind a word she says, Aunt Phoebe. She's just a mischief-making old hag, and she—oh, I'd like to beat her!"

Hagar shook her head violently, and her voice rose shrill and malicious, cutting short Evadna's futile defiance.

"Ka-a-ay bueno, yo'!" Her teeth gnashed together upon the words. "I no tellum lie. Good Injun him kill Man-that-coughs. All time I seeum creep, creep, through sagebrush. All time I seeum hoss wait where much rock grow. I seeum. I no speakum heap lie. Speakum true. I go tell sheriff mans Good Indian killum Man-that-coughs. I tellum—"

"Why didn't you, then, when the sheriff was in Hartley?" Evadna flung at her angrily. "Because you know it's a lie. That's why."

"Yo' thinkum Good Injun love yo', mebbyso." Hagar's witchgrin was at its malevolent widest. Her black eyes sparkled with venom. "Yo' heap fool. Good Injun go all time Squaw-talk-far-off. Speakum glad word. Good Injun ka-a-ay bueno. Love Squaw-talk-far-off. No love yo'. Speakum lies, yo'. Makum yo' heap cry all time. Makeum yo' heart bad." She cackled, and leered with vile significance toward the girl in the doorway.

"Don't you listen to her, honey." It was Phoebe's turn to reassure.

Good Indian took a step forward, his face white with rage. Viney saw him first, muttered an Indian word of warning, and the three sprang up and backed away from his approach.

"So you've got to call me a murderer!" he cried, advancing threateningly upon Hagar. "And even that doesn't satisfy you. You—"

Evadna rushed up the steps like a crisp little whirlwind, and caught his arm tightly in her two hands.

"Grant! We don't believe a word of it. You couldn't do a thing like that. Don't we KNOW? Don't pay any attention to her. We aren't going to. It'll hurt her worse than any kind of punishment we could give her. Oh, she's a VILE old thing! Too vile for words! Aunt Phoebe and I shouldn't belittle ourselves by even listening to her. SHE can't do any harm unless we let it bother us—what she says. *I* know you never could take a human life, Grant. It's foolish even to speak of such a thing. It's just her nasty, lying tongue saying what her

　　　B. M. Bower

black old heart wishes could be true." She was speaking in a torrent of trepidation lest he break from her and do some violence which they would all regret. She did not know what he could do, or would do, but the look of his face frightened her.

Old Hagar spat viciously at them both, and shrilled vituperative sentences—in her own tongue fortunately; else the things she said must have brought swift retribution. And as if she did not care for consequences and wanted to make her words carry a definite sting, she stopped, grinned maliciously, and spoke the choppy dialect of her tribe.

"Yo' tellum me shont-isham. Mebbyso yo' tellum yo' no ketchum Squaw-talk-far-off in sagebrush, all time Saunders go dead! Me ketchum hair—Squaw-talk-far-off hair. You like for see, you thinkum me tell lies?"

From under her blanket she thrust forth a greasy brown hand, and shook triumphantly before them a tangled wisp of woman's hair—the hair of Miss Georgie, without a doubt. There was no gainsaying that color and texture. She looked full at Evadna.

"Yo' like see, me show whereum walk," she said grimly. "Good Injun boot make track, Squaw-talk-far-off little shoe make track. Me show, yo' thinkum mebbyso me tell lie. Stoppum in sagebrush, ketchum hair. Me ketchum knife—Good Injun knife, mebbyso." Revenge mastered cupidity, and she produced that also, and held it up where they could all see.

Evadna looked and winced.

"I don't believe a word you say," she declared stubbornly. "You STOLE that knife. I suppose you also stole the hair. You can't MAKE me believe a thing like that!"

"Squaw-talk-far-off run, run heap fas', get home quick. Me seeum, Viney seeum, Lucy seeum." Hagar pointed to each as she named her, and waited until they give a confirmatory nod. The two squaws gazed steadily at the ground, and she grunted and ignored them afterward, content that they bore witness to her truth in that one particular.

"Squaw-talk-far-off sabe Good Injun killum Man-that-coughs, mebbyso," she hazarded, watching Good Indian's face cunningly to see if the guess struck close to the truth.

"If you've said all you want to say, you better go," Good Indian told her after a moment of silence while they glared at each other. "I won't touch you—because you're such a devil I couldn't stop short of killing you, once I laid my hands on you."

He stopped, held his lips tightly shut upon the curses he would not speak, and Evadna felt his biceps tauten under her fingers as if he were gathering himself for a lunge at the old squaw. She looked up beseechingly into his face, and saw that it was sharp and stern, as it had been that morning when the men had first been discovered in the orchard. He raised his free arm, and pointed imperiously to the trail.

"Pikeway!" he commanded.

Viney and Lucy shrank from the tone of him, and, hiding their faces in a fold of blanket, slunk silently away like dogs that have been whipped and told to go. Even Hagar drew back a pace, hardy as was her untamed spirit. She looked at Evadna clinging to his arm, her eyes wide and startlingly blue and horrified at all she had heard. She laughed then—did Hagar— and waddled after the others, her whole body seeming to radiate contentment with the evil she had wrought.

"There's nothing on earth can equal the malice of an old squaw," said Phoebe, breaking into the silence which followed. "I'd hope she don't go around peddling that story—not that anyone would believe it, but—"

Good Indian looked at her, and at Evadna. He opened his lips for speech, and closed them without saying a word. That near he came to telling them the truth about meeting Miss Georgie, and explaining about the hair and the knife and the footprints Hagar had prated about. But he thought of Rachel, and knew that he would never tell anyone, not even Evadna. The girl loosened his arm, and moved toward her aunt.

"I hate Indians—squaws especially," she said positively. "I hate the way they look at one with their beady eyes, just like snakes. I believe that horrid old thing lies awake nights just thinking up nasty, wicked lies to tell about the people she doesn't like. I don't think you ought to ride around alone so much, Grant; she might murder you. It's in her to do it, if she ever got the chance."

"What do you suppose made her ring Georgie Howard in like that?" Phoebe speculated, looking at Grant. "She must have some grudge against her, too."

"I don't know why." Good Indian spoke unguardedly, because he was still thinking of Rachel and those laboriously printed words which he had scattered afar. "She's always giving them candy and fruit, whenever they show up at the station."

"Oh—h!" Evadna gave the word that peculiar, sliding inflection of hers which meant so much, and regarded him unwinkingly, with her hands clasped behind her.

Good Indian knew well the meaning of both her tone and her stare, but he only laughed and caught her by the arm.

"Come on over to the hammock," he commanded, with all the arrogance of a lover. "We're making that old hag altogether too important, it seems to me. Come on, Goldilocks—we haven't had a real satisfying sort of scrap for several thousand years."

She permitted him to lead her to the hammock, and pile three cushions behind her head and shoulders—with the dark-blue one on top because her hair looked well against it—and dispose himself comfortably where he could look his fill at her while he swung the hammock gently with his boot-heel, scraping a furrow in the sand. But she did not show any dimples, though his eyes and his lips smiled together when she looked at him, and when he took up her hand and kissed each finger-tip in turn, she was as passive as a doll under the caresses of a child.

"What's the matter?" he demanded, when he found that her manner did not soften. "Worrying still about what that old squaw said?"

"Not in the slightest." Evadna's tone was perfectly polite—which was a bad sign.

Good Indian thought he saw the makings of a quarrel in her general attitude, and he thought he might as well get at once to the real root of her resentment.

"What are you thinking about? Tell me, Goldilocks," he coaxed, pushing his own troubles to the back of his mind.

"Oh, nothing. I was just wondering—though it's a trivial matter which is hardly worth mentioning—but I just happened to wonder how you came to know that Georgie Howard is in the habit of giving candy to the squaws—or anything else. I'm sure I never—" She bit her lips as if she regretted having said so much.

Good Indian laughed. In truth, he was immensely relieved; he had been afraid she might want him to explain something else—something which he felt he must keep to himself even in the face of her anger. But this—he laughed again.

"That's easy enough," he said lightly. "I've seen her do it a couple of times. Maybe Hagar has been keeping an eye on me—I don't know; anyway, when I've had occasion to go to

B. M. Bower

the store or to the station, I've nearly always seen her hanging around in the immediate vicinity. I went a couple of times to see Miss Georgie about this land business. She's wise to a lot of law—used to help her father before he died, it seems. And she has some of his books, I discovered. I wanted to see if there wasn't some means of kicking these fellows off the ranch without making a lot more trouble for old Peaceful. But after I'd read up and talked the thing over with her, we decided that there wasn't anything to be done till Peaceful comes back, and we know what he's been doing about it. That's what's keeping him, of course.

"I suppose," he added, looking at her frankly, "I should have mentioned my going there. But to tell you the truth, I didn't think anything much about it. It was just business, and when I'm with you, Miss Goldilocks, I like to forget my troubles. You," he declared, his eyes glowing upon her, "are the antidote. And you wouldn't have mo believe you could possibly be jealous!"

"No," said Evadna, in a more amiable tone. "Of course I'm not. But I do think you showed a—well, a lack of confidence in me. I don't see why *I* can't help you share your troubles. You know I want to. I think you should have told me, and let me help. But you never do. Just for instance—why wouldn't you tell me yesterday where you were before breakfast? I know you were SOMEWHERE, because I looked all over the place for you," she argued naively. "I always want to know where you are, it's so lonesome when I don't know. And you see—"

She was interrupted at that point, which was not strange. The interruption lasted for several minutes, but Evadna was a persistent little person. When they came back to mundane matters, she went right on with what she had started out to say.

"You see, that gave old Hagar a chance to accuse you of—well, of a MEETING with Georgie. Which I don't believe, of course. Still, it does seem as if you might have told me in the first place where you had been, and then I could have shut her up by letting her see that I knew all about it. The horrid, mean old THING! To say such things, right to your face! And—Grant, where DID she get hold of that knife, do you suppose—and—that—bunch of—hair?" She took his hand of her own accord, and patted it, and Evadna was not a demonstrative kind of person usually. "It wasn't just a tangle, like combings," she went on slowly. "I noticed particularly. There was a lock as large almost as my finger, that looked as if it had been cut off. And it certainly WAS Georgie's hair."

"Georgie's hair," Good Indian smilingly asserted, "doesn't interest me a little bit. Maybe Hagar scalped Miss Georgie to get it. If it had been goldy, I'd have taken it away from her if I had to annihilate the whole tribe, but seeing it wasn't YOUR hair—"

Well, the argument as such was a poor one, to say the least, but it had the merit of satisfying Evadna as mere logic could not have done, and seemed to allay as well all the doubt that had been accumulating for days past in her mind. But an hour spent in a hammock in the shadiest part of the grove could not wipe out all memory of the past few days, nor quiet the uneasiness which had come to be Good Indian's portion.

"I've got to go up on the hill again right after dinner, Squaw-with-sun-hair," he told her at last. "I can't rest, somehow, as long as those gentlemen are camping down in the orchard. You won't mind, will you?" Which shows that the hour had not been spent in quarreling, at all events.

"Certainly not," Evadna replied calmly. "Because I'm going with you. Oh, you needn't get ready to shake your head! I'm going to help you, from now on, and talk law and give advice and 'scout around,' as you call it. I couldn't be easy a minute, with old Hagar on the warpath the way she is. I'd imagine all sorts of things."

"You don't realize how hot it is," he discouraged.

B. M. Bower

"I can stand it if you can. And I haven't seen Georgie for DAYS. She must get horribly lonesome, and it's a perfect SHAME that I haven't been up there lately. I'm sure she wouldn't treat ME that way." Evadna had put on her angelic expression. "I WOULD go oftener," she declared virtuously, "only you boys always go off without saying anything about it, and I'm silly about riding past that Indian camp alone. That squaw—the one that caught Huckleberry the other day, you know—would hardly let go of the bridle. I was scared to DEATH, only I wouldn't let her see. I believe now she's in with old Hagar, Grant. She kept asking me where you were, and looked so—"

"I think, on the whole, we'd better wait till after supper when it's cooler, Goldenhair," Good Indian observed, when she hesitated over something she had not quite decided to say. "I suppose I really ought to stay and help the boys with that clover patch that Mother Hart is worrying so about. I guess she thinks we're a lazy bunch, all right, when the old man's gone. We'll go up this evening, if you like."

Evadna eyed him with open suspicion, but if she could read his real meaning from anything in his face or his eyes or his manner, she must have been a very keen observer indeed.

Good Indian was meditating what he called "making a sneak." He wanted to have a talk with Miss Georgie himself, and he certainly did not want Evadna, of all people, to hear what he had to say. For just a minute he wished that they had quarreled again. He went down to the stable, started to saddle Keno, and then decided that he would not. After all, Hagar's gossip could do no real harm, he thought, and it could not make much difference if Miss Georgie did not hear of it immediately.

CHAPTER XXIV

PEACEFUL RETURNS

That afternoon when the four-thirty-five rushed in from the parched desert and slid to a panting halt beside the station platform, Peaceful Hart emerged from the smoker, descended quietly to the blistering planks, and nodded through the open window to Miss Georgie at her instrument taking train orders.

Behind him perspired Baumberger, purple from the heat and the beer with which he had sought to allay the discomfort of that searing sunlight.

"Howdy, Miss Georgie?" he wheezed, as he passed the window. "Ever see such hot weather in your life? *I* never did."

Miss Georgie glanced at him while her fingers rattled her key, and it struck her that Baumberger had lost a good deal of his oily amiability since she saw him last. He looked more flabby and loose-lipped than ever, and his leering eyes were streaked plainly with the red veins which told of heavy drinking. She gave him a nod cool enough to lower the thermometer several degrees, and scribbled away upon the yellow pad under her hand as if Baumberger had sunk into the oblivion her temper wished for him. She looked up immediately, however, and leaned forward so that she could see Peaceful just turning to go down the steps.

"Oh, Mr. Hart! Will you wait a minute?" she called clearly

above the puffing of the engine. "I've something for you here. Soon as I get this train out—" She saw him stop and turn back to the office, and let it go at that for the present.

"I sure have got my nerve," she observed mentally when the conductor had signaled the engineer and swung up the steps of the smoker, and the wheels were beginning to clank. All she had for Peaceful Hart in that office was anxiety over his troubles. "Just held him up to pry into his private affairs," she put it bluntly to herself. But she smiled at him brightly, and waited until Baumberger had gone lumbering with rather uncertain steps to the store, where he puffed up the steps and sat heavily down in the shade where Pete Hamilton was resting after the excitement of the past thirty-six hours.

"I lied to you, Mr. Hart," she confessed, engagingly. "I haven't a thing for you except a lot of questions, and I simply must ask them or die. I'm not just curious, you know. I'm horribly anxious. Won't you take the seat of honor, please? The ranch won't run off if you aren't there for a few minutes after you had expected to be. I've been waiting to have a little talk with you, and I simply couldn't let the opportunity go by." She talked fast, but she was thinking faster, and wondering if this calm, white-bearded old man thought her a meddlesome fool.

"There's time enough, and it ain't worth much right now," Peaceful said, sitting down in the beribboned rocker and stroking his beard in his deliberate fashion. "It seems to be getting the fashion to be anxious," he drawled, and waited placidly for her to speak.

"You just about swear by old Baumberger, don't you?" she began presently, fiddling with her lead pencil and going straight to the heart of what she wanted to say.

"Well, I dunno. I've kinda learned to fight shy of swearing by anybody, Miss Georgie." His mild blue eyes settled attentively upon her flushed face.

"That's some encouragement, anyhow," she sighed. "Because he's the biggest old blackguard in Idaho and more treacherous than any Indian ever could be if he tried. I just thought I'd tell you, in case you didn't know it. I'm certain as I can be of anything, that he's at the bottom of this placer-claim fraud, and he's just digging your ranch out from under your feet while he wheedles you into thinking he's looking after your interests. I'll bet you never got an injunction against those eight men," she hazarded, leaning toward him with her eyes sparkling as the subject absorbed all her thoughts. "I'll bet anything he kept you fiddling around until those fellows all filed on their claims. And now it's got to go till the case is finally settled in court, because they are technically within their rights in making lawful improvements on their claims.

"Grant," she said, and her voice nearly betrayed her when she spoke his name, "was sure they faked the gold samples they must have used in filing. We both were sure of it. He and the boys tried to catch them at some crooked work, but the nights have been too dark, for one thing, and they were always on the watch, and went up to Shoshone in couples, and there was no telling which two meant to sneak off next. So they have all filed, I suppose. I know the whole eight have been up—"

"Yes, they've all filed—twenty acres apiece—the best part of the ranch. There's a forty runs up over the bluff; the lower line takes in the house and barn and down into the garden where the man they call Stanley run his line through the strawberry patch. That forty's mine yet. It's part uh the homestead. The meadowland is most all included. That was a preemption claim." Peaceful spoke slowly, and there was a note of discouragement in his voice which it hurt Miss Georgie to hear.

"Well, they've got to prove that those claims of theirs are lawful, you know. And if you've got your patent for the homestead—you have got a patent, haven't you?" Something in his face made her fling in the question.

"Y-es—or I thought I had one," he answered dryly. "It seems now there's a flaw in it, and it's got to go back to Washington and be rectified. It ain't legal till that's been done."

Miss Georgie half rose from her chair, and dropped back despairingly. "Who found that mistake?" she demanded. "Baumberger?"

"Y-es, Baumberger. He thought we better go over all the papers ourselves, so the other side couldn't spring anything on us unawares, and there was one paper that hadn't been made out right. So it had to be fixed, of course. Baumberger was real put out about it."

"Oh, of course!" Miss Georgie went to the window to make sure of the gentleman's whereabouts. He was still sitting upon the store porch, and he was just in the act of lifting a tall, glass mug of beer to his gross mouth when she looked over at him. "Pig!" she gritted under her breath. "It's a pity he doesn't drink himself to death." She turned and faced Peaceful anxiously.

"You spoke a while ago as if you didn't trust him implicitly," she said. "I firmly believe he hired those eight men to file on your land. I believe he also hired Saunders to watch Grant, for some reason—perhaps because Grant has shown his hostility from the first. Did you know Saunders—or someone—has been shooting at Grant from the top of the bluff for—well, ever since you left? The last shot clipped his hat-brim. Then Saunders was shot—or shot himself, according to the inquest—and there has been no more rifle practice with Grant for the target."

"N-no, I hadn't heard about that." Peaceful pulled hard at his beard so that his lips were drawn slightly apart. "I don't mind telling yuh," he added slowly, "that I've got another lawyer working on the case—Black. He hates Baumberger, and he'd like to git something on him. I don't want Baumberger should know anything about it, though. He takes it for granted I swallow whole everything he says and does—but I don't. Not by a long shot. Black'll ferret out any crooked work."

"He's a dandy if he catches Baumberger," Miss Georgie averred, gloomily. "I tried a little detective work on my own account. I hadn't any right; it was about the cipher messages Saunders used to send and receive so often before your place was jumped. I was dead sure it was old Baumberger at the other end, and I—well, I struck up a mild sort of flirtation with the operator at Shoshone." She smiled deprecatingly at Peaceful.

"I wanted to find out—and I did by writing a nice letter or two; we have to be pretty cute about what we send over the wires," she explained, "though we do talk back and forth quite a lot, too. There was a news-agent and cigar man—you know that kind of joint, where they sell paper novels and magazines and tobacco and such—getting Saunders' messages. Jim Wakely is his name. He told the operator that he and Saunders were just practicing; they were going to be detectives, he said, and rigged up a cipher that they were learning together so they wouldn't need any codebook. Pretty thin that—but you can't prove it wasn't the truth. I managed to find out that Baumberger buys cigars and papers of Jim Wakely sometimes; not always, though."

Miss Georgie laughed ruefully, and patted her pompadour absent-mindedly.

"So all I got out of that," she finished, "was a correspondence I could very well do without. I've been trying to quarrel with that operator ever since, but he's so darned easy-tempered!" She went and looked out of the window again uneasily.

"He's guzzling beer over there, and from the look of him he's had a good deal more than he needs already," she informed Peaceful. "He'll burst if he keeps on. I suppose I shouldn't keep you any longer—he's looking this way pretty often, I notice; nothing but the beer-keg holds him, I imagine. And when he empties that—" She shrugged her shoulders, and sat down facing Hart.

"Maybe you could bribe Jim Wakely into giving something away," she suggested. "I'd sure like to see Baumberger stub his toe in this deal! Or maybe you could get around one of those eight beauties you've got camping down on your ranch—but there isn't much chance of that; he probably took good care to pick clams for that job. And Saunders," she added slowly, "is eternally silent. Well, I hope in mercy you'll be able to catch him napping, Mr. Hart."

Peaceful rose stiffly,—and took up his hat from where he had laid it on the table.

"I ain't as hopeful as I was a week ago," he admitted mildly. "Put if there's any justice left in the courts, I'll save the old ranch. My wife and I worked hard to make it what it is, and my boys call it home. We can't save it by anything but law. Fightin' would only make a bad matter worse. I'm obliged to yuh, Miss Georgie, for taking such an interest—and I'll tell Black about Jim Wakely."

"Don't build any hopes on Jim," she warned. "He probably doesn't know anything except that he sent and received messages he couldn't read any sense into."

"Well—there's always a way out, if we can find it. Come down and see us some time. We still got a house to invite our friends to." He smiled drearily at her, gave a little, old-fashioned bow, and went over to join Baumberger—and to ask Pete Hamilton for the use of his team and buckboard.

Miss Georgie, keeping an uneasy vigil over everything that moved in the barren portion of Hartley which her window commanded, saw Pete get up and start listlessly toward the stable; saw Peaceful sit down to wait; and then Pete drove up with the rig, and they started for the ranch. She turned with a startled movement to the office door, because she felt that she was being watched.

"How, Hagar, and Viney, and Lucy," she greeted languidly when she saw the three squaws sidle closer, and reached for a bag of candy for them.

Hagar's greasy paw stretched out greedily for the gift, and placed it in jealous hiding beneath her blanket, but she did not turn to go, as she most frequently did after getting what she came for. Instead, she waddled boldly into the office, her eyes searching cunningly every corner of the little room. Viney and Lucy remained outside, passively waiting. Hagar twitched at something under her blanket, and held out her hand again; this time it was not empty.

"Ketchum sagebrush," she announced laconically. "Mebbyso yo' like for buy?"

Miss Georgie stared fixedly at the hand, and said nothing. Hagar drew it under her blanket, held it fumbling there, and thrust it forth again.

"Ketchum where ketchum hair," she said, and her wicked old eyes twinkled with malice. "Mebbyso yo' like for buy?"

Miss Georgie still stared, and said nothing. Her under lip was caught tightly between her teeth by now, and her eyebrows were pulled close together.

"Ketchum much track, same place," said Hagar grimly. "Good Injun makeum track all same boot. Seeum Good Injun creep, creep in bushes, all time Man-that-coughs be heap kill. Yo' buy hair, buy knife, mebbyso me no tell me seeum Good Injun. Me tell, Good Injun go for jail; mebbyso killum rope." She made a horrible gesture of hanging by the neck. Afterward she grinned still more horribly. "Ketchum plenty mo' dolla, me no tell, mebbyso."

Miss Georgie felt blindly for her chair, and when she touched it she backed and sank into it rather heavily. She looked white and sick, and Hagar eyed her gloatingly.

"Yo' no like for Good Injun be killum rope," she chuckled. "Yo' all time thinkum heap bueno. Mebbyso yo' love. Yo' buy? Yo' payum much dolla?"

Miss Georgie passed a hand slowly over her eyes. She felt numb, and she could not think, and she must think. A shuffling sound at the door made her drop her hand and look up, but there was nothing to lighten her oppressive sense of danger to Grant. Another squaw had appeared, was all. A young squaw, with bright-red ribbons braided into her shining black hair, and great, sad eyes brightening the dull copper tint of her face.

"You no be 'fraid," she murmured shyly to Miss Georgie, and stopped where she was just inside the door. "You no be sad. No trouble come Good Injun. I friend."

Hagar turned, and snarled at her in short, barking words which Miss Georgie could not understand. The young squaw folded her arms inside her bright, plaid shawl, and listened with an indifference bordering closely on contempt, one would judge from her masklike face. Hagar turned from berating her, and thrust out her chin at Miss Georgie.

"I go. Sun go 'way, mebbyso I come. Mebbyso yo' heart bad. Me ketchum much dolla yo', me no tellum, mebbyso. No ketchum, me tell sheriff mans Good Injun all time killum Man-that-coughs." Turning, she waddled out, jabbing viciously at the young squaw with her elbow as she passed, and spitting out some sort of threat or command—Miss Georgie could not tell which.

The young squaw lingered, still gazing shyly at Miss Georgie.

"You no be 'fraid," she repeated softly. "I friend. I take care. No trouble come Good Injun. I no let come. You no be sad." She smiled wistfully, and was gone, as silently as moved her shadow before her on the cinders.

Miss Georgie stood by the window with her fingernails making little red half-moons in her palms, and watched the three squaws pad out of sight on the narrow trail to their camp, with the young squaw following after, until only a black head could be seen bobbing over the brow of the hill. When even that was gone, she turned from the window, and stood for a long minute with her hands pressed tightly over her face. She was trying to think, but instead she found herself listening intently to the monotonous "Ah-h-CHUCK! ah-h-CHUCK!" of the steam pump down the track, and to the spasmodic clicking of an order from the dispatcher to the passenger train two stations to the west.

When the train was cleared and the wires idle, she went suddenly to the table, laid her fingers purposefully upon the key, and called up her chief. It was another two hours' leave of absence she asked for "on urgent business." She got it, seasoned with a sarcastic reminder that her business was supposed to be with the railroad company, and that she would do well to cultivate exactness of expression and a taste for her duties in the office.

She was putting on her hat even while she listened to the message, and she astonished the man at the other end by making no retort whatever. She almost ran to the store, and she did not ask Pete for a saddle-horse; she just threw her office key at him, and told him she was going to take his bay, and she was at the stable before he closed the mouth he had opened in amazement at her whirlwind departure.

CHAPTER XXV

"I'D JUST AS SOON HANG FOR NINE MEN AS FOR ONE"

Baumberger climbed heavily out of the rig,and went lurching drunkenly up the path to the house where the cool shade of the grove was like paradise set close against the boundary of the purgatory of blazing sunshine and scorching sand. He had not gone ten steps from the stable when he met Good Indian face to face.

"Hullo," he growled, stopping short and eying him malevolently with lowered head.

Good Indian's lips curled silently, and he stepped aside to pursue his way. Baumberger swung his huge body toward him.

"I said HULLO. Nothin' wrong in that, is there? HULLO— d'yuh hear?"

"Go to the devil!" said Grant shortly.

Baumberger leered at him offensively. "Pretty Polly! Never learned but one set uh words in his life. Can't yuh say anything but 'Go to the devil!' when a man speaks to yuh? Hey?"

"I could say a whole lot that you wouldn't be particularly glad to hear." Good Indian stopped, and faced him, coldly angry.

For one thing, he knew that Evadna was waiting on the porch for him, and could see even if she could not hear; and Baumberger's attitude was insulting. "I think," he said meaningly, "I wouldn't press the point if I were you."

"Giving me advice, hey? And who the devil are you?"

"I wouldn't ask, if I were you. But if you really want to know, I'm the fellow you hired Saunders to shoot. You blundered that time. You should have picked a better man, Mr. Baumberger. Saunders couldn't have hit the side of a barn if he'd been locked inside it. You ought to have made sure—"

Baumberger glared at him, and then lunged, his eyes like an animal gone mad.

"I'll make a better job, then!" he bellowed. "Saunders was a fool. I told him to get down next the trail and make a good job of it. I told him to kill you, you lying, renegade Injun—and if he couldn't, I can! Yuh WILL watch me, hey?"

Good Indian backed from him in sheer amazement. Epithets unprintable poured in a stream from the loose, evil lips. Baumberger was a raving beast of a man. He would have torn the other to pieces and reveled in the doing. He bellowed forth threats against Good Indian and the Harts, young and old, and vaunted rashly the things he meant to do. Heat-mad and drink-mad he was, and it was as if the dam of his wily amiability had broken and let loose the whole vile reservoir of his pirate mind. He tried to strike Good Indian down where he stood, and when his blows were parried he stopped, swayed a minute in drunken uncertainty, and then make one of his catlike motions, pulled a gun, and fired without really taking aim.

Another gun spoke then, and Baumberger collapsed in the sand, a quivering heap of gross human flesh. Good Indian stood and looked down at him fixedly while the smoke floated away from the muzzle of his own gun. He heard Evadna screaming hysterically at the gate, and looked over there inquiringly. Phoebe was running toward him, and the boys— Wally and Gene and Jack, from the blacksmith shop. At the corner of the stable Miss Georgie was sliding from her saddle, her riding whip clenched tightly in her hand as she hurried to him. Peaceful stood beside the team, with the lines still in his hand.

It was Miss Georgie's words which reached him clearly.

"You just HAD to do it, Grant. I saw the whole thing. You HAD to."

"Oh, Grant—GRANT! What have you done? What have you done?" That was Phoebe Hart, saying the same thing over and over with a queer, moaning inflection in her voice.

"D'yuh KILL him?" Gene shouted excitedly, as he ran up to the spot.

"Yes." Good Indian glanced once more at the heap before him. "And I'm liable to kill a few more before I'm through with the deal." He swung short around, discovered that Evadna was clutching his arm and crying, and pulled loose from her with a gesture of impatience. With the gun still in his hand, he walked quickly down the road in the direction of the garden.

"He's mad! The boy is mad! He's going to kill—" Phoebe gave a sob, and ran after him, and with her went Miss Georgie and Evadna, white-faced, all three of them.

"Come on, boys—he's going to clean out the whole bunch!" whooped Gene.

"Oh, choke off!" Wally gritted disgustedly, glancing over his shoulder at them. "Go back to the house, and STAY there! Ma, make Vad quit that yelling, can't yuh?" He looked eloquently at Jack, keeping pace with him and smiling with the steely glitter in his eyes. "Women make me sick!" he snorted under his breath.

Peaceful stared after them, went into the stable, and got a blanket to throw over Baumberger's inert body, stooped, and made sure that the man was dead, with the left breast of his light negligee shirt all blackened with powder and soaked with blood; covered him well, and tied up the team. Then he went to the house, and got the old rifle that had killed Indians and buffalo alike, and went quickly through the grove to the garden. He was a methodical man, and he was counted slow, but nevertheless he reached the scene not much behind the others. Wally was trying to send his mother to the house with Evadna, and neither would go. Miss Georgie was standing near Good Indian, watching Stanley with her lips pressed together.

It is doubtful if Good Indian realized what the others were doing. He had gone straight past the line of stakes to where Stanley was sitting with his back against the lightning-stricken apricot tree. Stanley was smoking a cigarette as if he had heard nothing of the excitement, but his rifle was resting upon his knee in such a manner that he had but to lift it and take aim. The three others were upon their own claims, and they, also, seemed unobtrusively ready for whatever might be going to happen.

Good Indian appraised the situation with a quick glance as he came up, but he did not slacken his pace until he was within ten feet of Stanley.

"You're across the dead line, m' son," said Stanley, with lazy significance. "And you, too," he added, flickering a glance at Miss Georgie.

"The dead line," said Good Indian coolly, "is beyond the Point o' Rocks. I'd like to see you on the other side by sundown."

Stanley looked him over, from the crown of his gray hat to the tips of his riding-boots, and laughed when his eyes came back to Good Indian's face. But the laugh died out rather suddenly at what he saw there.

"Got the papers for that?" he asked calmly. But his jaw had squared.

"I've got something better than papers. Your boss is dead. I shot him just now. He's lying back there by the stable." Good Indian tilted his head backward, without taking his eyes from Stanley's face—and Stanley's right hand, too, perhaps. "If you don't want the same medicine, I'd advise you to quit."

Stanley's jaw dropped, but it was surprise which slackened the muscles.

"You—shot—"

"Baumberger. I said it."

"You'll hang for that," Stanley stated impersonally, without moving.

Good Indian smiled, but it only made his face more ominous.

"Well, they can't hang a man more than once. I'll see this ranch cleaned up while I'm about it. I'd just as soon," he added composedly, "be hanged for nine men as for one."

Stanley sat on his haunches, and regarded him unwinkingly for so long that Phoebe's nerves took a panic, and she drew Evadna away from the place. The boys edged closer, their hands resting suggestively upon their gun-butts. Old Peaceful half-raised his rifle, and held it so. It was like being compelled to watch a fuse hiss and shrivel and go black toward a keg of gun-powder.

"I believe, by heck, you would!" said Stanley at last, and so long a time had elapsed that even Good Indian had to think back to know what he meant. Stanley squinted up at the sun, hitched himself up so that his back rested against the tree more comfortably, inspected his cigarette, and then fumbled for a match with which to relight it. "How'd you find out Baumberger was back uh this deal?" he asked curiously and without any personal resentment in tone or manner, and raked the match along his thigh.

Good Indian's shoulders went up a little.

"I knew, and that's sufficient. The dead line is down past the Point o' Rocks. After sundown this ranch is going to hold the Harts and their friends—and NO ONE ELSE. Tell that to your pals, unless you've got a grudge against them!"

Stanley held his cigarette between his fingers, and blew smoke through his nostrils while he watched Good Indian turn his back and walk away. He did not easily lose his hold of himself, and this was, with him, a cold business proposition.

Miss Georgie stood where she was until she saw that Stanley did not intend to shoot Good Indian in the back, as he might have done easily enough, and followed so quickly that she soon came up with him. Good Indian turned at the rustling of the skirts immediately behind him, and looked down at her somberly. Then he caught sight of something she was carrying in her hand, and he gave a short laugh.

"What are you doing with that thing?" he asked peremptorily.

Miss Georgie blushed very red, and slid the thing into her pocket.

"Well, every little helps," she retorted, with a miserable attempt at her old breeziness of manner. "I thought for a minute I'd have to shoot that man Stanley—when you turned your back on him."

Good Indian stopped, looked at her queerly, and went on again without saying a word.

CHAPTER XXVI

"WHEN THE SUN GOES AWAY"

"I wish," said Phoebe, putting her two hands on Miss Georgie's shoulders at the gate and looking up at her with haggard eyes, "you'd see what you can do with Vadnie. The poor child's near crazy; she ain't used to seeing such things happen—"

"Where is she?" Good Indian asked tersely, and was answered immediately by the sound of sobbing on the east porch. The three went together, but it was Grant who reached her first.

"Don't cry, Goldilocks," he said tenderly, bending over her. "It's all right now. There isn't going to be any more—"

"Oh! Don't TOUCH me!" She sprang up and backed from him, horror plain in her wide eyes. "Make him keep away, Aunt Phoebe!"

Good Indian straightened, and stood perfectly still, looking at her in a stunned, incredulous way.

"Chicken, don't be silly!" Miss Georgie's sane tones were like a breath of clean air. "You've simply gone all to pieces. I know what nerves can do to a woman—I've had 'em myself. Grant isn't going to bite you, and you're not afraid of him. You're proud of him, and you know it. He's acted the man, chicken!—the man we knew he was, all along. So pull yourself together, and let's not have any nonsense."

"He—KILLED a man! I saw him do it. And he's going to kill some more. I might have known he was like that! I might have KNOWN when he tried to shoot me that night in the orchard when I was trying to scare Gene! I can show you the mark—where he grazed my arm! And he LAUGHED about it! I called him a savage then—and I was RIGHT—only he can be so nice when he wants to be—and I forgot about the Indian in him—and then he killed Mr. Baumberger! He's lying out there now! I'd rather DIE than let him—"

Miss Georgie clapped a hand over her mouth, and stopped her. Also, she gripped her by the shoulder indignantly.

"'Vadna Ramsey, I'm ashamed of you!" she cried furiously. "For Heaven's sake, Grant, go on off somewhere and wait till she settles down. Don't stand there looking like a stone image—didn't you ever see a case of nerves before? She doesn't know what she's saying—if she did, she wouldn't be saying it. You go on, and let me handle her alone. Men are just a nuisance in a case like this."

She pushed Evadna before her into the kitchen, waited until Phoebe had followed, and then closed the door gently and decisively upon Grant. But not before she had given him a heartening smile just to prove that he must not take Evadna seriously, because she did not.

"We'd better take her to her room, Mrs. Hart," she suggested, "and make her lie down for a while. That poor fellow—as if he didn't have enough on his hands without this!"

"I'm not on his hands! And I won't lie down!" Evadna jerked away from Miss Georgie, and confronted them both pantingly, her cheeks still wet with tears. "You act as if I don't know what I'm doing' and I DO know. If I should lie down for a MILLION YEARS, I'd feel just the same about it. I couldn't bear him to TOUCH me! I—"

"For Heaven's sake, don't shout it," Miss Georgie interrupted, exasperatedly. "Do you want him—"

"To hear? *I* don't care whether he does or not." Evadna was turning sullen at the opposition. "He'll have to know it SOME TIME, won't he? If you think can forgive a thing like that and let—"

"He had to do it. Baumberger would have killed HIM. He had a perfect right to kill. He'd have been a fool and a coward if he hadn't. You come and lie down a while."

"I WON'T lie down. I don't care if he did have to do it—I couldn't love him afterward. And he didn't have to go down there and threaten Stanley—and—HE'LL DO IT, TOO!" She fell to trembling again. "He'll DO it—at sundown."

Phoebe and Miss Georgie looked at each other. He would, if the men stayed. They knew that.

"And I was going to marry him!" Evadna shuddered when she said it, and covered her face with her two hands. "He wasn't sorry afterward; you could see he wasn't sorry. He was ready to kill more men. It's the Indian in him. He LIKES to kill people. He'll kill those men, and he won't be a bit sorry he did it. And he could come to me afterward and expect me—Oh, what does he think I AM?" She leaned against the wall, and sobbed.

"I suppose," she wailed, lashing herself with every bitter thought she could conjure, "he killed Saunders, too, like old Hagar said. He wouldn't tell me where he was that morning. I asked him, and he wouldn't tell. He was up there killing Saunders—"

"If you don't shut up, I'll shake you!" Miss Georgie in her fury did not wait, but shook her anyway as if she had been a ten-year-old child in a tantrum.

"My Heavens above! I'll stand for nerves and hysterics, and almost any old thing, but you're going a little bit too far, my lady. There's no excuse for your talking such stuff as that, and you're not going to do it, if I have to gag you! Now, you march to your own room and—STAY there. Do you hear? And don't you dare let another yip out of you till you can talk sense."

Good Indian stood upon the porch, and heard every word of that. He heard also the shuffle of feet as Miss Georgie urged Evadna to her room—it sounded almost as if she dragged her there by force—and he rolled a cigarette with fingers that did not so much as quiver. He scratched a match upon the nearest post, and afterward leaned there and smoked, and stared out over the pond and up at the bluff glowing yellow in the sunlight. His face was set and expressionless except that it was stoically calm, and there was a glitter deep down in his eyes. Evadna was right, to a certain extent the Indian in him held him quiet.

It occurred to him that someone ought to pick up Baumberger, and put him somewhere, but he did not move. The boys and Peaceful must have stayed down in the garden, he thought. He glanced up at the tops of the nodding poplars, and estimated idly by their shadow on the bluff how long it would be before sundown, and as idly wondered if Stanley and the others would go, or stay. There was nothing they could gain by staying, he knew, now that Baumberger was out of it. Unless they got stubborn and wanted to fight. In that case, he supposed he would eventually be planted alongside his father. He wished he could keep the boys and old Peaceful out of it, in case there was a fight, but he knew that would be impossible. The boys, at least, had been itching for something like this ever since the trouble started.

Good Indian had, not so long ago, spent hours in avoiding all thought that he might prolong the ecstasy of mere feeling. Now he had reversed the desire. He was thinking of this thing and of that, simply that he might avoid feeling. If someone didn't kill him within the next hour or so, he was going to feel something—something that would hurt him more than he had been hurt since his father died in that same house. But in the meantime he need only think.

The shadow of the grove, with the long fingers of tho poplars to point the way, climbed slowly up the bluff. Good Indian smoked another cigarette while he watched it. When a certain great bowlder that was like a miniature ledge glowed rosily and then slowly darkened to a chill gray, he threw his cigarette stub unerringly at a lily-pad which had courtesied many a time before to a like missile from his hand, pulled his hat down over his eyes, jumped off the porch, and started around the house to the gate which led to the stable.

Phoebe came out from the sitting-room, ran down the steps, and barred his way.

"Grant!" she said, and there were tears in her eyes, "don't do anything rash—don't. If it's for our sakes—and I know it is— don't do it. They'll go, anyway. We'll have the law on them and make them go. But don't YOU go down there. You let Thomas handle that part. You're like one of my own boys. I can't let you go!"

He looked down at her commiseratingly. "I've got to go, Mother Hart. I've made my war-talk." He hesitated, bent his head, and kissed her on the forehead as she stood looking up at him, and went on.

"Grant—GRANT!" she cried heartbrokenly after him, and sank down on the porch-steps with her face hidden in her arms.

Miss Georgie was standing beside the gate, looking toward the stable. She may not have been waiting for him, but she turned without any show of surprise when he walked up behind her.

"Well, your jumpers seem to have taken the hint," she informed him, with a sort of surface cheerfulness. "Stanley is down there talking to Mr. Hart now, and the others have gone on. They'll all be well over the dead-line by sundown. There goes Stanley now. Do you really feel that your future happiness depends on getting through this gate? Well—if you must—" She swung it open, but she stood in the opening.

"Grant, I—it's hard to say just what I want to say—but—you did right. You acted the man's part. No matter what—others—may think or say, remember that I think you did right to kill that man. And if there's anything under heaven that I can do, to—to help—you'll let me do it, won't you?" Her eyes held him briefly, unabashed at what they might tell. Then she stepped back, and contradicted them with a little laugh. "I will get fired sure for staying over my time," she said. "I'll wire for the coroner soon as I get to the office. This will never come to a trial, Grant. He was like a crazy man, and we all saw him shoot first."

She waited until he had passed through and was a third of the way to the stable where Peaceful Hart and his boys were gathered, and then she followed him briskly, as if her mind was taken up with her own affairs.

"It's a shame yon fellows got cheated out of a scrap," she taunted Jack, who held her horse for her while she settled herself in the saddle. "You were all spoiling for a fight—and there did seem to be the makings of a beautiful row!"

Save for the fact that she kept her eyes studiously turned away from a certain place near by, where the dust was pressed down smoothly with the weight of a heavy body, and all around was trampled and tracked, one could not have told that Miss Georgie remembered anything tragic.

But Good Indian seemed to recall something, and went quickly over to her just in time to prevent her starting.

"Was there something in particular you wanted when you came?" he asked, laying a hand on the neck of the bay. "It just occurred to me that there must have been."

She leaned so that the others could not hear, and her face was grave enough now.

"Why, yes. It's old Hagar. She came to me this afternoon, and she had that bunch of hair you cut off that was snarled in the bush. She had your knife. She wanted me to buy them—the old blackmailer! She made threats, Grant—about Saunders. She says you—I came right down to tell you, because I was afraid she might make trouble. But there was so much more on hand right here"—she glanced involuntarily at the trampled place in the dust. "She said she'd come back this evening, 'when the sun goes away.' She's there now, most likely. What shall I tell her? We can't have that story mouthed all over the country."

Good Indian twisted a wisp of mane in his fingers, and frowned abstractedly.

"If you'll ride on slowly," he told her, at last straightening the twisted lock, "I'll overtake you. I think I'd better see that old Jezebel myself."

Secretly he was rather thankful for further action. He told the boys when they fired questions at his hurried saddling that he was going to take Miss Georgie home, and that he would be back before long; in an hour, probably. Then he galloped down the trail, and overtook her at the Point o' Rocks.

The sun was down, and the sky was a great, glowing mass of color. Round the second turn of the grade they came upon Stanley, walking with his hands thrust in his trousers pockets and whistling softly to himself as if he were thinking deeply. Perhaps he was glad to be let off so easily.

"Abandoning my claim," he announced, lightly as a man of his prosaic temperament could speak upon such a subject. "Dern poor placer mining down there, if yuh want to know!"

Good Indian scowled at him and rode on, because a woman rode beside him. Seven others they passed farther up the hill. Those seven gave him scowl for scowl, and did not speak a word; that also because a woman rode beside him. And the woman understood, and was glad that she was there.

From the Indian camp, back in the sage-inclosed hollow, rose a sound of high-keyed wailing. The two heard it, and looked at each other questioningly.

"Something's up over there," Good Indian said, answering her look. "That sounds to me like the squaws howling over a death."

"Let's go and see. I'm so late now, a few minutes more won't matter, one way or the other." Miss Georgie pulled out her watch, looked at it, and made a little grimace. So they turned into the winding trail, and rode into the camp.

There were confusion, and wailing, and a buzzing of squaws around a certain wikiup. Dogs sat upon their haunches, and howled lugubriously until someone in passing kicked them into yelping instead. Papooses stood nakedly about, and regarded the uproar solemnly, running to peer into the wikiup and then scamper back to their less hardy fellows. Only the bucks stood apart in haughty unconcern, speaking in undertones when they talked at all. Good Indian commanded Miss Georgie to remain just outside the camp, and himself rode in to where the bucks were gathered. Then he saw Peppajee sitting beside his own wikiup, and went to him instead.

"What's the matter here, Peppajee?" he asked. "Heap trouble walk down at Hart Ranch. Trouble walk here all same, mebbyso?"

Peppajee looked at him sourly, but the news was big, and it must be told.

"Heap much trouble come. Squaw callum Hagar make much talk. Do much bad, mebbyso. Squaw Rachel ketchum bad heart along yo'. Heap cry all time. No sleepum, no eatum—all time heap sad. Ketchum bad spirit, mebbyso. Ketchum debbil. Sun go 'way, ketchum knife, go Hagar wikiup. Killum Hagar—so." He thrust out his arm as one who stabs. "Killum himself—so." He struck his chest with his clenched fist. "Hagar heap dead. Rachel heap dead. Kay bueno. Mebbyso yo' heap bad medicine. Yo' go."

"A squaw just died," he told Miss Georgie curtly, when they rode on. But her quick eyes noted a new look in his face. Before it had been grave and stern and bitter; now it was sorrowful instead.

CHAPTER XXVII

LIFE ADJUSTS ITSELF AGAIN TO SOME THINGS

The next day was a day of dust hanging always over the grade because of much hurried riding up and down; a day of many strange faces whose eyes peered curiously at the place where Baumberger fell, and at the cold ashes of Stanley's campfire, and at the Harts and their house, and their horses and all things pertaining in the remotest degree to the drama which had been played grimly there to its last, tragic "curtain." They stared up at the rim-rock and made various estimates of the distance and argued over the question of marksmanship, and whether it really took a good shot to fire from the top and hit a man below.

As for the killing of Baumberger, public opinion tried—with the aid of various plugs of tobacco and much expectoration—the case and rendered a unanimous verdict upon it long before the coroner arrived. "Done just right," was the verdict of Public Opinion, and the self-constituted judges manifested their further approval by slapping Good Indian upon the back when they had a chance, or by solemnly shaking hands with him, or by facetiously assuring him that they would be good. All of which Grant interpreted correctly as sympathy and a desire to show him that they did not look upon him as a murderer, but as a man who had the courage to defend himself and those dear to him from a great danger.

With everything so agreeably disposed of according to the

B. M. Bower

crude—though none the less true, perhaps—ethics of the time and the locality, it was tacitly understood that the coroner and the inquest he held in the grove beside the house were a mere concession to red tape. Nevertheless a general tension manifested itself when the jury, after solemnly listening, in their official capacity, to the evidence they had heard and discussed freely hours before, bent heads and whispered briefly together. There was also a corresponding atmosphere of relief when the verdict of Public Opinion was called justifiable homicide by the coroner and so stamped with official approval.

When that was done they carried Baumberger's gross physical shell away up the grade to the station; and the dust of his passing settled upon the straggling crowd that censured his misdeeds and mourned not at all, and yet paid tribute to his dead body with lowered voices while they spoke of him, and with awed silence when the rough box was lowered to the station platform.

As the sky clears and grows blue and deep and unfathomably peaceful after a storm, as trees wind-riven straighten and nod graciously to the little cloud-boats that sail the blue above, and wave dainty finger-tips of branches in bon voyage, so did the Peaceful Hart ranch, when the dust had settled after the latest departure and the whistle of the train—which bore the coroner and that other quiet passenger—came faintly down over the rim-rock, settle with a sigh of relief into its old, easy habits of life.

All, that is, save Good Indian himself, and perhaps one other.

. . . .

Peaceful cleared his white mustache and beard from a few stray drops of coffee and let his mild blue eyes travel slowly around the table, from one tanned young face to another.

"Now the excitement's all over and done with," he drawled in his half-apologetic tones, "it wouldn't be a bad idea for you boys to get to work and throw the water back where it belongs. I dunno but what the garden's spoiled already; but the small fruit can be saved."

"Clark and I was going up to the Injun camp," spoke up Gene. "We wanted to see—"

"You'll have to do some riding to get there," Good Indian informed them dryly. "They hit the trail before sunrise this morning."

"Huh! What were YOU doing up there that time of day?" blurted Wally, eying him sharply.

"Watching the sun rise." His lips smiled over the retort, but his eyes did not. "I'll lower the water in your milk-house now, Mother Hart," he promised lightly, "so you won't have to wear rubber-boots when you go to skim the milk." He gave Evadna a quick, sidelong glance as she came into the room, and pushed back his chair. "I'll get at it right away," he said cheerfully, picked up his hat, and went out whistling. Then he put his head in at the door. "Say," he called, "does anybody know where that long-handled shovel is?" Again he eyed Evadna without seeming to see her at all.

"If it isn't down at the stable," said Jack soberly, "or by the apple-cellar or somewhere around the pond or garden, look along the ditches as far up as the big meadow. And if you don't run across it there—" The door slammed, and Jack laughed with his eyes fast shut and three dimples showing.

Evadna sank listlessly into her chair and regarded him and all her little world with frank disapproval.

"Upon my WORD, I don't see how anybody can laugh, after what has happened on this place," she said dismally, "or— WHISTLE, after—" Her lips quivered a little. She was a distressed Christmas angel, if ever there was one.

Wally snorted. "Want us to go CRYING around because the row's over?" he demanded. "Think Grant ought to wear crepe, I suppose—because he ain't on ice this morning—or in jail, which he'd hate a lot worse. Think we ought to go around with our jaws hanging down so you could step on 'em, because Baumberger cashed in? Huh! All hurts MY feelings is, I didn't get a whack at the old devil myself!" It was a long speech for Wally to make, and he made it with deliberate malice.

"Now you're shouting!" applauded Gene, also with the intent to be shocking.

"THAT'S the stuff," approved Clark, grinning at Evadna's horrified eyes.

"Grant can run over me sharp-shod and I won't say a word, for what he did day before yesterday," declared Jack, opening his eyes and looking straight at Evadna. "You don't see any tears rolling down MY cheeks, I hope?"

"Good Injun's the stuff, all right. He'd 'a' licked the hull damn—"

"Now, Donny, be careful what language you use," Phoebe admonished, and so cut short his high-pitched song of praise.

"I don't care—I think it's perfectly awful." Evadna looked distastefully upon her breakfast. "I just can't sleep in that room, Aunt Phoebe. I tried not to think about it, but it opens right that way."

"Huh!" snorted Wally. "Board up the window, then, so you can't see the fatal spot!" His gray eyes twinkled. "I could DANCE on it myself," he said, just to horrify her—which he did. Evadna shivered, pressed her wisp of handkerchief against her lips, and left the table hurriedly.

"You boys ought to be ashamed of yourselves!" Phoebe scolded half-heartedly; for she had lived long in the wild, and had seen much that was raw and primitive. "You must take into consideration that Vadnie isn't used to such things. Why, great grief! I don't suppose the child ever SAW a dead man before in her life—unless he was laid out in church with flower-anchors piled knee-deep all over him. And to see one shot right before her very eyes—and by the man she expects—or did expect to marry—why, you can't wonder at her looking at it the way she does. It isn't Vadnie's fault. It's the way she's been raised."

"Well," observed Wally in the manner of delivering an ultimatum, "excuse ME from any Eastern raising!"

A little later, Phoebe boldly invaded the secret chambers of Good Indian's heart when he was readjusting the rocks which formed the floor of the milk-house.

"Now, Grant," she began, laying her hand upon his shoulder as he knelt before her, straining at a heavy rock, "Mother Hart is going to give you a little piece of her mind about something that's none of her business maybe."

"You can give me as many pieces as you like. They're always good medicine," he assured her. But he kept his head bent so that his hat quite hid his face from her. "What about?" he asked, a betraying tenseness in his voice.

"About Vadnie—and you. I notice you don't speak—you haven't that I've seen, since that day—on the porch. You don't want to be too hard on her, Grant. Remember she isn't used to such things. She looks at it different. She's never seen the times, as I have, where it's kill or be killed. Be patient with her, Grant—and don't feel hard. She'll get over it. I want," she stopped because her voice was beginning to shake "—I want my biggest boy to be happy." Her hand slipped around his neck and pressed his head against her knee.

Good Indian got up and put his arms around her and held her close. He did not say anything at all for a minute, but when he did he spoke very quietly, stroking her hair the while.

"Mother Hart, I stood on the porch and heard what she said in the kitchen. She accused me of killing Saunders. She said I liked to kill people; that I shot at her and laughed at the mark I made on her arm. She called me a savage—an Indian. My mother's mother was the daughter of a chief. She was a good woman; my mother was a good woman; just as good as if she had been white.

"Mother Hart, I'm a white man in everything but half my mother's blood. I don't remember her—but I respect her memory, and I am not ashamed because she was my mother. Do you think I could marry a girl who thinks of my mother as something which she must try to forgive? Do you think I could go to that girl in there and—and take her in my arms—and love her, knowing that she feels as she does? She can't even forgive me for killing that beast!

"She's a beautiful thing—I wanted to have her for my own. I'm a man. I've a healthy man's hunger for a beautiful woman, but I've a healthy man's pride as well." He patted the smooth cheek of the only woman he had ever known as a mother, and stared at the rough rock wall oozing moisture that drip-dripped to the pool below.

"I did think I'd go away for awhile," he said after a minute spent in sober thinking. "But I never dodged yet, and I never ran. I'm going to stay and see the thing through, now. I don't know—" he hesitated and then went on. "It may not last; I may have to suffer after awhile, but standing out there, that day, listening to her carrying on, kind of—oh, I can't explain it. But I don't believe I wes half as deep in love as I thought I was. I don't want to say anything against her; I've no right, for she's a thousand times better than I am. But she's different. She never would understand our ways, Mother Hart, or look at life as we do; some people go through life looking at the little things that don't matter, and passing by the other, bigger things. If you keep your eye glued to a microscope long enough, you're sure to lose the sense of proportion.

"She won't speak to me," he continued after a short silence. "I tried to talk to her yesterday—"

"But you must remember, the poor child was hysterical that day when—she went on so. She doesn't know anything about the realities of life. She doesn't mean to be hard."

"Yesterday," said Grant with an odd little smile, "she was not hysterical. It seems that—shooting—was the last little weight that tilted the scale against me. I don't think she ever cared two whoops for me, to tell you the truth. She's been ashamed of my Indian blood all along; she said so. And I'm not a good lover; I neglected her all the while this trouble lasted, and I paid more attention to Georgie Howard than I did to her—and I didn't satisfactorily explain about that hair and knife that Hagar had. And—oh, it isn't the killing, altogether! I guess we were both a good deal mistaken in our feelings."

"Well, I hope so," sighed Phoebe, wondering secretly at the decadence of love. An emotion that could burn high and hot in a week, flare bravely for a like space, and die out with no seared heart to pay for the extravagance—she shook her head at it. That was not what she had been taught to call love, and she wondered how a man and a maid could be mistaken about so vital an emotion.

"I suppose," she added with unusual sarcasm for her, "you'll be falling in love with Georgie Howard, next thing anybody knows; and maybe that will last a week or ten days before you find out you were MISTAKEN!"

Good Indian gave her one of his quick, sidelong glances.

"She would not be eternally apologizing to herself for liking me, anyway," he retorted acrimoniously, as if he found it very hard to forgive Evadna her conscious superiority of race and upbringing. "Squaw."

"Oh, I haven't a doubt of that!" Phoebe rose to the defense of her own blood. "I don't know as it's in her to apologize for anything. I never saw such a girl for going right ahead as if her way is the only way! Bull-headed, I'd call her." She looked at Good Indian afterward, studying his face with motherly solicitude.

"I believe you're half in love with her right now and don't know it!" she accused suddenly.

Good Indian laughed softly and bent to his work again.

"ARE you, Grant?" Phoebe laid a moist hand on his shoulder, and felt the muscles sliding smoothly beneath his clothing while he moved a rock. "I ain't mad because you and Vadnie fell out; I kind of looked for it to happen. Love that grows like a mushroom lasts about as long—only *I* don't call it love! You might tell me—"

"Tell you what?" But Grant did not look up. "If I don't know it, I can't tell it." He paused in his lifting and rested his hands upon his knees, the fingers dripping water back into the spring. He felt that Phoebe was waiting, and he pressed his lips together. "Must a man be in love with some woman all the time?" He shook his fingers impatiently so that the last drops hurried to the pool.

"She's a good girl, and a brave girl," Phoebe remarked irrelevantly.

Good Indian felt that she was still waiting, with all the quiet persistence of her sex when on the trail of a romance. He reached up and caught the hand upon his shoulder, and laid it against his cheek. He laughed surrender.

"Squaw-talk-far-off heap smart," he mimicked old Peppajee gravely. "Heap bueno." He stood up as suddenly as he had started his rock-lifting a few minutes before, and taking Phoebe by the shoulders, shook her with gentle insistence.

"Put don't make me fall out of one love right into another," he protested whimsically. "Give a fellow time to roll a cigarette, can't you?"

B. M. Bower

Choose from Thousands of 1stWorldLibrary Classics By

A. M. Barnard
Ada Leverson
Adolphus William Ward
Aesop
Agatha Christie
Alexander Aaronsohn
Alexander Kielland
Alexandre Dumas
Alfred Gatty
Alfred Ollivant
Alice Duer Miller
Alice Turner Curtis
Alice Dunbar
Allen Chapman
Alleyne Ireland
Ambrose Bierce
Amelia E. Barr
Amory H. Bradford
Andrew Lang
Andrew McFarland Davis
Andy Adams
Angela Brazil
Anna Alice Chapin
Anna Sewell
Annie Besant
Annie Hamilton Donnell
Annie Payson Call
Annie Roe Carr
Annonaymous
Anton Chekhov
Archibald Lee Fletcher
Arnold Bennett
Arthur C. Benson
Arthur Conan Doyle
Arthur M. Winfield
Arthur Ransome
Arthur Schnitzler
Arthur Train
Atticus
B.H. Baden-Powell
B. M. Bower
B. C. Chatterjee
Baroness Emmuska Orczy
Baroness Orczy
Basil King
Bayard Taylor
Ben Macomber
Bertha Muzzy Bower
Bjornstjerne Bjornson

Booth Tarkington
Boyd Cable
Bram Stoker
C. Collodi
C. E. Orr
C. M. Ingleby
Carolyn Wells
Catherine Parr Traill
Charles A. Eastman
Charles Amory Beach
Charles Dickens
Charles Dudley Warner
Charles Farrar Browne
Charles Ives
Charles Kingsley
Charles Klein
Charles Hanson Towne
Charles Lathrop Pack
Charles Romyn Dake
Charles Whibley
Charles Willing Beale
Charlotte M. Braeme
Charlotte M. Yonge
Charlotte Perkins Stetson
Clair W. Hayes
Clarence Day Jr.
Clarence E. Mulford
Clemence Housman
Confucius
Coningsby Dawson
Cornelis DeWitt Wilcox
Cyril Burleigh
D. H. Lawrence
Daniel Defoe
David Garnett
Dinah Craik
Don Carlos Janes
Donald Keyhoe
Dorothy Kilner
Dougan Clark
Douglas Fairbanks
E. Nesbit
E. P. Roe
E. Phillips Oppenheim
E. S. Brooks
Earl Barnes
Edgar Rice Burroughs
Edith Van Dyne
Edith Wharton

Edward Everett Hale
Edward J. O'Biren
Edward S. Ellis
Edwin L. Arnold
Eleanor Atkins
Eleanor Hallowell Abbott
Eliot Gregory
Elizabeth Gaskell
Elizabeth McCracken
Elizabeth Von Arnim
Ellem Key
Emerson Hough
Emilie F. Carlen
Emily Bronte
Emily Dickinson
Enid Bagnold
Enilor Macartney Lane
Erasmus W. Jones
Ernie Howard Pie
Ethel May Dell
Ethel Turner
Ethel Watts Mumford
Eugene Sue
Eugenie Foa
Eugene Wood
Eustace Hale Ball
Evelyn Everett-green
Everard Cotes
F. H. Cheley
F. J. Cross
F. Marion Crawford
Fannie E. Newberry
Federick Austin Ogg
Ferdinand Ossendowski
Fergus Hume
Florence A. Kilpatrick
Fremont B. Deering
Francis Bacon
Francis Darwin
Frances Hodgson Burnett
Frances Parkinson Keyes
Frank Gee Patchin
Frank Harris
Frank Jewett Mather
Frank L. Packard
Frank V. Webster
Frederic Stewart Isham
Frederick Trevor Hill
Frederick Winslow Taylor

Friedrich Kerst
Friedrich Nietzsche
Fyodor Dostoyevsky
G.A. Henty
G.K. Chesterton
Gabrielle E. Jackson
Garrett P. Serviss
Gaston Leroux
George A. Warren
George Ade
Geroge Bernard Shaw
George Cary Eggleston
George Durston
George Ebers
George Eliot
George Gissing
George MacDonald
George Meredith
George Orwell
George Sylvester Viereck
George Tucker
George W. Cable
George Wharton James
Gertrude Atherton
Gordon Casserly
Grace E. King
Grace Gallatin
Grace Greenwood
Grant Allen
Guillermo A. Sherwell
Gulielma Zollinger
Gustav Flaubert
H. A. Cody
H. B. Irving
H.C. Bailey
H. G. Wells
H. H. Munro
H. Irving Hancock
H. R. Naylor
H. Rider Haggard
H. W. C. Davis
Haldeman Julius
Hall Caine
Hamilton Wright Mabie
Hans Christian Andersen
Harold Avery
Harold McGrath
Harriet Beecher Stowe
Harry Castlemon
Harry Coghill
Harry Houidini

Hayden Carruth
Helent Hunt Jackson
Helen Nicolay
Hendrik Conscience
Hendy David Thoreau
Henri Barbusse
Henrik Ibsen
Henry Adams
Henry Ford
Henry Frost
Henry James
Henry Jones Ford
Henry Seton Merriman
Henry W Longfellow
Herbert A. Giles
Herbert Carter
Herbert N. Casson
Herman Hesse
Hildegard G. Frey
Homer
Honore De Balzac
Horace B. Day
Horace Walpole
Horatio Alger Jr.
Howard Pyle
Howard R. Garis
Hugh Lofting
Hugh Walpole
Humphry Ward
Ian Maclaren
Inez Haynes Gillmore
Irving Bacheller
Isabel Cecilia Williams
Isabel Hornibrook
Israel Abrahams
Ivan Turgenev
J.G.Austin
J. Henri Fabre
J. M. Barrie
J. M. Walsh
J. Macdonald Oxley
J. R. Miller
J. S. Fletcher
J. S. Knowles
J. Storer Clouston
J. W. Duffield
Jack London
Jacob Abbott
James Allen
James Andrews
James Baldwin

James Branch Cabell
James DeMille
James Joyce
James Lane Allen
James Lane Allen
James Oliver Curwood
James Oppenheim
James Otis
James R. Driscoll
Jane Abbott
Jane Austen
Jane L. Stewart
Janet Aldridge
Jens Peter Jacobsen
Jerome K. Jerome
Jessie Graham Flower
John Buchan
John Burroughs
John Cournos
John F. Kennedy
John Gay
John Glasworthy
John Habberton
John Joy Bell
John Kendrick Bangs
John Milton
John Philip Sousa
John Taintor Foote
Jonas Lauritz Idemil Lie
Jonathan Swift
Joseph A. Altsheler
Joseph Carey
Joseph Conrad
Joseph E. Badger Jr
Joseph Hergesheimer
Joseph Jacobs
Jules Vernes
Julian Hawthrone
Julie A Lippmann
Justin Huntly McCarthy
Kakuzo Okakura
Karle Wilson Baker
Kate Chopin
Kenneth Grahame
Kenneth McGaffey
Kate Langley Bosher
Kate Langley Bosher
Katherine Cecil Thurston
Katherine Stokes
L. A. Abbot
L. T. Meade

L. Frank Baum
Latta Griswold
Laura Dent Crane
Laura Lee Hope
Laurence Housman
Lawrence Beasley
Leo Tolstoy
Leonid Andreyev
Lewis Carroll
Lewis Sperry Chafer
Lilian Bell
Lloyd Osbourne
Louis Hughes
Louis Joseph Vance
Louis Tracy
Louisa May Alcott
Lucy Fitch Perkins
Lucy Maud Montgomery
Luther Benson
Lydia Miller Middleton
Lyndon Orr
M. Corvus
M. H. Adams
Margaret E. Sangster
Margret Howth
Margaret Vandercook
Margaret W. Hungerford
Margret Penrose
Maria Edgeworth
Maria Thompson Daviess
Mariano Azuela
Marion Polk Angellotti
Mark Overton
Mark Twain
Mary Austin
Mary Catherine Crowley
Mary Cole
Mary Hastings Bradley
Mary Roberts Rinehart
Mary Rowlandson
M. Wollstonecraft Shelley
Maud Lindsay
Max Beerbohm
Myra Kelly
Nathaniel Hawthrone
Nicolo Machiavelli
O. F. Walton
Oscar Wilde
Owen Johnson
P.G. Wodehouse
Paul and Mabel Thorne

Paul G. Tomlinson
Paul Severing
Percy Brebner
Percy Keese Fitzhugh
Peter B. Kyne
Plato
Quincy Allen
R. Derby Holmes
R. L. Stevenson
R. S. Ball
Rabindranath Tagore
Rahul Alvares
Ralph Bonehill
Ralph Henry Barbour
Ralph Victor
Ralph Waldo Emmerson
Rene Descartes
Ray Cummings
Rex Beach
Rex E. Beach
Richard Harding Davis
Richard Jefferies
Richard Le Gallienne
Robert Barr
Robert Frost
Robert Gordon Anderson
Robert L. Drake
Robert Lansing
Robert Lynd
Robert Michael Ballantyne
Robert W. Chambers
Rosa Nouchette Carey
Rudyard Kipling
Saint Augustine
Samuel B. Allison
Samuel Hopkins Adams
Sarah Bernhardt
Sarah C. Hallowell
Selma Lagerlof
Sherwood Anderson
Sigmund Freud
Standish O'Grady
Stanley Weyman
Stella Benson
Stella M. Francis
Stephen Crane
Stewart Edward White
Stijn Streuvels
Swami Abhedananda
Swami Parmananda
T. S. Ackland

T. S. Arthur
The Princess Der Ling
Thomas A. Janvier
Thomas A Kempis
Thomas Anderton
Thomas Bailey Aldrich
Thomas Bulfinch
Thomas De Quincey
Thomas Dixon
Thomas H. Huxley
Thomas Hardy
Thomas More
Thornton W. Burgess
U. S. Grant
Upton Sinclair
Valentine Williams
Various Authors
Vaughan Kester
Victor Appleton
Victor G. Durham
Victoria Cross
Virginia Woolf
Wadsworth Camp
Walter Camp
Walter Scott
Washington Irving
Wilbur Lawton
Wilkie Collins
Willa Cather
Willard F. Baker
William Dean Howells
William le Queux
W. Makepeace Thackeray
William W. Walter
William Shakespeare
Winston Churchill
Yei Theodora Ozaki
Yogi Ramacharaka
Young E. Allison
Zane Grey